Every Block Boy Needs A Little Love 3

TINA J

Disclaimer:

Please be advised that there will be drug use, drinking, discussions regarding incest, and comedy.

MARIAH

Finally, someone put that bitch out of her misery. How do you come to a hospital with a man and your pimp, called you out? Arabia wasn't gonna be happy hearing her new bestie was sleeping with her man at the time.

River must've been a low budget ho because she damn sure didn't come up off whatever money he gave her. The bitch was still broke as fuck.

"I'm not going to jail." Huff shouted, and continued firing off shots.

The cops were trying to get him but he ran through the hospital doors. All of sudden there was a lock down being put in place. People were hiding, nurses and doctors didn't know what to do and that stupid bitch was gargling on her blood. I'm not saying I wish death on her, but she ran her mouth and got what she got.

"Shit. Stay here." Onyx said. He had pushed me in the bathroom that was next to the nurses station where we were standing before the shooting took place.

"Onyx—" I stepped out to regain his attention.

"Not right now, Mariah. My cousin was shot and—" He stopped when he noticed my pants were wet.

"What the fuck? This can't be happening." I was a week overdue so it was definitely happening.

"Yo, this woman's water just broke." Did he just make it seem as if we weren't together? He rushed to the nurses desk and pulled one of the ground.

"We need a wheelchair. Ma'am did you have any contractions yet?" I shook my head no. Someone brought a chair and Onyx helped me sit.

"Ahhhh!" I screamed when a pain shot through my body. It felt like someone had a knife inside my stomach and was dragging it across the lining.

"Ok. I'm going to assume that was a contraction. We're going to start counting how far apart they are now." I took breaths in and out to keep me from panicking. That did not help one bit. When the next one came, the pain was even more intense. My stomach was hard and I could feel more liquid seeping down my leg.

"We have to deliver in one of the rooms since the hospital was locked down." A doctor said, closing the door. At least there was a curtain as well and I has some sort of privacy.

"We have everything down here for emergencies so you and the baby will be fine." Glancing around the tight room, Onyx was nowhere to be found. Where did he go?

As the nurses scrambled around in the room to prepare me for birth, Onyx stepped back in. He had a devastated look on his face. Not caring what happened out there, I reached my hand out for him to come closer. He can be mad all he wanted but this baby was coming and he was going to be here for support.

Two hours later, our daughter Heaven Lucille Buggs was born at seven pounds, six ounces. Onyx smiled after she came out and was the first person to hold her. Once the doctor left, the nurse helped clean me up by having the tech move me into a wheelchair to go in the bathroom. The lockdown was lifted an hour into my delivery but it was too late for me to move upstairs.

"Onyx, I'm sorry about everything between us." I managed to get out. I was exhausted and wanted to sleep but my conscience wouldn't allow me to until he knew my feelings.

"Having my daughter is the only thing I'm worried about right now." Respecting his answer, I slowly rolled over, pulled the covers up and went to sleep. I'm not about to argue with him right now.

"Wake up, Bitch." A male voice spoke in my ear. Slowly opening my eyes, some man stood there I've never seen before. The hospital room was different too. They must've brought me up when I was asleep.

"Who the hell are you?" He was handsome, dressed nice and resembled someone I knew.

"Where the fuck is my brother?"

"Your brother? I don't even know who you are; how would I know where your brother was?" He laughed as I sat up.

"You were the last one seen with, Sean. Where the fuck is he?" My mouth fell open hearing Sean was missing and even more, seeing his brother in my hospital room.

"How do you even know me and what are you doing in my room?" Obviously, Onyx wasn't here because this would not be happening.

"Your friend told me."

"I don't have any friends so whoever told you anything, lied." I'm not admitting to nothing. Especially, when this man could be unstable.

"Bitch, where the fuck is my brother?" Gripping my hair tight, I felt this situation was about to get out of hand. Pressing the nurses button, I waited for someone to answer. Just my luck, it kept making the noise to call the nurse station, yet no one answered. Where the hell were they?

"I'm not gonna ask you again." He gripped it tighter making my eyes go into slits where I could barely see.

"I don't know. The last time we saw one another, we broke it off. Feelings were involved so we stopped seeing each other." I cried out.

"You're lying."

"I swear. I haven't seen or heard from Sean in months." I was trying my hardest to pry his hands from my hair.

"Now, Mariah. Why you lying about being with that man's brother?" Salina stepped in with a smirk on her face. I should've known her trifling ass was behind this. But who told her about Sean?

"You know damn well, I been with Onyx." The guy let go and slammed my head against the bed.

"Speaking of him, where is he? Y'all just had a baby and he's not here." She put her index finger under her chin.

"Oh wait. He probably at my house waiting for me to ride that dick again." That was always her get back at me. I blame Onyx for backtracking. The least he could've done was search elsewhere for pussy.

"Really?" The guy was aggravated.

"Can I help you?" Now the nurse wanted to get on the intercom.

"Please call the cops and have them come to my room for unwanted guests." Outta nowhere the man backslapped the shit out of me. Trying to get off the bed, I fell and hit my head on the heater by the wall. He kneeled down next to me.

"If I find out you had anything to do with my brother's disappearance, I'm gonna kill you." He banged my head on the heater twice before walking out.

"Tsk. Tsk. Tsk. Trying to get one over on, Onyx was your downfall."

"What?" I rubbed the back of my head and felt something wet. Pulling my hand away, it showed blood.

"You and I both know he found out and took that man's life. When his brother finds out, you're gonna be on his most wanted list."

"What you mean Onyx did something to him?" She laughed.

"You really are dumb. Even I know when we were together he had eyes on me at all times. I couldn't take a piss without him knowing about it." She backed up as I put my hands on the bed to help me stand. I saw the specks of blood on the sheet that must've rubbed off my hand when I felt my head.

"Onyx knew when you stepped out the first time even though he may not have said it. Depending on how many times you did it, trust and believe he knew about each rendezvous." Was she right? Did Onyx know more than he led on?

"Anyway, I'm only here to let you know me and Onyx fucked." I laid in the bed on my side.

"He told me, Salina." She got off on relaying bad news to me.

"I guess he mentioned our new bundle of joy coming in nine months." She rubbed her stomach to be funny.

"Onyx would never fuck you without a condom." She threw her head back and cackled. That's when I remembered him saying, he'd never use a condom with his baby mama.

"Whether you want to admit it or not, his dick was addicted to this pussy. Hence the reason we kept fucking while you two were together." Her words were cutting me deep as hell. I refused to let her know and let her finish speaking.

"My question to you is, who is the father to that baby you

just had? If my calculations were correct, you and Sean stopped soon as you told Onyx you were pregnant." This bitch knew too much information. Where was she getting it from? Before I was able to kick her out, Onyx stepped in.

"Are you gonna answer her, Mariah because I wanna know too." Was he here the whole time?

Fuck my life!

"Why didn't you talk to him?" Chana asked, strapping Jasir in the back seat. We were in her Kia Sorrento. It was nice as hell and put my van to shame. As much as I would love to get a new car, my finances aren't enough for me to afford a car note.

"He saw me, Chana. He could've spoken to me." She hopped in the front seat.

"Why would he speak to someone who told him she couldn't be around him if his cousin was there?" She made sense but still, he didn't say hi or anything.

"He looked so damn good." I smiled as she pulled out the lot where the baby shower was held. Block had on a pair of jeans, Jordan's as usual and a T-shirt. There was nothing fancy about his attire but then again, he turned me on no matter what he wore.

"What's going on there?" She stopped short. The street was

blocked off by cars and trucks. People were running but we couldn't see why.

"Oh wow. It looks like a bunch of cars shooting at each other. Let me get the heck out of here. We do not need to get caught up in that." As she drove to get us home, Block was on my mind heavy. Going through my phone, I went into the photos.

"Chanaaaaaa." I sang closing out the app.

"What?" She took turns looking at me and then the road.

"Do you mind keeping, Jasir?" Ryan had to work which was why he wasn't here. Block's family was cool with him and now that we were related to Onyx, we kinda meshed the family ourselves.

"For?"

"I have to get my man back." She smiled.

"You want me to drop you off?" I thought about it and decided not to make her go out the way. Block lived forty minutes away from me.

"No, I'll take my van." Once we got to the house, I ran in to grab an overnight bag for me and Jasir. She waited with him in the truck.

I kissed him goodnight, gave her a hug and hopped in my van. Not wanting to hear him tell me no, I went to Block's house without so much as a text to let him know I'm coming. He doesn't allow women there so I wasn't worried about that.

Parking at his house, I saw his truck was there as well as a brand new corvette looking car. The temp tags were still on and the dark blue was beautiful. Unlocking the door with the key he gave me, I heard music coming from the sound system. Running up the stairs to change into nothing, I caught him coming out the bathroom with a towel wrapped around his waist.

"What's up?" Cracking a smile because he didn't ask why I was there, I removed my clothes and stood there naked.

Not wasting any time, Block lifted me on the dresser and spread my legs wide. His hands roamed the top of my legs and one found its way in between. Sticking his finger in my mouth with his free hand, I slowly guided it down my chest, onto my stomach and placed it inside my love nest.

"Sssss." My head went back when he took over.

"Don't stop. Yessss." Just that fast, I encountered my first orgasm. It felt so good, my body shook for a few seconds.

"Now, tell me why you here." Lifting my head, my eyes met his and all the love he had for me showed.

"I missed you." Helping me off the dresser with one hand, he let the towel drop and in a swift motion, made us one.

"Shit, River. You wet as fuck." I had him lie back on the bed, stood on my feet and rode the heck out of him. I made sure to drop harder, to feel his dick deeper. Not sure why I did that when he was busting me wide open.

"Fuck, Block." He sat up and pulled me in for a kiss. Our pelvises were in sync as we continued fucking the hell out of one another.

"Don't leave me again." He squeezed my ass and moved my lower half in circles.

"I won't." He flipped me over, opened my legs wide as they could go and had me begging for mercy.

"Ain't nobody ever feeling inside this pussy, River. We clear on that!"

"Yessss. Oh gawdddd. Yesss." His finger was plucking my clit gently, driving me insane.

"Make that pussy squirt for me." Pulling out and ramming himself in had my eyes rolling. I couldn't move or do what he asked. The euphoric feeling had me on cloud nine. When he let my legs go, and substituted his dick for his mouth, my body shook uncontrollably. I have never in my life felt anything like this.

"Ain't no man gonna do your body like this." He kissed my stomach, turned me over to get on my knees, stuck his dick inside my pussy and once that one finger went in my ass, that was it. Block had total control over me and he knew. That man could ask me for an orgy right now and I'd say yes.

"Fuck! Got dammit, Block." I was pounding on his bed while he continued fucking both of my holes with his dick and finger.

SMACK! His free hand went to my clit and another orgasm overtook my body. He removed his finger out my ass, spread my cheeks wide and fucked me even harder. He was teaching me a lesson and I was here for it.

"Get the fuck up." My body was weak as hell. Moving me off the bed, he bent me over to touch my toes, bent his knees too dig deeper and my whole body collapsed from the orgasm. He didn't stop and got on the floor with me. Turning me back over, he placed one leg on his shoulder and pushed himself in. Our tongues met and we were once again in sync.

"I'm about to cum." Moving faster inside me, my nails dug into his back making him yelp like a wounded animal.

"That's right, River. Fuck me back." Sliding my hands under my ass to give me a boost, I pumped from the bottom and shortly after, Block released everything he had. We both laid there breathing heavy.

"That was intense as fuck." He whispered with his arm over his face.

"I'm sorry."

"River, I can't control what Mariah says or does but I will always make it my business to make sure she doesn't overstep."

"Why did you let her say you settled with me?" I was becoming upset laying there.

"I was gonna say, you're right she wasn't like any woman I've ever met, but she was mine and ain't no changing that." Rolling onto his body, he held me tight.

"I told you, your broke ass had me stuck. I'm not a fake nigga and if you had let me finish speaking, you would've heard me correct Mariah." Block was right. He never got the chance to respond due to me barging in on the conversation.

"I'm not gonna hurt you, River." His hands were on my back.

"I won't hurt you either but I don't want you battling with your family over me." He made me stare in his eyes.

"I'll battle anyone over you." Kissing his juicy lips got us aroused and we were back at it. This time we had sex in the shower and the bathroom floor. When it was time to sleep, we passed out; at least I know I did.

* * *

"What?" Block shouted, waking me out my sleep. It felt like I just closed my eyes. Sitting up to wait for him to get off the phone, I rubbed his back.

"I'm on the way." He disconnected the call.

"You ok?" Hopping out the bed, he rushed to get dressed.

"Someone ambushed Deray and Arabia when they left the baby shower."

"Oh my God!" Jumping out the bed, I threw on some sweats and a shirt that I had over here. He passed me a pair of Air Max he purchased me. He never removed any of my stuff from his house.

"We have to get to the hospital." We got in the truck and I had to hold on to the door handle due to how fast he was going. Once we got there, Block grabbed my hand and we basically ran in. His parents were there and so was Mariah, Onyx and more family walked in behind us.

"Well, well, well." The voice made me cringe. What was he doing here? He was texting me nonstop for the last two months threatening to tell my man about us. Ignoring him in hopes he would go away, he had a smirk on his face. Please don't let him announce what we've done.

"Just the nigga we been looking for?" Onyx had his gun on Brandon but why. Did they know one another?

"Fuck y'all."

"What nigga?" Block let go of my hand and walked straight toward him until Brandon pulled a gun out.

"Y'all turned on me for that nigga, who was supposed to be dead."

"Turned on you? Nigga we didn't even know about him. We stopped fucking with you for putting hands on my sister." Block said making me very confused.

"Then, y'all killed my parents." He sounded like he was about to cry.

"You can't be mad at the repercussions when you're the one causing it." Block was right. People always wanted you to take it easy on them no matter how bad the situation was that they caused.

"Whatever." He focused his attention on me.

"If that's the only reason, then why you fucking my bitch. Block, we ain't never slept with the same woman." You could hear a pin drop when he said that. All eyes were on me.

"You fucking my sister's ex?" The hate on his face made me upset. His sisters ex name was Huff. How did he figure we were sleeping with the same guy? Unless, Huff was... oh my God!

"Block, can we speak in private?"

"Nah, tell him, River how me and you hooked up twice a week. That's my top bitch and she gets paid very well for what we do behind closed doors. Ain't that right, River. That pussy A1 too ain't it, Block." Was he making a joke out of it?

"Oh, that bitch a ho." Mariah said and before I could hit her, Onyx stopped me. She was talking shit but knew not to move from behind him. Pregnant or not I was ready to knock her fucking head off. I walked over to Block.

"Babe. Please let me talk to you." He snatched away when I grabbed his hand.

"Get the fuck out!" His tone was loud and everyone was staring.

"Please. It's not what he's saying." Block looked up at me.

"Did you fuck him?"

"Will you let me explain?" He wasn't hearing anything I had to say.

"All I need to know is, did he pay you to fuck?" My head went down in shame. There was no getting through to him so I stopped trying and accepted defeat.

"Where's Arabia? Did they say if she was ok?" He left me standing there.

"Fuck that bitch, Block. River for everybody. Let's finish what we started." I couldn't believe he was in the hospital with a gun challenging Block to a fight. His father pulled him outside.

"I'm a bitch, Brandon." I walked towards him pretending the gun didn't bother me but he wasn't about to disrespect me.

"Brandon?" I heard someone sound as confused as me when they called him, Huff.

"You wasn't saying that when your ass was moaning, were you." He focused back on me. They all knew we had sex, wasn't no use in trying to hide it.

"The only reason you're really mad is because I wouldn't let you and that nigga run a train on me." I stood directly in front of him.

"You beat my ass that night too. Now you're mad I'm with someone else." How dare him even bring up what we did when he was sleeping with various women?

"Nobody cares about you and him. I know his money long so he paying you better than me." I slapped fire from his ass.

"Bitch."

POW! My body collapsed when the bullet hit me.

"FREEZE!" Was all I heard before feeling myself choking on my own blood.

Chapter One

BLOCK

"**D**id you fuck that nigga? Nah, did he pay you to fuck him?" When River put her head down that gave me the answer.

I don't give a fuck how strong a nigga was, to hear the woman you loved let niggas hit for money was enough to break him. I left her standing there and walked out to calm myself down. I wanted to kill both of them; him for putting my sister through so much and River, for not respecting herself enough to stoop that low. Money was tight for her and I get it, but damn.

BOOM! Standing outside when the gun when off, I ran back in only to find River on the ground bleeding to death. Huff was going back and forth with the cops but my only focus

1

was River. How did this happen? Who shot her? Was it a mistake?

Dropping to my knees to cradle her, blood was pouring out her mouth. No idea where the bullet pierced her at, I turned her on the side to try and keep her from swallowing her own blood.

"Sir, we need to take her." I'm not sure who it was speaking nor did I care at the moment.

"River. River. You're gonna be ok." She was trying to speak but no words were coming out.

"Son, they can't help her if you don't let go." My mom was yelling behind me.

"River. Don't you fucking die. We not done talking about this. FUCK!!!!!" I shouted when her eyes began rolling.

"Move." My father removed my hands from her body. I watched people lift and rush her in the back. Getting off the floor, I stood with River's blood on my clothes.

"Who did this?" It may have seemed obvious being Huff had a gun. Then again, so did Onyx and some of the guys who were friends with Deray.

"Get him outta here." My Uncle Montell yelled. My parents were at the nurses station for some reason and Onyx was calling out for help. Mariah had gone into labor amidst all the chaos going on.

"Let's go, nephew." My Uncle Trevor walked me through the revolving door. Walking in complete silence to his car, my mind overflowed with visions of River dying. Seeing the woman you love possibly taking her last breath was killing me.

"You have to tell her family." My uncle said, unlocking the

door to his car. Still remaining quiet, I sat down, put the seat back and tried to relax.

"Block."

"I can't do it." Closing my eyes only made me vision River dying. Opening them back up, my uncle was staring over at me.

"Give me the number to at least one of her family members. They'll do the rest once I'm done explaining."

"Onyx has their information." It felt inappropriate for me to have Chana's information. I know they may not look at it as such, but unless River gave me her sister's number for emergency purposes, I didn't need it.

"He ok?" Speaking of Onyx, the door unlocked and he hopped in the back.

"Can you make the call to her sister?" He asked Onyx to do what I refused.

"Shit, I don't want to." Onyx knew what I did and that's, that Chana was about to lose it. Since their first introduction they've become very tight. You wouldn't even know they were separated at birth.

"Make the call and I'll talk." Uncle Trevor was always the calm one out of the elders. Onyx dialed and put the phone on speaker.

"Hello." Chana's voice was very groggy. I'm sure she was asleep because it was late when me and River left my house to get here. Onyx passed him the phone in order to make sure she heard him carefully.

"Hi, Chana."

"Hi. Who is this?" The confusion was expected being the call came from Onyx phone and someone else spoke.

"This is Block's uncle. There's been an accident."

"What? Where's my sister?" You could hear noise in her background.

"You and your family need to get to the hospital right away." He spoke very calm to her.

"Why? Is she ok? I have my nephew here. Let me call my father."

"Chana, drive safe." She hung up and five minutes later, my phone rang from Ryan. I passed the phone to my uncle and let him relay the same message.

"Block, you ok? Where's River? I'm on my way down to emergency room." He didn't let my uncle get a word in.

"The hospital is on lockdown right now and Onyx's wife went into labor. Can you get him back inside and we'll explain the rest then?" After finding out it wasn't me on the phone, he agreed. My uncle made Onyx wait by the door and not too long after, Ryan was allowing him entry. When he walked over to where Onyx pointed to find us, I stepped out the car.

"What the hell? Do not tell me that's River's blood." Clearing my throat to speak, I opened my mouth but no words would come out.

"River was shot by someone she used to mess with."

"Fuck! Was it the guy sending her threatening messages?" That piqued my interest.

"What guy?" He started pacing and talking.

"Chana mentioned some guy she used to mess with had

been stalking her for a few months. He would send messages saying if she didn't sleep with him anymore, he was going to tell her man. She ignored and even blocked him but he would reach out from unknown numbers. Just last week she was scared to go home because he sent her a picture sitting outside her house."

"Say what?"

"River didn't tell you about him. Me and Chana both told her to let you handle it." I felt like shit hearing Huff was stalking her. We've been searching for him and the whole time he was right under our nose. Granted, he only made himself noticeable when he wanted but still, he never left town.

"She didn't tell me anything."

"His name was Brandon, I think. Did he do this?" My uncle answered.

"Where did she get hit? That's a lot of blood. Did they say she would be ok?" He questioned us as if we had the answers.

"We have no idea what's going on or where she was hit. I was outside when it took place. When I ran in, River was on the floor choking—" I stopped speaking.

"I know you're a street dude but it's ok to show emotion. You're in love with her and to watch that happen was hard to see." My uncle patted my shoulder.

"Let me go inside and see what I can find out. In the meantime, go get changed and come back up. She will be pissed seeing you in clothes full of her blood." He gave me a man hug and walked back in.

"That's a good dude." My uncle said what I already knew.

I had him take me home and once we got there, I took a

deep breath. Me and River were just here together. Going in, I didn't want to step inside the room but had no choice. Her scent was all over, the bed we rushed out of was unmade, the clothes she came in were on the floor from her stripping right away and her phone was on the nightstand. Leaving in such a rush, she must've forgotten it.

Against my better judgement, I put the code in which was Jasir's birthday and searched for Huff's number in her messages. She had him listed as Brandon. It didn't dawn on me then but now that I'm finding things out, he never told her his street name. That's why she had no idea how we knew him at the hospital, or that him and Arabia used to be a couple.

Finding his name, I clicked on the message and I'll be damned. There were texts from months ago in here. As I read through them, Huff asked why she wasn't answering him, did she miss him, could they have sex again and he would pay her more than three hundred dollars. That shit threw me because River had some fire between her legs and he low balled her. Not that I'd pay for it but still, what she had was worth way more than he offered.

Stumbling across some photos there were some of her new place as well as her old place. How long had he been stalking her? Was he doing the same to Arabia and that's how he learned of Deray? The last message was sent yesterday from a phone number with no name. It read:

Bitch, I know you're fucking that Block, nigga. How you think he gonna feel knowing you sell your pussy to the highest bidder? She didn't respond. He sent her another one.

That nigga can't do you like me. Stop playing and answer the phone. I'm trying fuck all night. Again, she didn't respond. Scrolling down, I noticed he kept going all the way up until she arrived here. Why didn't she say anything? Closing out the messages, a new one popped up from her mother.

Louise. *River? Are you ok? Your twin sent me a message saying you were hurt. Are you?"* Louise was dumb as hell. How you ask that when someone told you? Did she really expect an answer? Without responding, I went in the bathroom, removed my clothes, and started the water. Blood residue from my hand seeped onto the shower handle and then the floor.

Stepping in once the water reached the hot temperature that I wanted, more blood slid down my body and into the drain. I hadn't realized that it soaked through my clothes.

"Block, we gotta get back to the hospital if we want Ryan to get us in." I heard my uncle yell.

"A'ight." After washing up, I grabbed a towel to dry off. Wrapping the towel around me, I opened the bottom cabinet, found the Lysol with bleach cleaner, and sprayed the shower down. I didn't have time to scrub it but at least it can sit in the shower until I return. The blood went down the drain but still. It would be unsanitary as hell to not spray anything on it.

Once I put my clothes on, I placed hers in the laundry basket, removed the sheets we rumbled in hours before and replaced them with new ones. When she got out the hospital she'll want to sleep on clean linen. Taking them down to the laundry room, I started the washer and told my uncle we could go.

"Block." I stopped at the door. He was standing behind me.

"If it's bad, I don't wanna hear it right now. Just take me to the hospital. We still don't know what happened with Arabia." Assuming it was bad since he didn't speak on it, I locked up and we left.

* * *

"Hey, you ok?" Chana hugged me when we arrived. Evidently, Huff ran out the hospital so the lockdown was lifted. Cops and detectives were lingering in the waiting room and asking questions.

"I'm cool. Do we know anything?" She gave me a weird look.

"Your uncle didn't tell you?" Chana asked. Looking around the waiting room at my family and hers, the mood was somber and most of the women were crying or had been.

"No. Where's Arabia?" I headed to my parents. If there was bad news about River, I wanted to make sure my sister was good first.

"Her and Deray are ok. They'll be discharging her soon. The doctor wanted to make sure the baby was fine."

"Did he say what happened?"

"Just that some of Huff's people ambushed them. His boys took them out but Huff got away which we know that." She explained.

"Block, Arabia doesn't know anything."

"What you mean?" I asked my mother.

"I had one of Deray's friends call him on the phone. I explained what went on down here and asked that he take her home. His friend will pick them up from the front entrance to avoid her from seeing this." She ran her hand down my face. My mother doesn't show emotion so it always felt weird when she did.

"How are you doing?" I kissed the side of her hand.

"I'm a'ight. Just waiting to hear." I took a seat.

"Uncle Trevor didn't tell you?" She looked over at him talking to my aunt.

"I wouldn't let him." She took a seat next to me.

"Honey, River died." I don't know what happened after those words left her mouth because everything went black.

Chapter Two

MARIAH

"Are you gonna answer?" Onyx questioned me while Salina stood there waiting for an answer.

"First off, when have we ever discussed our business in front of your, ho?" I snapped.

"Ho? Bitch, I got your ho." Salina had the nerve to get mad.

"What you mad for? At the end of the day; Onyx was still my husband when you slept with him. You think that's a flex? Tuh! It's the exact reason he doesn't respect you now." He always told me, she'd never be an option whether we stayed together or not.

"He respected me enough." She sassed.

"Yea, to allow you to suck him off in the parking lot of a

club, oh and fuck. But that's love in your eyes right." She didn't respond.

"And Onyx, don't question me on the paternity of my child when you just put one in her. You couldn't fucking wait to hurt me." I hated that she was in here during this conversation. Then again, it was his fault for not putting her out when he walked in.

"Ain't nobody do that on purpose." His attitude caught me off guard. How he mad at me for what he did?

"Oh no. So, you couldn't wear a condom? Wait, I forgot you'll never fuck your baby mother without one. Well, guess what, you did and now look." I pointed to Salina being extra by rubbing her stomach. The bitch probably wasn't even a week yet and acting dramatic.

"Now, here we are with your baby mother bragging about sleeping with my husband. The same husband who swore she wouldn't break us. The same husband who walked down the aisle and promised to never hurt me again." He stood there looking dumbfounded.

"I know we weren't seeing eye to eye lately but damn, I just had our fucking daughter. It hasn't even been twenty four hours and you got your top bitch in here antagonizing me. She did the same shit at my wedding. What the fuck, Onyx?" I shouted at the end.

"Get out, Salina." She sucked her teeth and flipped me the finger on her way out.

"You can go with her." I thought he was leaving until he showed his face after closing the door.

"Just go, Onyx. Tell the nurse you want to have a DNA test done on your way out and when I get home, the annulment papers will be signed and sent to your lawyer. I can't do this no more." It was at that very moment I knew we were never going to be the same again.

"I know Heaven is my daughter." I stared at him.

"Sean lost his life after the last time y'all had sex." I shook my head. I guess his brother won't ever find him.

"It was well over a year ago. Dude begged for his life but no man could walk this earth saying he laid with my woman." I laughed.

"But all the bitches in the world can brag about having my man; my husband. You sound like a hypocrite." He sat on the edge of the bed. Onyx mentioned getting rid of any woman he slept with that bothered me but why. If he hadn't cheated all those times, they would've never been in a position to do it. Then I remember him admitting not being happy with me.

"Did you get Salina pregnant?" When he blew his breath in the air, that gave me the answer.

"You know, the entire time I slept with Sean, not once did I ever consider not using protection. I'd never hurt you that way by allowing a man to impregnate me." I couldn't stop the tears even if I tried.

"No, we went through some things but you were the only man I'd ever have kids by. But you, you went back to being the same Onyx who didn't give a fuck about anyone but himself. It's why we ended up in that situation from the start." I sat there so disappointed in him.

"I'll admit saying some mean things to you about your family. Yes, I was jealous they were getting more attention from you than me. I wasn't used to anyone making you laugh or going out with you but me. So yes, I was being an evil bitch but never would I go sleep with another man and have his baby."

"Mariah."

"I know, you sent me the papers but did it ever occur to you that maybe we could go to counseling, talk to each other; communicate in general? Or were you that angry that all you saw was hurting me?" I was devastated hearing that he slept with other women but learning about the pregnancy was breaking me down.

"There's no coming back from that. You can get Heaven whenever you want, I'd never keep her away from you. But us —" He turned around to see me pointing between the two of us.

"We will never be us again." His eyes were sad.

"I allowed so much in the beginning of our relationship just because I refused to allow another woman to have you. Yet and still, they did. Then, I stepped out of the relationship for revenge and all that did was put more of a strain on us. Lastly, you may not have purposely got her pregnant but had you not searched elsewhere for pussy, that wouldn't have happened." I pressed the button for the nurse to come in. She did when Sean's brother first left and Onyx walked in but I waved her off. Instead of responding to the intercom one walked in.

"Can you help me get cleaned up? Also, I fell off the bed and hit my head." He had a surprised look on his face.

"Ma'am, you shouldn't be getting out the bed alone yet. You just had a baby."

"I know but I needed the bathroom." Lying to the nurse, I lifted the covers and noticed a massive amount of blood on the bed.

"Oh my, what happened. Let me get the doctor." Onyx jumped up.

"You ok?" Was he really pretending to be concerned.

"Honestly, Onyx. It would be better if you just left."

"Mariah, I'm—"

"Just go, dammit. I'm possibly hemorrhaging and all you're worried about is sitting in here. You can't help me. Just go, please." Just staring at him was hurting my heart. We just birthed a child and in nine months he would be in this exact position again but with someone else. The doctor stepped in with two nurses.

"Let's check you out. Sir, can you step out for a moment."

"Don't worry, he's leaving." Lying back in the bed, I watched him walk out and prayed this wasn't me dying.

"How's mommy's baby?" I cooed at Heaven. She was the prettiest baby I've ever seen dressed in her little pink Tu-Tu, I found online. Who knew they had one in a newborn size.

We were still in the hospital after the hemorrhaging incident which ended up not being that at all. Evidently, when I fell, the sanitary napkins must've shifted so when I bled, nothing was there to catch it. My body was in pain but I was ok. My parents stopped by the house to bring me clothes for today and I'm thankful because I had nothing.

"Aww, don't cry stinky butt." Her scream was loud for a baby when changing her.

"Hey, Honey. You ready to go home?" My father walked in and so did Onyx. He called and texted me all night and each time I ignored it. There was nothing to speak about because anything that needed to be spoken on, was said yesterday.

"Yes. This food was nasty and I can't wait to put her in the bassinet." Thankfully all of Heaven's main items like the crib, bassinet and highchair were put together prior to. Otherwise, I'd have my father do it.

"Can you hold her while I use the bathroom?" Handing her to Onyx, I went to clean myself up. I didn't want to bleed in my parent's car on the way home.

"Get it together, Mariah." Speaking to myself as I sat down on the toilet, tears flooded my face again. This breakup with Onyx was killing me and now I have a baby. It was too much for one person to handle.

"You ok in there?" I heard knocking and then the door opened. My mom closed it and smiled.

"It's gonna be ok." She hugged me while I sat on the toilet.

"Let's get you cleaned up and home. You need some rest." I nodded. She waited for me to do what needed to be done. I wasn't embarrassed at all because my mother knew what was going on between me and my husband, and all women bleed after birth.

Standing after using the bathroom, I washed my hands and used one of the rags to wash my face. You could see the redness from crying and how puffy my eyes were. It was no use trying to hide the inevitable. My family knew we were over, well my mom did because she let me cry on the phone to her last night. She didn't judge or make any rude comments.

"I'm ready." Onyx and my dad turned around. Neither said a word.

Walking slow to grab my bag, the nurse rolled in a wheelchair. The pain was bad at times and plopping down would make it worse so I sat down slowly.

"Daddy can you make sure, Heaven's blanket is out the closet? I don't want the sun in her eyes." Her father had her in the car seat following behind.

When we got downstairs, I was confused. Onyx car was parked in the front and my parents wasn't. Looking at my dad, he told me Onyx was taking me because he wanted to spend time with Heaven. This was not the plan but I didn't have the energy to argue or debate.

I sat in silence the whole way and once we arrived at the house that he left me, I went inside, signed the annulment papers on my dresser, got in bed and went to sleep. We said all that needed to be at the hospital. The relationship had run its course and all I could do was accept it.

Chapter Three

ONYX

Lying my daughter in the bassinet next to her mother made me smile. I loved both of them with everything I had but Mariah was right. We couldn't come back from what took place. There was too much hurt and pain inflicted on both of us to know where to try and fix it. Her admitting to being a bitch and childish threw me for a loop because Mariah didn't ever take accountability.

However, she was absolutely correct when she spoke on what we could've done to fix us. There was counseling, communicating with one another or just walking away before instilling that kinda hurt on the other. Granted, she didn't step out after the first time but I did without thinking of the effects it would have on her, our relationship and now marriage.

Kissing Heaven goodbye, I quietly headed to the door.

Mariah was staring, yet neither of us felt the need to speak. Cracking the bedroom door, I went downstairs to leave. There was other business that needed to be handled, such as dealing with Salina and her shit.

The fact she thought it was ok to pop in Mariah's room after her delivery, was mind boggling. I blame myself in a sense because being petty, I entertained that comment if Heaven was mine, knowing there was no way she could be someone else's.

Leaving the house, I called Block to check on him. It's been a few days now since River was shot and he hadn't spoken to anyone. In all the time we've known one another, this had to be the first I've witnessed him cry, and get emotional. From what Montell said, when he heard River died, he passed out. Evidently, his pressure was so high he could've had a stroke.

When he woke up, they kept him overnight until they could get it under control. Twice, they had to sedate him because he was adamant about seeing her. In the short amount of time they knew one another, the impact she had on him was like nothing I'd ever seen.

His phone went to voicemail so after stopping by Salina's house, I'll go check on him. Parking in front of my ex's house, I lit a blunt and took a few pulls before exiting the car. She was a handful and I already know her mouth would be reckless.

"What you doing here?" She had snatched the door open before I could knock. Pushing her out the way, I made my way inside. The house was clean for the most part.

"We need to have a conversation." The door slammed behind me.

"About what? I hope not about your soon to be ex-wife."

"Who told you she's about to be my ex-wife?"

"Duh, at the hospital she told you to leave and that she couldn't do it no more, which means—" Salina stopped speaking to wrap her arms around my neck.

Falling back on the couch, she maneuvered her way onto my lap. I'm not gonna lie, those spandex shorts and the tank top with no bra was enticing the hell out of me. Salina always had a nice body.

"Where's Laila?" Looking around her in order not to be caught, she removed her shirt and started feeling herself up.

"I'm not here for that Salina and where is, Laila?"

"She's not here and you and Mariah are over." Salina stood to remove her clothes and my dick started to rise.

"What the hell is that smell?" Moving my face close to her pussy, I almost gagged at the sour aroma.

"What crawled up inside you and died?" She put her hands on her hips.

"Excuse me. That's the new lotion I got from Victoria Secret. It's called Japanese Cherry Blossom."

"Ain't no way in hell anything out that store smell like that."

"Onyx, every woman's body won't smell the same." Pushing her away, I stood up.

"Say what you want but that's not lotion smelling that way. And when did you start putting lotion in your pussy?" She didn't know what to say.

"How long you been smelling that way? Fuck! I don't even

remember if you did when we fucked. I was drunk and the door was opened." She caught me at the club, came to the car and rode me in the front seat.

"Whatever. Are we having sex?"

"Hell no." Making my way to the door, I turned around.

"I just stopped by to tell you stop fucking with Mariah. If she beats your ass I'm not stopping her."

"I'm not worried about her. What, she mad that nigga smacked her and knocked her head against the heater." I ran up on Salina.

"What nigga and he did what?" I was clueless about what she spoke about.

"Before you arrived at the hospital, Sean's brother was there threatening her. She didn't know what he was talking about so he back slapped her. She tried to get out the bed and fell and his brother banged her head against the heater. He walked out right before you walked in." Why didn't I see that man when he left? Did he walk the other way?

"Ain't no way a nigga put his hands on her. I don't even do that shit." She folded her arms.

"Well, he did."

"Why didn't you say anything when I walked in?"

"That ain't my business and besides, it was fun watching y'all argue. That bitch don't have you like she thinks." She shrugged, picking her clothes up off the ground. The whole living room was beginning to smell.

"He wouldn't know shit about Mariah unless you told him since that's the same nigga you was outside the bodega with."

Her eyes grew wide. I didn't know who he was at first but after doing my research, it was brought to my attention that he was Sean's brother. I'm aware of what he looked like that's why I was confused hearing her say he walked out before I entered.

"I saw you with him and now I know why." Staring at Salina made her uncomfortable. My ex probably thought he would do something to Mariah and I'd end up with her.

"I knew something was up but didn't know what it was. What else did he want?" She didn't want you to say.

"What else did he say?" I spoke through gritted teeth trying to keep my composure. Salina had a tendency of playing scary when she didn't want to answer.

"Nothing. Just that if he found out anything happened to his brother, he would take it out on her."

"Bitch, and you led that nigga to her room?" Salina hated Mariah, it was no secret but to lead someone there to hurt her was where I had the problem.

"Onyx, I don't care if the bitch died. I'm who you should be with." When she tried to hug me again, I twisted her arm back. As bad as I wanted to knock her teeth out for saying that about Mariah, I kept my composure. I'm not sure where my daughter was at the moment and didn't want her to walk in on her deceased mother. Salina will pay dearly for that dumb shit.

"You don't ever gotta fuck with her but don't wish death on her because I'm telling you now." I made sure my face was close to hers.

"If anything happened to Mariah, I'm gonna throw you off a bridge and that's after I put a bullet in your chest." She backed up fast as hell. I've never spoken to Salina like that and seeing her terrified made me smile.

"Mariah will always be my wife and there's nothing you or any other bitch can do to take her spot." I headed to her door.

"The next time you see that nigga, tell him he a dead man walking just like his brother was." I slammed the door and went to my car. Mariah may have despised Salina but she had never wished death on her. What type of woman says some shit like that?

* * *

"It's been a long time." My mother hugged Raymond and wouldn't let go. He barely reciprocated the gesture.

"Ma, he can't breathe." I pulled her back and smiled seeing how happy she was to have him in her presence. It took me offering his ass a seafood dinner at my house to get him here. Hopefully, Mariah would be ok making it.

It's been a week since she delivered our daughter and she's been moving around more. We only speak about Heaven and neither of us text nor call one another. The marriage had definitely taken a hit and I'm not sure we'll ever be back to the way we were.

"Why did you want to see me? You know I don't wanna be here?" He was straight to the point.

Raymond was my younger brother who no one knew about, not even Mariah. He was never a secret but he begged me not to mention him being a part of the family. I never understood why until one day he sat me down and explained what happened to him.

"Onyx, did daddy kill, Auntie?" Raymond asked. At the age of seven he knew more than most kids would.

"What? Who told you that?" After witnessing the murder, my pops told me not to mention it. How was it that Raymond knew? It just happened a few days ago.

"Daddy told me, he was going to do it."

"Did he tell you why?" My father tried to get my aunt to tell me but she never did. Raymond pulled me in our room and closed the door. Watching him turn his video game on for the noise, I knew it had to be serious. We sat on his bed.

"It's my fault." Still confused on why he made that assumption, I questioned it.

"Auntie, came in my room." He was fiddling with his fingers.

"Ok. She always does." My aunt came over all the time. He looked behind me to make sure no one was coming.

"Yea but she was touching my private part and daddy caught her." Hearing that as a kid had me at a loss for words. Why would my aunt touch him where our parents always said not to let anyone touch?

"Are you sure?" He nodded. No wonder my aunt wouldn't say why my dad was going to kill her.

That night it took me a long time to fall asleep after hearing him explain more in depth of what our aunt did.

Evidently, Charlene had gotten caught by my father as well watching us in the bathroom but I didn't know. She actually did the same thing to my brother that my aunt did. My parents argued a lot over it because my mother didn't believe Raymond.

He kicked Charlene out the house and she was never allowed back. Even though my father didn't live with us he made it known that my grandmother better not ever come over. I don't even know what happened to her at the time and why she didn't lose her life then too.

Anyway, when Mariah confronted Charlene about watching us at the pool, my mother begged her to tell me. Eventually, it came out and that's when my mom felt worse for not believing Raymond. In her eyes, she wasn't the one who caught her mother touching her son so therefore it couldn't have happened. However, she believed that my aunt did.

Growing up, he wanted nothing to do with my mother but because he was a kid, he had to stay put. Raymond went to school and locked himself in his room until dinner. Anytime it was shower time, my father told him to keep the door locked. He knew my mother didn't believe him and wasn't sure if Charlene would come over at night.

When Montell offered me the house in Rhode Island, we moved there. My mother did redecorate and reside there for a couple of years. Once her and Julio became a couple, she spent more time at his house and decided it was best to move in together, Since my brother moved out the minute he turned eighteen, he was staying in a one bedroom apartment at the time, I offered the house to him. He only agreed if the deed was in my name and my mother couldn't come over. He's been living there ever since but I transferred the deed to him.

"I'm sorry for not believing you. I was in denial about a lot that happened when you two were kids." She backed away wiping her tears.

"You said that a million times already." He reminded her.

"Can you ever forgive me?" Raymond blew his breath.

"You want to be forgiven now because the truth of your mother was revealed." I told him what happened and he was just as shocked as the rest of us.

"Crazy thing about all of this is, had her siblings not come forward, you'd still be in denial. You still would've been believing her story over mine as if a seven year old had a reason to lie about someone touching him." Raymond was getting upset. My mother had her head down in shame as he spoke.

"Now we have family members who were born through incest." My mother tried to speak up but he stopped her.

"No, it wasn't your fault but you knew Charlene was sleeping with young boys so it should've never been questioned when I told you what she did." I agreed with everything Raymond said.

"Forgiving you for not believing me would do what for you, huh? Will it ease your mind? Relax your conscience or make you feel better about being a piece of shit mother to me after finding out because you were in denial? Tell me what forgiving you would do for me?" Raymond hadn't spoken to my mother in years because of the situation and like I said, back then he never came out of his room except for school and eating.

"Raymond, I'm sorry. Charlene was my mother and—"

"And I'm tired of hearing the same story. *"She was my mom*

and I didn't want to believe it? Why would she touch a child? She wouldn't do that to me, blah, blah, blah." He mocked her.

"Everything ok?" Julio walked in the house from work.

"I wanted to see Raymond but it's clear that he doesn't want anything to do with me." My brother chuckled.

"Just like you to try and gain sympathy. I'm ready, Bro." I waited to follow his lead because it didn't feel as if he was finished venting.

"Oh yea." I knew it. Raymond was by the door.

"Don't make any more requests to see me. If I want to see you, then I'll find my way here. Otherwise, keep your distance like you have been and I'll do the same." Raymond walked out. I started the car from inside the house and unlocked the door for him to get in.

"Onyx, why does he speak to me that way?" Julio and I looked at one another. Was she serious?

"Charlene and our aunt did horrible things to him so if he doesn't want to forgive or speak to you then that's his choice. The more you try and force a relationship, the worse it will get."

"But he's my son." I headed to the door.

"And he was your son when Charlene did those things to him too." She gave me a surprised look.

"What happened to him didn't happen to me. Therefore, I can't explain how he's feeling but I do know, he is who he is." And with that I left her there to bask in her own thoughts.

Raymond had every right to feel the way he did. My mother let him down and he wasn't trying to relive the past by going down memory lane with her. I'm not saying she was doing that but asking for forgiveness over the past that a person was trying to move on from was almost the same.

"You good?" I asked getting in the car.

"Yup. Where's my seafood?" He made both of us laugh. Instead of taking him to the house with Mariah, we went to a different spot. As long as Raymond was good, so was I. My mother would most likely question me on it later and I'd tell her the same thing I've always did. Let my brother be. If he doesn't want to come around you, then that's how it had to be.

Chapter Four

BLOCK

"You gotta eat something." My mother handed me a take-out tray of food she made at the house. Ever since the shooting, she's been by my side and I'm grateful as fuck for it.

Janetta Winston was soft as a teddy bear on the inside, but her exterior was like bricks. You couldn't break her for nothing unless it had something to do with family; mainly her kids. That woman went to war with any and every one over me and Arabia; including my pops. Yes, she was a daddy's girl, yet Arabia could do no wrong in my mother's eyes either.

"I'm not hungry." Pushing the tray away, she placed it on the nightstand in the room and sat next to me. Intertwining her hand in mine, she squeezed it before speaking.

"What happened to River was devastating for you, her

family and mainly her son, Jasir." I turned my head and cracked a smile seeing him sitting on Chana's lap close to the bed. He had his iPad and earphones on. All of us have been around one another every day.

When Chana arrived to the hospital, my pops told me, she could barely see from the tears coming down. Ryan must've told her over the phone after we called him that night because I couldn't even believe it myself. Why would Huff shoot her? It couldn't have been over her smacking him. There had to be more to his reasoning.

"You know a long time ago when you and Arabia were kids, someone shot your father." I sat there listening because we've been told the story a million times and he showed the scars from the three spots the bullets went in. There was a drug deal gone bad and a shootout occurred in which he suffered.

"The truth of the story was that some woman, he cheated on me with did it." I swung my head in her direction.

"I know. We told you a different story and let me tell you why." I slouched down in my chair and removed my hand from hers.

"Your dad did cheat on me a few times and to be honest, I deserved it." I looked at her.

"Yea. Your father would get on my nerves by staying out all night hustling and to me, it was taking away from his family." She explained how she always knew where he was so there was never a moment she suspected him stepping out.

"Long story short, trying to teach him a lesson and prove

other men wanted me, I slept with someone else." I hated that she was telling me this. The original story sounded better.

"Your father found out, most likely killed the guy and decided to give me a taste of my own medicine." I shook my head.

"The woman he cheated with fell in love but the feelings weren't returned from your father. She saw him out and said if he wasn't gonna be with her, then he wouldn't be with anyone." My mother started demonstrating how the woman was allegedly shooting blindly and what she looked like doing it. Chana was laughing while I was turning my face up at her pretending to be the lady from Terminator.

"I stayed by your father's side until he was better. We talked things out and never stepped out on the other since."

"Wow, Mrs. Winston, that sounds like one heck of a story." My mom cut her eyes at Chana.

"Just because I said you resembled Aaliyah and not Velma like your sister didn't mean butt in on our conversation." Chana definitely resembled her.

"I'm just saying, why lie to your kids?" She shrugged.

"The same reason your daddy lied about who he was." Ernie gave Chana little information about the incest. She knew about Louise being her aunt and mother but he never told her how it all happened until that day at my mother's house. After hearing it myself, I wouldn't have wanted to tell anyone either.

"He didn't lie, he just kept things away from me."

"Sounds like a lie." My mother rolled her eyes.

"Anyway, before I was rudely interrupted by Changing

Faces." My mother was just saying anything at this point. I asked Chana not to respond to anything else.

"All I'm saying is you have to take care of yourself. River wouldn't want this." She handed me the tray again. I opened it to see fried chicken, baked mac and cheese, yams, fresh string beans and a piece of cornbread. Jasir hopped off Chana's lap to come where I was on the other side.

"Mmm, Grandma Netta." That's what he called her. They only met a few times but from the very first day, she told him to call her that. My father had him use Pop Pop. It was as if they knew me and River would be together.

"Where's my food?"

"Who said I was bringing you food? You haven't skipped a meal." She poked at his belly.

"Grandma." He pouted.

"Fine. It's on the counter over there. You're very greedy." She walked over to remove it from the bag. Jasir sat at the table with his iPad propped up while my mom got him comfortable. Realizing there was no plastic ware, her and Jasir went down the hall to get some. Chana stepped out to use the phone so it only left me and River. Placing the tray on the seat, I stood to fix her covers. Jasir laid in the bed with her for a while and the bottom half of the blanket was off her legs.

"You gotta get up, River. Jasir misses you, we all miss you. Shit, Arabia been up here a lot even though the doctor placed her on strict bed rest." My sister had grown a tight bond with her so she was taking it just as hard.

River was shot in the chest by Huff at close range. She fell

31

face first on the ground, breaking her nose and causing two black eyes. We had no idea that when River hit the floor it was worse than we thought. She had a brain bleed and evidently a heart attack as well. Sadly, with so much trauma to her body at once, she slipped into a coma.

When my mother first told me she died, I couldn't take it. I've never had any health problems but hearing those words made my blood pressure skyrocket. The doctors thought I'd have a stroke and had me taken into a room. Once I opened my eyes, they had to sedate me because I wanted to see River's body before going to the morgue. The shit Arabia went through not laying eyes on Deray wasn't something I wanted to deal with.

My pops and both uncles waited for me to relax and told me the truth. I'll admit, learning that River was alive, made me feel better but knowing she was in a coma fucked me up. That woman had gone through so much and still stood strong after hearing who her parents were. It wasn't fair what she was going through.

"I'm supposed to get you pregnant so I can get corrective eye surgery for the baby." Making jokes made me crack a smile.

"You better not ask me to wear a condom either when you wake up." I felt movement and looked down to see one of her fingers moving. She had been in a coma for three and a half weeks and this was the first time she moved.

"Come on, River. I know you hear me. Walk to the light."

"Bro, she not supposed to go in the light. That's when people die." Onyx said, walking in.

"Whatever. I don't know what to say in order for her to wake up. What if the light is waking her up?"

"How she see it if she sleep? Think, bro, think." Onyx used his pointer finger to touch my temple.

"Oh shit." My mother yelled making me and Onyx look. River had her eyes opened and seconds later closed them back.

"Open them back up. Stay awake, River." I sat on the bed trying to wake her up but it wasn't working. Chana pressed the nurses button after we told her what happened.

Twenty minutes later, the doctor stepped in and did an exam. He explained that patients can hear family members speaking and when they're trying to come out of the coma, their eyes may open and close a few times. He did reassure us that her wound was healing perfectly but feeling on her right side may have been affected. Meaning movement can be limited for River due to nerves being damaged with the shooting. He also said, gunshot victims could have chronic pain in the future.

"When will my mommy wake up?" Jasir asked, trying to get on the bed. Onyx lifted him up and we all watched him get under the covers.

"Soon." The doctor responded. We asked a few more questions before he left.

"I hope she wakes up soon. I'm tired for feeding her greedy ass son."

"Grandma, you love feeding me."

"What I tell you about being in grown folks business?" She scolded him in a sarcastic type of way.

"You said, listen to everything and come back to tell you." We all started laughing.

"That's right and don't you forget it." She kissed his cheek and went home for the night. Chana and Onyx left a few hours later and she dropped Jasir off on the way. His grandmother, Ms. Rogers was waiting for him. She had been up here daily as well and from how close they were, she wasn't taking it well either.

"What up? I heard she opened her eyes." Ryan stepped in. I checked the time and it was after midnight. He did his regular walk through when on duty and stopped by for about two hours to sit. I'd go home to change and come right back. He may not be hood but I knew he wouldn't allow anyone in the room that wasn't family.

"Yea. Next time we're hoping it would be longer." He nodded.

"Jasir's birthday is next week. I'm gonna hold off on the party since it was at your place." River asked me if she could throw it there due to all the backyard space.

She wanted to have animals, clowns, an ice cream truck, a bouncy house, some damn Power Ranger characters he loved was coming and she brought a bunch of fireworks for the end. To me it was dramatic but she wanted it. Her father was footing the bill so she spared no expense.

"That's cool. You still taking him to Dave & Busters?" His birthday fell during the week and they always took him out on that day.

"Yea. Chana's brothers are coming too. That way he'll have someone to play with."

"Make sure you tell those motherfuckers not to teach Jasir how to cuss." We started laughing. I hadn't met them yet but River gave me an earful of who they were.

"She's gonna be ok, Block." That came outta nowhere.

"The doctor said it was a good thing the shooting happened in the hospital, otherwise she wouldn't have made it." I leaned my head against the wall as he reminded me.

"Just make sure I'm the first one you call so Jasir can see her. Between Chana, her stepmother, and your mom, they're all in a race to be here." He wasn't lying. Each of them called me at least four or five times a day asking if she had woken up and that's after they left.

"You got it." We spoke a little longer and he went back to work. Soon as he walked out the room, River opened her eyes again. Instead of getting excited, I waited to see how long it would last. Her eyes went from side to side as she slowly lifted one of her hands to wipe the tears. I'm not even sure why she was crying or when it happened. After two or three minutes of staring, I made myself known. The smile on her face was barely there because of the tube in her mouth but I saw the corners of her mouth turned up. Pressing the button for a nurse because I didn't want to leave and she go back to sleep, River reached for my hand.

"It's about time you woke up." I kissed her forehead.

"Jasir is with Ms. Rogers for the night and everyone else just left." She didn't ask but I'm sure she wanted to know.

"Welcome back, Miss Thomas." The doctor walked in and proceeded to do an exam. He held the light to her eyes, and checked the monitors over for her pressure and heart rate.

"Ok, Miss Thomas, I'm going to use this reflex hammer on your knees and elbows. Then I'm going to run this pen up and down your right side. Nod your head if you feel anything." When she nodded her head, I was relieved.

"That's great. Now, I'm going to send you down for some Cat Scans and a MRI of your brain to make sure there's no bleeding." He explained how they hadn't seen any the last time he checked but because she was awake, he wanted to look again. After walking out, I called up Ryan.

"What up?" Placing him on speaker so River could hear, she grabbed my hand.

"She's awake."

"Really? That's great. I'll be right there." He hung up.

"You need anything?" River turned her head side to side.

"I'm happy as hell you woke up." She lifted her hand slow to wipe the few tears streaming down my face. Hell yea, I was crying. River was definitely my other half and like Ryan said before, it's ok to show emotion for the woman you love.

"It's about damn time you woke up." My mother barged in the room talking shit.

When River opened her eyes, Ryan was the only one told. He and I both felt it necessary for Jasir to be the first one to see her. It would become very chaotic once the family found out. I have to admit, the joy on her face seeing her son put a smile on everyone in the room. He couldn't jump and hug her the way he used to and he damn sure wouldn't leave her side.

"Hey." Her voice was very raspy and dry ever since the tube was removed.

She did ask the doctor to leave the catheter in until she felt comfortable getting out of bed. It had only been a day but she was adamant about getting up sooner than later. The occupational therapist popped in earlier and explained the exercises she'd be doing to help get her stronger.

"Listen here, Heffa. Your son greedy as hell. You need to get better and feed him before people start saying he malnourished." River laughed.

After about an hour, River said she was in pain and asked the nurse to give her some medication. That was everyone's cue to leave; including mine. I wanted to run home and change.

"I'll be back."

"Please don't leave me."

"Ryan has one of his friends watching the door. No one can get in and there's a nurse I'm cool with who's down for whatever." She was engaged to one of my boys and carried her weapon everywhere. It didn't matter if it was an open carry state or not; she did what she wanted.

"I'll be back in an hour." She finally agreed when the medicine kicked in. I wasn't comfortable leaving, yet I'm not worried about anyone coming up here either.

Chapter Five

RIVER

"**G**ood Morning." The therapist was cheery as heck today. Block came out the bathroom after brushing his teeth and washing his face.

After he left the other day, panic struck and I made him stay on the phone with me until he walked back in the room. I was afraid Huff would return and regardless of the nurse he had on standby, the guard outside, it only felt safe when he was around.

"Good morning." I let the bed go lower, slid my legs to the side and sat up. This would be the third day she'd been here.

On day one, she had me lifting my right arm and the pain was out of this world. She decided on working my other limbs to make sure the stiffness wouldn't limit any movement.

Day two, there was still pain, yet I allowed her to do a few exercises with me. The initial discomfort could've been because my arm hadn't moved in weeks.

Today she was supposed to have me do some lifting on my own. I had to be strong because the doctor already said, he wouldn't discharge me until he saw me able to move. He also made plans to have the catheter removed only if the therapist could get me to at least stand, if not walking. Standing was ok because I could get in a wheelchair to use the bathroom.

However, this too would be my first which was why she brought an extra person. I've never been one to take anything for granted and this shooting allowed me to see that in a split second your life can be taken.

"Ok, Miss Thomas. Me and Mark." He was the guy with her.

"We are going to have you stand. You don't have to move right away." I nodded and looked over at Block.

He was standing in the corner watching. Before they came he helped me put a sweater on because this hospital was very cold. I couldn't put pants on yet but the sweater and the ties in back of the gown was able to keep me from exposing myself.

"How do you feel?" Soon as she asked, my legs buckled.

"Shit!" I yelled. They sat me on the bed.

"It's ok. This was your first time. Your legs have to get used to the weight of your body."

"Give me a minute and I want to try again." They nodded.

"Take your time, River. Don't stress yourself out trying to walk." Block was now on the opposite side of the bed talking to me.

"But I wanna go home." I whined.

"I want you to come home too. Shit, I'm horny as fuck." The therapist fell into a fit of laughter and the guy's face was beet red.

"Really?"

"What you mean really? You been down for a minute and ain't nobody fucking me like you. The way you used—"

"Ok. I get it, Block." I had to cut him off.

"You know that was rude of you not to let me finish talking." I swung my neck in his direction and gave him a dirty look.

"Whatever." He backed himself up to the wall.

"Miss Thomas, are you ready to try again?" I nodded. As they assisted me to stand, it felt like all my weight was overpowering me. Instead of telling them, I stood there trying to take it in. If I continue to sit each time, I'll never walk.

"We're going to let go in order for you to stand alone." When they removed their arms, my body started to shake. Grabbing the side rail of the bed gave me some support.

"That's good, Miss Thomas. Do you want to take a step?" Looking over at Block, he smiled which gave me confidence.

"One, two, three, four..." As they held onto me and counted, my legs kept going. I'm nowhere near ready to walk regularly but being up and out the bed was refreshing.

"Let's walk back." They allowed me to walk to the door with their assistance.

"You did great. Tomorrow, I'll come in with a walker."

"A walker? She not going to be a handicapped person

forever; is she?" Why was Block like this? I can't really blame him when his momma the same way.

"No, Sir. The walker would allow Miss Thomas to move on her own without our help. If she does well, we can take it away and she'd walk alone."

"Oh, a'ight. I was about to say we ain't using no walker when I bend you over. Or when we role playing the…"

"BLOCK!"

"It's ok, Miss Thomas. A lot of the boyfriends and husbands are like that. They want to make sure sexual activity won't be limited."

"Yea, what she said."

"Why didn't you just say that?" I retorted making myself comfortable in the bed.

"I did. You just didn't like the way I said it." All I could do was shake my head.

"So, we'll see you in two days." She explained her day off was tomorrow and since I'm comfortable with her and the guy, she wanted to keep me as her patient. I'm ok with that because walking took a lot out of me.

They had the leg compressions on me when I was in a coma to keep the blood circulating, but not being on your feet for weeks can be hard.

"Bye." They stepped out leaving me and Block alone. He went to the door and put a chair in front of it. He better not assume we having sex because ain't no way.

"You gotta do something." Block started unbuckling his belt and pulled his dick out.

"Pass me, my phone." It wasn't much I could do with a weak arm. The catheter was still inside me and my mouth was in no condition to give head. After asking him to help me remove my shirt and the gown, I laid there completely naked with the sheet covering my pussy and the catheter. Thankfully, no poop was in it.

"Here." He sat on the bed next to me. If we couldn't have sex there was other things to do.

"What's this?" Block hit play and let a grin creep on his face.

"When did you do this?" It was a recording of us having sex the night of the shooting. I pressed record on the way in his room and placed the phone on the dresser.

"Damn, you look sexy as fuck naked." His dick started to get hard.

"Kiss me." He leaned down to do what I asked and started to jerk himself off. I'm not gonna lie, he was turning me on.

"You feel so good, baby. Right there." Hearing myself moaning over the phone had me sliding my own hand in between my legs. Using two of my fingers to rub my clit while we kissed, had both of us getting hot.

"Mmmm, I wish you were inside me right now. I miss feeling your dick go in and out." Our kissing became aggressive.

"I'm about to cum, Block. Go faster so we can cum together." He stopped kissing me, went faster on himself as he watched me doing the same thing.

"Shit."

"Keep playing with that pussy." His dick was hard as hell and as much as I wanted to give him head, I couldn't.

"Block, I'm about to." My body became hot and the blood was rushing through my veins.

"Me too."

"Cum on my body the way I like. I want to feel all that warm cum." He stood and turned to me. Me and Block did a lotta freaky things in the bedroom.

"You sure? It's gonna be a lot."

"Yessssss. Fuck yes." My orgasm was right there. When cum coated my chest, my body jerked at the same time from releasing myself.

"Damn." He leaned down to kiss me.

"I fucking love you, girl. Shit, I needed that." His hands cupped my breasts and once again, we were back at it. This time, I had him turn the lights off, close the blind and get in bed with me. Block removed all his clothes and got in.

He mounted me on top, spread my ass cheeks and guided me down slow. I'm not sure why we didn't think of doing it this way first.

"Got damn, River. I ain't never leaving you." His hands were massaging my breasts from behind as I took the pain from having anal sex like a pro. It didn't matter that the catheter was moving around on the bed or that it could possibly burst. The only thing on either of our minds was pleasuring one another.

"That ass getting wetter. Fuck!" He used his strength to move me up and down like I was riding him.

"Block, make me cum hard." Anal sex had a way of making

a person hot and once that orgasm started to brew, the feeling was inexplainable. My eyes were fluttering and my stomach was tightening up. I had him pass me a pillow to stifle my moans.

"That ass looks real good, River." He gently bit down on my back and both of us released. Lying on top of him with my back pressed to his chest, he wrapped his arm as around me. Our breathing was slowing down.

"I can't believe we just fucked with that shit in your pussy." I started laughing.

"Whatever my man wants, he'll get." As he moved me, I could feel his dick sliding out.

"Let me start the shower."

"Babe, I can't walk in there."

"I'm gonna carry you." Watching him get up made me smile. He was not the only handsome with an amazing body, he was my rock and I'd do anything for him.

"Let's go." He carried me in and had me sit in the shower seat. The water felt good beating down on me, especially since I've been doing the sponge bath thing. A few minutes later, he stepped in and locked the door.

"I grabbed my clothes, and took the sheets and blankets off. When we're done, I'll contact housekeeping." He got in the shower, and started to wash me up.

Being extra careful around the chest wound, he cleaned me up well. The bandages were gone but this was my first time in the shower. When he finished washing himself, he turned the shower off and grabbed our towels.

"Chana brought you some more clothes." He placed lotion

on my body, put a black T-shirt on and a pair of sweats. I'm not comfortable trying to wear a bra again yet so my breasts will be free. Helping me put the sweats on, he lifted the urine bag. It felt a little uncomfortable from the tube but it was better than only sitting in that gown.

"You ready?" He asked after putting clean clothes on. Block kept his own stuff here too, so he didn't have to leave as much.

"Yea." Opening the door, he lifted me up and carried me to the recliner. Afterwards, he pressed the button for house-keeping to come and asked the nurse to change my bag.

"Wow, you look different." The older nurse spoke coming in the room.

"My man gave me a shower."

"Good job, young man. Most would leave her until we came in." If she only knew what we did to need that shower she'd laugh.

"Yea, he's pretty good to me." The nurse smiled. She went to get some things to remove the catheter. Evidently, the doctor felt since I'm doing therapy it was better to start using the bathroom on my own. Block had to lay me on the bed and pulled my sweats down for the nurse to get the catheter out. It was a slight discomfort but I'm happy it was removed. Block placed me back on the recliner.

"Shit, I could've waited to fuck. That way, I would've been able to put my son or daughter in you."

"We have more than enough time for that." He leaned down to kiss me.

"Hell yea, we do." For the rest of the day, he stayed with me.

I even had him walk with me every hour to get used to it. Of course I held him tight but he was a great help. Hopefully, I'll be able to go home soon.

* * *

"Mommy!" Jasir yelled, running toward me. He sat next to me with a smile on his face. The doctor discharged me a week later and Block forced me to stay with him until Brandon, Huff or whoever his name was, was found. I didn't mind because he had a huge place and since they waited for me to get better for my son's party, I could plan from here.

"Hey, Baby. What you doing here?" Ryan and Chana were supposed to take him to the party store. They went to order the balloons, and pick up the paper products because they store had every color.

"I wanted to see you. Didn't you want to see me?"

"Of course. I always want to see you." I hugged him and watched as he ran in the kitchen where Block and Onyx were talking.

"Clearly, he didn't want to really see me." I joked with Chana and Ryan who had a weird look on their face.

"What?" Chana stared at me.

"Louise wanted me to ask if you would stop by her house?"

"For what?"

"I'm not sure but when I went by, she had cleaned the entire place. It actually smelled like bleach." We laughed.

"One day, just not right now. I'm still healing and Jasir's party is coming up. I don't want any bad aura around me."

"I understand and I'll tell her."

"When did you two become friends?" I felt a tad bit jealous because my mother barely said two words to me, my entire life. Now her and Chana are close.

"When you were shot, I told her." I rolled my eyes.

"Regardless of the past, she was our mother. I've kept her updated on your status and she was happy to learn how well you were doing." That sounded like a lie.

"Believe it or not, she apologized for leaving me at the hospital."

"What?"

"I think it's what she wanted you to stop by for."

"I'm in no need of an apology." Chana nodded her head as if she understood.

"You didn't grow up with her. You didn't see your child lying on the floor dying or had him removed from your life. Do you know what that did to me watching my son get raised by his father?" Ryan sat there quiet.

"I'm thankful as hell to have the best baby father in the world but what she did, I could never forget or forgive. Especially when she admitted to wanting us to die." Chana came to sit next to me.

"You don't have to ever forgive or forget; shit you don't even have to go over there. I only mentioned it because I'm a woman of my word and told her I would." Chana lifted my face.

"She was very aware that you would be reluctant after what you went through." She hugged me.

"So, when are you and Block giving me a niece or nephew?" She changed the subject and rubbed my stomach.

"Whenever she stopped being stingy." Block stood behind me. I hadn't noticed him come from the kitchen.

"Block, don't start." Once we came home from the hospital, all I've been doing was sleeping and doing exercises the therapist gave me. Walking was better, yet still slow and my right side was very weak at times.

"Whatever. I'm taking it tonight." I laughed because there was no doubt that he would.

"Well, we didn't plan on staying long. Jasir wanted his mommy." Chana responded to Block.

"Since y'all have plans we're gonna take him. My mom made spaghetti."

"Oh, he's gonna be ecstatic." Jasir loved spaghetti; especially when his grandmother made it. After they left, Onyx stayed a little while longer and Block and I ate dinner and retired to the bedroom.

Chapter Six

ARABIA

"Waa, waa!" Hearing my baby cry had me wanting to rush down the stairs and snatch him up from those people but I promised my husband, I'd be nice.

I had my son two weeks after River slipped into a coma. My due date was approaching, yet it wasn't time. The doctor said the stress from being shot at outside the baby shower, and the constant back and forth to the hospital checking on my brother and River could've been the reason. I still get nervous leaving the house after going through that.

"Who the hell is shooting?" I panicked when Deray shouted as he sped off the street.

"Get down, Arabia." Doing what he said the best way I could,

I pressed the button for the seat to lean back and covered my eyes. There was no way I'd fit on the floor, nor could I climb in the back.

"You ok?" The truck stopped shortly after and it's when I noticed we were at the hospital.

"Fuck! I'm gonna kill that nigga." He jumped out the truck and ran to the passenger side.

"What... how was I not hit?" Looking around the truck on the inside there wasn't any bullet holes. However, when Deray helped me out, there were dents all over.

"The truck is bulletproof." He closed the door.

"Then why did you have me ducking?"

"Regardless if it were bulletproof or not, I had to make sure if by some chance they had bullets that could go through metal, you weren't hit."

"But I wasn't really covered." He grabbed my hand.

"That's why I pulled off quick and let my boys handle those niggas." Deray stopped for a second and looked down at me.

"If it came down to me or you, I would've took more bullets to save you and my son." His lips gently touched mine.

"Shoot." I bent over in pain. We rushed inside and one of the nurses had a tech come out to take me upstairs.

Thankfully, they did because not too long after, my family arrived and it was pure chaos in the emergency room. River was shot, my brother passed out, Mariah had her daughter and secrets were told. It was best for me not to exit out the way we came in because that would've been a lot to take in.

The following day, Deray had the mayor stop by to marry us. Don't ask me how he got it done, but we were Mr. and Mrs. Smith by noon. My parents and one of his friends were the witnesses. Once we said, I do and signed the paperwork, all of us went to the hospital to check on River, my brother and Mariah.

My little cousin was so pretty and I can't deny being aggravated hearing the shit that took place with Salina and Sean's brother.

My aunt told Mariah plenty of times to tell Onyx about Sean as did I. Mariah was stubborn and hardheaded which put her in the exact situation she was in. Now her and Onyx were legally separated but then again, I'm not sure he filed the paperwork after she signed it.

"Can I talk to you for a minute?" I looked toward the door and saw Tricia standing there along with his mother.

"Where is my son?" I snapped because Deray left and they were the only two here that I'm aware of.

"His grandfather downstairs feeding him." I rolled back over to finish watching television.

"Arabia, I'm sorry for not telling you about Deray, but he asked me to keep it quiet." Tricia spoke first. I closed my eyes taking a deep breath. This conversation was a long time coming.

"Arabia." His mom called my name.

"What!" I turned over to see both of them standing there shocked at my response.

"Mrs. Smith, I'm aware that your son requested you not inform me of him being alive. But did it ever occur to either of you to make him tell me? Huh? Both of you knew how devastated I was." Neither of them said a word.

"Tricia, you had him on FaceTime at my fucking doctor's appointment and when he wanted to come in both of you told him not to; why?"

"We didn't think it was a good idea." His mom answered.

"You didn't think it was a good idea." I chuckled.

"Why would you? Both of you were able to be around him so why tell me, right. There was no need for me to know." I was getting more and more aggravated.

"Y'all let me mourn a man who wasn't dead and the entire time y'all spent every moment with him." I shook my head.

"What's crazy was after the doctor's appointment and besides me coming by to visit, neither of you called to check on me. You didn't send me a message asking if I were ok or needed anything. My family was the only one who gave me the support I needed and you had the fucking audacity to come in my house questioning me on why I'm not speaking to you." His mother turned her face up.

"That's right, my house. My name is on that deed and all his bank accounts." Tricia sucked her teeth.

"You come here wondering why I'm not speaking when the whole time he was pretending to be dead, you had no problem not contacting me."

"Arabia." I cut his mother off.

"Deray felt my wrath as well for what he did so don't think I'm only confronting you two because the entire situation was uncalled for." Again, no response from them, not that I expected one.

"As a woman, Tricia, you didn't think to tell him what he was doing wasn't right." She rolled her eyes.

"I guess not being he was around you and your daughter, and the fact you was tryna fuck him." His mother gasped.

"Yea, Deray showed me the messages you sent about being upset that he chose me to marry and spend the rest of his life with. What was it you said, *You and him belong together and I can't satisfy him the way you could.*" I reminded her of the text she sent.

"Tricia."

"You wanted to know why he chose me to be his wife. Oh, yea and since I assumed you were dead, I'd never know. That about summed it up, right Tricia." His mom was shocked to say the least. Shit, I was too when he told me. To my knowledge, Tricia was into her partner but evidently the chick left her after finding out she wanted Deray.

"Deray never had any issues with someone trying to kill him until you. Damn right I felt we belonged together. My daughters father almost died because of you and hell no I didn't feel bad for you mourning. No, I didn't feel sad that he wanted you to think he was dead, and you damn right I stayed at his parents' house and fucked him." Now that was unexpected but not a surprise. Deray told me everything when we started speaking but I promised not to say a word. He didn't want Tricia to try and keep their daughter away..

"What the hell?" His mom must not have known.

"What's crazy is my husbanddddd." I drug out the word.

"Already told me about you waking him up by sucking his dick. It happened two weeks after he came home. He was heavily medicated and his body wasn't even healed, yet you hopped on his dick." I shook my head. I was pissed hearing that and it made me look at her different. Who sexually assaults someone while they're incapable of fighting them off.

"That was a savage move knowing how weak he was, but what's more crazy was to know he called you my name the entire time and you continued." Mrs. Smith turned her face up. Deray knew it wasn't me and only laid there due to being weak. I still say he should've pushed her off but I wasn't in the position to know how incapacitated he really was.

"You even let him cum inside you in hopes he got you pregnant. Maybe you should tell Mrs. Smith what happened afterwards." Complete silence from Tricia but the hateful look let me know I had that bitch.

"I'll tell her." I smiled.

"He called you over the next day when his parents left. You thought it was to fuck again until he put that gun to your head and threatened to pull the trigger if you didn't take a plan b." Mrs. Smith gasped again. He was still weak and refused to take any medication for the pain until he dealt with her that day.

"His boy brought it for him and stayed to make sure you

took it as well. If I'm not mistaken he had you take an abortion pill too, right. Granted it was too early for it but my husband made sure you would never birth another one of his kids."

"Fuck you, bitch." I smirked at her response.

"That nigga should've killed you at the McDonald's. How you think he found your stupid ass at Deray's other house? That's right, I knew all about you. I'm the one who told Huff that you were fucking my man and where you'd be."

"Say what?" Was she admitting to setting Deray up.

"I was mad as hell watching them shoot Deray at the door. You were supposed to answer it and die." I've answered his door many times so it could've been me that was shot.

"What the fuck you just say?" None of us knew Deray was standing at the door. It didn't matter at this point, I jumped on Tricia.

"Oh my, God!" I heard his mom say.

"That's enough, Arabia." Deray was pulling me off Tricia. I was mad because she didn't deserve to live any longer. Banging her head on the ground one last time before he managed to get me off completely, I was able to stomp on her face.

"Calm down."

"Deray... she admitted... she set up..." I was outta breath still trying to speak.

"I heard her. Are you ok?" He checked over me.

"Yes. Babe, let me finish." He leaned down to kiss me and just like that, I started relaxing.

"You're upsetting our daughter." He placed his hand on my

belly. We hadn't mentioned the pregnancy to anyone yet. I'm not sure if the baby was a girl but it's what he wanted.

"What's going on up here?" Deray's father stepped in the room.

"Tricia set up Arabia to be killed. She's the reason our son was shot and—" Mrs. Smith was distraught trying to explain.

"Are you ok, Arabia?" He asked, hugging his wife.

He came over after the shooting at the baby shower and explained why he didn't mention Deray being alive. His reason was the same as theirs and he did apologize and asked me to forgive him. Unlike his mother and Tricia who had a get over it type of attitude from what I gathered.

"I'm fine."

"You need to handle Tricia." He spoke directly to Deray. We all turned to where she was laying and noticed the bitch left. When did she get up?

"I'm gonna find her." I nodded because it was up to him to handle her. Going into my son's room, I smiled down at him sleeping peacefully. With so much going on I was surprised he slept through it.

After checking the house to make sure she left and the security cameras, it was confirmed. Deray made a few calls to have people searching for her. His mom did apologize again but I remained quiet because I wasn't sure if forgiving her right now was what I wanted to do. Eventually, I will but right now finding both of our ex's was at the top of our list. They needed to be found expeditiously because no one wanted enemies lurking.

Deray took me to the hospital to get checked out. His parents watched DJ at their house because he wasn't sure if Tricia would return. He had gates all around this new house but he wanted to take extra precaution.

We found out the baby was fine but the doctor did suggest no more fighting. On the way home, we stopped at a diner to grab some food. Afterwards, we pick DJ up, drove home, put him to sleep, showered and Deray made love to me for as long as I could take it.

* * *

"I know you beat that bitch ass." Mariah joked, handing DJ back to me. She stopped by because Onyx was at the house with their daughter. They still weren't on speaking terms and in a way I don't blame her. Salina was too comfortable coming around when she wasn't asked.

We haven't spoken much either after that fiasco she caused with River. It was jealousy but I admit, I missed talking to my cousin all the time.

"Hell yea."

"That bitch nasty as hell for sleeping with him while he was damn near sleep himself." I agreed and pulled my boob out to breastfeed. I was slowly weening DJ off because I didn't like the feeling.

I only tried it due to the damn nurse saying it was healthy and kids don't get sick which I knew was a lie. It's plenty of women who breastfed their kids and they still got sick. I'm thankful he loved the formula too because it would've been a lot harder.

Mariah stayed over a little longer and decided to run some errands before going home. Once Deray came home, he took the baby and gave me time to myself. I really enjoyed being married as well as being a mom.

Chapter Seven

MARIAH

"**D**o I really want to go inside? If I'm trying to do better, then this had to be done." I spoke to myself getting out the car. This was the last place I'd ever think to show up at.

Walking toward the house, I noticed the outside door was opened. You could hear a woman screaming and glass breaking. Not sure which house I'm actually looking for, I took slow steps in case someone came out swinging. I waited a few minutes before going inside, and proceeded since there wasn't any more screaming.

"Hello." I wasn't loud just in case this was the wrong place.

"Help me." A low voice could be heard inside the apartment with the door opened. Being nosy, I popped my head in and didn't see anyone. The coffee table was broke in half, there was glass all over the floor and the television was face down. The sight only proved there was some sort of altercation.

"Help me." The voice spoke again only this time, I saw some legs moving on the opposite side of the couch. Still not aware if this was the correct place, I stayed put until a photo on the wall caught my attention.

"Hello. River." I called out. Making my way inside the apartment and to where she was, I found her on the ground with blood gushing out the side of her head. Well, that's what it seemed.

"What the fuck?" Quickly grabbing my phone, I dialed Onyx number. Block wasn't speaking to me so he was the only one I knew would answer and get here.

"What's up?" He answered and for a moment I smiled hearing his voice.

"Yo, Mariah. You there?" He yelled.

"Oh, yea. Onyx, I'm at River's house and—" He cut me off immediately.

"What the fuck are you doing there? Mariah, I swear you better not be starting no shit." He instantly went into defense mode.

"Onyx, listen. Something bad happened to her."

"What you mean?"

"She needs an ambulance from what I see and it wasn't me who did it." I looked around for a towel or something for her head but nothing was visible.

"Fuck! Is she ok?"

"I don't know. She's barely breathing and it's a lot of blood but I'm not sure where it's coming from."

"A'ight. Your mom stopped by so I'm leaving Heaven with her. You good?" I loved that he still worried about me.

"Yes but I don't know where the person went." After saying that, there was a noise in the other room.

"Shit, the person still here." I whispered.

"Get out the house, Mariah. I'm on the way." He yelled making me drop the phone. As I picked it up, there was a grip on my wrist.

"My son. Please get my son." River had tears streaming down her face.

"Where is he?" Jasir was a sweet kid and my family loved him.

"My son. Get my son." Was all she said before passing out. Not knowing anything about this place, I went in the kitchen, no Jasir. Both bedrooms were empty but the bathroom door was closed.

"No. No. Stop it. My mommy said no." I could hear Jasir. When the door opened, my eyes couldn't believe what they were seeing. Charlene had Jasir in the bathroom naked. He was in the corner covering his private area and this bitch was recording or taking pictures of him on her phone.

"Bitch, are you fucking crazy?" I hit her so hard, she dropped her phone and fell in the bathtub. I lifted my foot and stomped her in the stomach a few times. Remembering Jasir was in here, I looked over and saw him shaking and crying.

"Jasir."

"Don't touch me. No one can touch me there." I was tearing up myself hearing him say that. Did Charlene touch him? How long was she here? What did she do to him?

"I'm not going to hurt you. Block and Onyx are on the way." I put my hand out for him to grab it but he refused.

"I want my daddy." His lips were trembling.

"Jasir, I'm not going to hurt you. I promise help is on the way. Can you come with me to get dressed?" It took him a few minutes to believe me and that hurt because had I not been a bitch to his mother, he'd know I'm here to help.

"Where's my mommy?" Grabbing one of the towels to wrap him up, I removed him from the bathroom. Charlene was laid out in the bathtub with her feet in the air.

"Is this your room!" He nodded.

"Ok. I'm going to close the door. Put some clothes on and meet me out here." I went to close it and he stopped me.

"Don't leave. What if she touched me again?" Those words stung like crazy because it confirmed what I hoped wasn't true.

"She won't. I beat her up and Block is coming."

"Please don't leave me here." As much as I wanted to hug him, it was best to give him space. Jasir only had a towel on and he may think otherwise.

"I'm not. I'll be right here when you get dressed." I closed the door and called 911 first and then Onyx. Grabbing Charlene's phone out the bathroom, I rushed back to Jasir's door. I didn't want him to think I left.

"I'm almost there. Block will probably beat me. Do me a favor and keep your smart remarks to yourself."

"Onyx."

"I don't know why you're there but if something happened to her, Block will ask questions."

"I'm dressed. Where's my mommy?" Jasir interrupted me before I could answer. He had on sweats, a shirt and sneakers. The iPad was in his hands as well.

"I'll be there soon." He hung up. I put the phone in my pocket and had him sit on the couch. River was on the opposite side laid out and I didn't want him to see her.

"Stay right here. Ok. Don't move." He nodded. I ran in the kitchen to grab paper towels. Running them under the water, I made my way to where River was laying. There was blood coming from the side of her head. I almost gagged seeing the thick clots.

"My son." River spoke very low with her eyes closed. This chick had to be superwoman because it seemed like she was going to hell and back every other month.

"He's ok." I responded hoping she heard me.

"What the fuck happened?" Block barked, pushing me out the way. When he saw the blood, I could see rage in his eyes.

"It wasn't me." I told him to go check the bathroom.

"Ain't nobody in there."

"What? It has to be. That's where I left her." Rushing in to see for myself, Charlene was indeed missing.

"The bitch must've left when I had Jasir get dressed." The bathroom was down the hall from his room. She must've crept out after I grabbed the phone off the floor. The bitch was quiet as hell because I didn't hear her.

"Dressed? Why was she here and did she—?" He couldn't even finish his sentence. My eyes gave him the answer to a question he couldn't ask.

"Did someone call for an ambulance?" We turned to see a cop and two EMT's standing there. I pointed to where River was lying and explained to them what I walked in on. They carefully put her on a stretcher after wrapping her head up in guaze to stop the bleeding.

"Why were you here?" Onyx questioned when they took River out. He arrived when the EMT's were on their way outside with her. Block followed behind the ambulance. He must've called Ryan on the way too because he showed up and took Jasir.

"I got her address from Arabia." He walked behind me to my car.

"For what?"

"To apologize." That was my intention. Unfortunately, it didn't happen.

"Apologize?"

"I wanted my husband back and I knew in order for it to happen, there could be no animosity between me and your family. I was trying to make it right but your grandmother got here before me and... and..." He hugged me.

"Jasir was terrified and I'm mad at myself for not getting here sooner to save him. River was bleeding really bad and... Onyx, he was so scared. Why did she do that? Why was she here?" I broke down thinking about what took place. To hear what Charlene did in the past was one thing but to see it for myself was another.

"He's gonna be fine. You got here in enough time."

"I don't know how much she did but—"

"It's ok, Mariah. She won't get to him again." I looked up at him wiping my face.

"She'll be staying with Block permanently She was only here to pick up more of her and Jasir's things." That made me feel better knowing Charlene won't bother Jasir again.

"She will be found." He kissed my lips and once his tongue entered my mouth, both of us fought to find out who was the better kisser.

"Y'all fucking out here or what because I could've stayed home for this." Onyx laughed. I turned to see a guy sitting in his car looking at what appeared to be his phone.

"Who is that?"

"My brother." I was surprised, especially since I've only known his mom to have one child.

"I'll explain later. Let's get to the hospital." He had me walk to his car.

"Raymond drive Mariah's car so she can ride with me."

"Nigga, ain't y'all divorced?" He retorted but opened the car door to get out.

"Mind your business."

"Well don't leave your separation paperwork lying around and I won't know." He extended his hand to mine.

"By the way, that punk is my brother; same mother and father. Our grandmother was a pervert and my mother knew which is why no one knew about me. I wanted it to stay that way but his cry baby ass brought me here to meet my niece, who looks just like me by the way." He joked.

"Anyway, I don't know how long you two been at odds but he definitely needs some pussy. Maybe he'll leave me the fuck alone and take me home." I started laughing and got in Onyx car.

"Just drive her car, damn. You stay with the drama."

"Fuck you. I hope she give you blue balls." The way those two went back and forth made me laugh. It also had me wondering why he wanted to remain a secret. Then again, it could be because Charlene was around. Whatever the case, I'm just happy Onyx and I were speaking.

"What they saying?" Onyx asked Block after walking in the emergency room. I know the doctors and nurses are tired of seeing us because we're tired of seeing them.

"Nothing yet. The doctor sent her for a MRI of the brain and some Cat scans."

"What the hell you doing here? You don't even like her." Onyx squeezed my hand when Chana approached me.

"I'm the one who found her."

"And why were you at her house? Onyx did you send her there to fight River?" This chick was beside herself.

"Chana, you're upset right now and I get it. But don't ask me no dumb shit like that."

"Why not? She can't stand River and we're supposed to

believe she didn't do this. You know what, you're no longer pregnant. Let me whoop your ass real quick like my sister did." Chana started removing her earrings.

"First off, you not whooping shit. Second, go sit the fuck down. Ain't nobody got time for your attitude either." Onyx answered for me.

"Whatever. If River wakes up and says she did this, she will see me." Chana went to walk away.

"Oh, and I'm gonna beat the fucking brakes off you." As bad as I wanted to respond, Onyx asked me not to. She had every right to be mad, especially since me and River didn't speak. I'd be asking the same exact questions.

"Is she ok?" All of us turned to see the woman known as River's mother. Now that's who Chana should ask why she's there. She did appear to be worried.

"They're running tests on her." Block responded which shocked me.

"Why is this happening to her? Once she got away from me, her life was supposed to be better. This is all my sister's fault. Had she not forced me to do those horrible things, I could've been a better mother; a better grandmother." Her mother started pacing the hospital waiting room.

"River will be fine." Block walked over and hugged her. Again, that shocked me as well. Then again, I'd probably know they spoke if I hadn't shut everyone out.

After staying for another four hours, the doctor finally emerged from the back. He called everyone in a room to keep the others out of her business.

"Miss Thomas suffered head trauma that caused some minor bleeding on her brain. There was a huge knot and a large gash on her forehead. We had to give her twenty five stitches. The black eye will go away and so will the bruises on her back. Does anyone know if she was attacked because she had all the signs."

"Yes she was." I answered and explained what I walked in on; leaving out the part with her son.

"Oh, well lucky for her the baby survived." Everyone directed their attention to Block who had a smile on his face. Onyx told me after she lost the first baby, he wanted to get her pregnant again.

"She will be in a lot of pain for the next few weeks and most likely suffer from constant headaches. I'm keeping her for a few days to make sure her and the baby are ok. In the meantime, she's asleep and visiting hours are over. One person can stay the night with her but everyone else can return tomorrow."

Block asked if River's mom could see her and told him, he'll be staying the night. Onyx let Block know he'd be up in the morning to sit with her so he could go home and change. What a damn day.

!!!!!! Trigger Warning !!!!!!

Please be advised that the content in the following
chapter may be disturbing due to a sensitive subject
regarding incest, abuse, & sexual assault. It will contain
traumatic scenarios that some may not want to read.
If you do decide to skip this chapter, it won't take away
from the book.
The story will continue with no lapse in it.

Thanks!!

Chapter Eight

RIVER

"**W**hat are you doing here and how the hell did you know where I lived?" I barked at Charlene.

"You're my niece and I think it's time we get to know one another." Was she serious? We're not even acquainted with one another. I've seen Charlene before but never really conversated with her.

"No thanks." I went to close the door and she pushed it open. Not trying to get into an altercation, I moved out the way.

"This is nice. Did Block buy you this furniture?" She walked around the living room being nosy. I don't recall her being this big, she gained weight.

"What do you want?" My arms were folded across my chest as she stood in front of the television observing.

"I know your mother gave you her side of the story. It's time I tell you mine."

"To be honest, Charlene, I'm ok not hearing anything else about the past. You can go." Turning my back to walk by the door she left open, I felt a hard push to my back. Being I just found out I'm pregnant minutes before she got here, I didn't react. Block and I wanted a baby. He didn't know yet; my plan was to tell him tonight.

"You are just as beautiful as your mom used to be." She stood behind me whispering with that hot breath. I turned around so now she was directly in front of me.

"Louise had some amazing pussy and my brother, your father had a big dick." I started gagging.

"After making them have sex, I'd make sure to indulge as well and I must say, they both enjoyed me pleasing them." I couldn't believe she was bragging about the things she did.

"They didn't even know you were doing that."

"Not the point. They both came so it must've felt good." When she slid her tongue down my neck, I punched her in the face.

"You're fucking disgusting." Pushing me back into the wall, I became dazed for a minute after hitting my head.

"I'm going to have some of you too." Using all my strength, I managed to push her off. We started fighting. She fell into the TV and then rushed me. Both of us were now fighting over top the coffee table. Once I heard it crack, I knew it was going to buckle.

"Get off me." I yelled and prayed Jasir had his headphones on. This was not a good time for him to come out his room.

"Get the fuck up." Charlene pulled me by the shirt and threw *me on the ground. This woman was strong as hell and after hitting my head and damn near breaking my back on the coffee table, I could barely fight her. Let alone I was still weak from the shooting. Because of my small frame it was taking a lot longer to recover.*

"Stop moving." She grabbed the lamp off the coffee table and hit me over the head with it. The shit hurt like hell and I instantly felt blood.

"At least I don't have to drug you." She slid her hand inside my sweats and forced her finger in between my legs.

"Mmmmmm you taste just as good as your mother. Let me see what it taste like when you cum in my mouth." All I could do was cry. She had the nerve to place kisses down my leg as if she was trying to get me turned on. I've never been assaulted like this in my life except for Brandon and it wasn't like this.

"Mommy." And just like that, Charlene stopped. Jasir was calling me from his room.

"Oh, it's my lucky day." When she got off of me, I pulled my sweats up and the second, I tried to get up, Charlene hit me with something harder, making me pass out. When I came to, Mariah was there which I assumed was a dream. I mean it had to be a dream because why would she be here. All I remember asking was her to get my son.

"Get my son. Please get my son." I woke up sweating profusely.

"River. River." I heard Block calling my name.

"My son. Where's my son?" My eyes popped open. Where am I? Where's Jasir?"

"River." He called my name again.

"Block, did you get Jasir? Please tell me that he's ok." The monitors were going berserk on the side of my head.

"Relax. He's ok." He sat on the bed and kissed my lips.

"Where is he? Did she—?" The words would not come out.

"Mariah arrived in time and called Onyx. By the time we got there, Charlene was gone." Tears cascaded down my face once he mentioned Jasir being ok.

"How you feeling?" He ran his hand down the side of my face. I held onto it tight.

"How did she find me?"

"I'm not sure but between her and Huff those two are hiding well." I laid there in a zone wondering if Charlene did anything inappropriate to my son, yet didn't want you to ask. At the moment, I'm incapable of doing anything but trust and believe I will find Charlene.

"Louise was here."

"Who told her?" We weren't really on speaking terms but she was still my mother. When Chana mentioned her wanting to see me, I refused. One day I'll get the strength to go over but not right now.

"Chana and she was very worried."

"Block, please be honest with me when I ask this next question." He nodded.

"Did we lose another baby?"

"No. You're still pregnant but I did ask the doctor if he could check the baby's eyes in your stomach." It hurt to laugh.

"I'm serious. I can't have my kid out here with fishbowl glasses." I shook my head listening to him. He was my man and I'm gonna stick by him.

* * *

"Mommy, why do you keep getting hurt?" Jasir questioned, sitting on my lap. It was three days after the attack and we were chilling at the house. There wasn't a need to fight Block on moving in because truth be told, I felt the need to have some sort of security.

"Mommy's strong, Jasir so even though she may be hurt, she always gets better." Chana answered for me.

"Grandma Netta said she's going to beat that lady up who touched me." My heart dropped hearing him say that. Up until this very moment no one said a word about Charlene doing anything to him. When me and Chana's eyes met, her head went down.

"Jasir let me talk to mommy for a minute." Maribel had one of my brothers take him in the room to play Xbox. Block brought him that and the PlayStation.

"Before you hyperventilate, let me fill you in."

"Ma." Chana interrupted.

"The only way she'll be able to deal with this is to hear what happened. If you keep things away from her, she'll never be able to move on." I agreed but did I want to hear.

"Honey." Maribel took my hand in hers. Block and Onyx

put their heads down while my father kept a mean mug on his face.

"Charlene made Jasir take his clothes off in the bathroom. When Mariah walked in, he was standing in the corner covering his private area." I started crying.

"Mariah beat her up, but she left before Onyx and Block arrived." She took a deep breath.

"Per the video she recorded, she did catch him fully naked. She touched him there a few times but he kept smacking her hand away and telling her to stop."

"I don't want to hear anymore." I covered my ears. Maribel removed them.

"That's all she did because Mariah walked in. After she beat her up, you could hear Mariah telling him she wouldn't hurt him and that he needed to get dressed." She put her hands on both sides of my face.

"I know you and her don't get along but she saved him and you. Whether you thank her or not, she was the one who stopped it from going further." I hugged her tight and my body shook.

"How could I let that happen? I was so weak. I couldn't even stop her from touching me."

"Say what?" My father shouted. Pulling away from Maribel, I explained what she did to me. They all had a sad look on their faces.

"I wanna go lay down." Maribel wiped my face and kissed my forehead. Block lifted me in his arms and carried me upstairs. After pulling the covers over me, he stared down at me.

"She will be taken care of."

"I hope so."

"River, she won't hurt you, Jasir or anyone else again." Before I could ask him to elaborate, he kissed my lips and walked out. *Did that mean she was dead?*

Chapter Nine

ONYX

"You still my wife?" I asked Mariah, holding one leg over my shoulder as the other laid flat on the bed. This position allowed me to dig deeper inside and touch spots she never knew existed.

"Yes. Oh, God, yes." Her nails were puncturing my skin with each stroke.

"Then tell me." I slowly pulled out.

"I'm still your wife, Onyx."

"Ahhhh, shit. Dammit." She pounded her fist on the bed when I rammed back in.

"Get your shit together because if you behave that way again, I'll fuck you one last time and take your life." Her closed eyes popped open to see the expression on my face.

"No other man will have you again and if I have to kill you, then it is what it is." My words struck a chord with her because she knew I meant every word. Putting her leg down and pulling out, I flipped her over, stuck my dick in her pussy and my finger in her ass.

"Fuck me." I smacked her ass with the other hand.

"Go faster." I was sliding my finger in and out, watching her body jerk.

"You love this nasty shit, don't you." Mariah turned to me and smirked. My wife was a certified freak.

"I'm about to cum." Mariah moved away, turned around and stuck my dick in her mouth.

"Got damn." My shit was disappearing, driving me in fucking sane. My hands were behind my head as her hands pushed me deeper down her throat.

"Oh shit." Her fingers tickled under my balls and I lost control. She made my body shake and once I fell back, she hopped on my face. Her juices were dripping on the sides but I refused to be outdone.

"Ride my face faster." Squeezing her ass, I moved her up and down.

"Onyx, don't stop baby. Fuck, I'm about to—" Her body shook before she could finish the sentence.

Gently biting her clit, she fell back but I kept ahold of her legs. No matter how she tried to get me to stop, I had control.

"Onyx, I can't take no more." Releasing one arm from under her thigh, I let two of my fingers go inside her tunnel as I continued flickering her clit.

"Babyyyyyyyy. Oh gawdddddd. I'm cumming." She sang

and this time her body flopped like a fish over and over. Letting her roll over, I smacked her ass a few times.

"Ain't no nigga ever gonna fuck you like me." Hell yea I always bragged about how good my stroke and tongue game were.

"And no bitch ever gonna fuck you like me." Mariah finally calmed down, mounted herself on top and rode me so good, not only did she have me moaning and calling her name, she put my ass straight to fucking sleep. Her words were definitely true that no bitch would do me like her, and I didn't want one too.

* * *

"All that fucking and moaning last night was like listening to a damn porno. I had to blast the tv just to drown the noise out." My brother complained when I went into the kitchen.

He had been staying in town since I brought him to see our mother. Now that I'm back home and not at the condo, I felt more than comfortable making love to my wife.

"I didn't know you were here. Me and Block left you at the club."

"Ok but I got here at three this morning."

"Well shit, me and my wife go off and on all night; especially when we making up." He stuck his finger down his throat.

Ding! Dong!

"There's someone at your front door." Alexa spoke over the

speaker. Walking to the door, I smiled watching Mariah coming down looking beautiful as ever.

"It's probably, Mommy. She's bringing Heaven back so her and my dad can go out for brunch." It was Sunday and her parents did that faithfully since I've known them. Opening the door, shock was on my face.

"You gonna let us in nigga or what?" Block always had something smart to say. Pushing me to the side, he barged in. River handed me a bouquet of flowers before hugging me. She was still moving slow from the shooting which was another reason she couldn't fight off Charlene the way she wanted.

"Move, Punk." Chana bumped into me hard and Ryan said, "Excuse me."

"Why y'all motherfuckers couldn't be nice like Ryan?" I slammed the door and made my way to the living room where they were.

"I keep telling him to be mean but he don't listen." Block shrugged.

"Who the fuck are y'all?" My brother was ignorant as hell. I told him about the girls but he hadn't physically met them.

"Who the hell are you?" Chana snapped back while Block helped River take a seat on the plush couch. It was soft as hell and felt as if you were falling in.

"None of your got damn business. Onyx, who this, Ho?" He pointed to her.

"Ho? I got your, Ho." Chana be ready to pop off at the drop of a dime. You could tell she was the dangerous twin even though they grew up separate.

"Raymond, this is Chana, River, and Chana's fiancé, Ryan." He stared for a minute.

"Y'all don't look special needs or like conjoined twins." That nigga ignorant as hell.

"What?" River yelled.

"Kids born from incest are supposed to have a birth defect. Which one y'all got?" Raymond stood in front of Chana and turned her head side to side.

"Boy, get off me." She slapped his hand.

"You do look like, Aaliyah tho." He focused back on River.

"Anyone ever tell you, you resemble Velma from Scooby Doo?" Me and Block fell into a fit of laughter. I will never understand why River wore the color orange when she knew that was Velma's color, and someone would mention the resemblance.

"I mean, those glasses thick as FUCK!" The way he said fuck had us laughing harder.

"Block, no disrespect but I hope you have her take those glasses off in the bedroom. She probably sees double of you when y'all doing it." I thought Block was gonna pee on himself.

"Wait a minute. Wait a minute." Raymond shouted.

"Are you the one with the Mystery Machine van?" He ran to look out the window.

"Block, I swear if you don't stop laughing you'll be using your hand for the next month." That nigga stopped fast as hell.

"Anyway, we're not here to see you, Loser. We're here for, Mariah." Chana chimed in. She walked in from the kitchen. Knowing my wife, she needed a moment before joining in the conversation. There was no need for me to ask why when I'm sure it's due to the incident with Charlene.

"What's up?" Mariah stood next to me. She wasn't scared at all but I'm sure she wanted to be close in case things got outta hand. I'll never support my wife and family fighting and I'll never support one tryna disrespect the other. River cleared her throat.

"I had Block bring me here to say, Thank you for saving me and my son. Had it not been for you showing up, I'm not sure I'd be here or that she wouldn't have violated my son more."

"Hold the hell up. Charlene got to you and your son?" I didn't tell Raymond about it because he hated our grandmother. To be honest, I'm shocked he stuck around town this long.

"Who are you again?" Chana asked. Neither of us answered the first time they asked because those two were busy arguing.

"Onyx is my brother so guess what that makes us." Chana and River looked at me.

"That's right, cousins. Blood cousins and won't be no fucking going on between us." I thought Chana was going to rip his eyes out. Ryan had to hold her back. That's how mad she was.

"I stopped by your house to apologize for being a bitch. None of you knew about your family's past and instead of helping my husband through it, I turned my back on him." I stood Mariah in front of me as she spoke.

"I wasn't even mad at you more than I was myself for not understanding the magnitude of what y'all family had to deal with. I took my anger out on you because Onyx made me feel like I wasn't his main concern." I hugged her waist from behind.

"I'm sorry I didn't get there sooner. It took a lot for me to go; better yet get out the car." She looked at Block.

"I'm sorry for breaking our bond too. I love you, Cousin." She walked over to hug him.

"Now that you're done being a pitiful loser, let's get back to what Charlene did." Raymond was disgusted after hearing the story Mariah told as was everyone else. River did say she signed Jasir up for counseling just in case. She wanted him to speak with someone about it so he knows it wasn't his fault. A lot of kids do believe they did something wrong for adults to do bad things to them and she didn't want that.

"We don't ever have to be friends but I do want you to know, I won't disrespect you anymore." River nodded.

"As far as the shit with Charlene, I wish she didn't get away." The room fell quiet for a minute.

"Well, I still don't like you, and as long as you and my sister not beefing, I won't say a word." Chana responded making it known how she felt.

"Chana." Ryan attempted to keep her quiet.

"Mariah, while I understand your ignorance toward the situation, there was never a need for you to disrespect me." River shocked us because none of us thought she would say anything.

"Any issues you had should've been taken up with, Onyx." She asked Block to help her stand.

"I may not be the woman you expected Block to fall in love with but just know, he's my man and nothing you or anyone else can say to make me leave him." She smiled at him.

"And for future reference, never go out your way to put another woman down to make yourself feel good. All it did was show your insecurities and honestly, you have nothing to be insecure about." River told Block she was ready to go.

"Oh." River turned around at the door.

"Block's home is now my house and yes, we're in the process of adding me to the deed. Therefore, if you still feel a way about me after today, don't come there. You can meet him elsewhere for all I care. My home will always be my sanctuary and anyone threatening it won't be welcomed." She walked out.

"I guess she told you, Mariah. And just in case you didn't get it, she said, don't bring your ass to her house with your bull-shit." Raymond was a clown. Chana walked over to Mariah who was in front of me.

"River is a forgiving person but I'm not. What you did was fucked up and uncalled for. She didn't deserve that, hell no woman did but she is who she is and I am who I am. Like I said before, I don't have no problem with you as long as you don't have one with her." Chana stood firm with her words.

"We may have just found one another but I'll be damned if anyone treated her like shit. She is my twin, my sister and now my best friend, and I will go to war behind her." Those were Chana's last words before walking out. I told Mariah I'd be right back.

"Hold up." River was about to get in the car.

"That needed to be done and I'm proud of you." I hugged her.

"I really am very thankful for Mariah. I'll always be in debt to her for saving Jasir. Make sure she gets those flowers."

"She's doesn't look at it like that." Mariah wasn't the type to throw something in your face.

"I just wish we were on better terms so we could hang out. She seems like a cool person but the way her attitude set up, I'll pass." We both laughed.

After they left, I went inside and her and Raymond were talking. He asked if she knew where Charlene could be so he could take her life. If he only knew that would happen sooner than later. In the meantime, I'm gonna enjoy making up with my wife.

Chapter Ten

BLOCK

"You feel better." I stood behind River in the shower. We came home after the sit down with Mariah that she wanted to have. I told her have Onyx say, Thank you but she said it was impersonal. She wanted Mariah to know just how thankful she really was.

What's crazy was, I was on my way to help River grab more stuff when Onyx called to tell me something happened. She called me a few times asking what was taking me so long. She had some good news and couldn't wait to see my face when she told me.

Deep down, I knew River was pregnant because after we had sex when she left the hospital from being shot, I never pulled out.

After hearing what Charlene did to her and tried to do with

Jasir, my body filled with rage and murder. I went to the house she occupied and burned it down. All her bank accounts were depleted thanks to knowing people in high places, and she too was on my most wanted list. Between her and Huff they were able to keep me off their trail but not for long. Both of them will be dealt their fate very soon.

"Yea. We may not speak but the respectful thing to do was say, Thank you." I placed my hands on top of her shoulder and slid them down her arms.

"I'm happy as fuck you're having my kid." She turned around.

"You sure?"

"Positive." Leaning down to kiss her, she pushed me back.

"I have to properly thank you too for saving me."

"River, you're my woman. Saving you is part of the job and there's no need to thank me. You've already done it by keeping the baby. That debt can never be repaid." She smiled.

"I'm gonna always be here for you and the kids." Taking her hands in mine, I turned her around, arched her back and licked my lips when her pussy opened wide. River by far was the best I've ever had.

"Shit." I moaned when my dick went into her tight pussy. Her walls clenched down instantly and the wetness had me ready to cum. Moving my hands to the top of her shoulders to go deeper, I heard a moan escape her lips. The fact we were always in sync during sex let me know I made the right choice choosing her.

"Block."

"Yea." I was enjoying the sight of my dick disappearing in her pussy.

"I love you."

"I love you, too." I placed a few kisses on her spine and the two of us did some freaky shit in the shower. By the time we finished, all I wanted to do was sleep.

"Block, look. Someone gave me money for my birthday." Jasir showed me a hundred dollar bill.

Today was his birthday party and it was hella kids here. Some from his school and a few who came with their parents that worked with River. I made sure she let everyone know not to bring no purses or big bags. If they had babies, then I needed to check inside and make sure there was no weapons. Because this party was at my house, I took every precaution to keep River and Jasir safe, as well as everyone else.

Huff was still on the run and even though I doubt he'll return, I wasn't taking any chances. It's unfortunate that he's hiding because his family members are being killed and they will be until he is produced.

"Who gave it to you?"

"That guy." He pointed to Deray. Him and Arabia were walking in.

"Oh ok. You want me to hold it until the party over?"

"Yes. I don't want to lose it." And just like that, he was gone to play with the other kids. Walking over to my sister and brother in law, I noticed River looking sad as she stood by the bouncy house.

"What's wrong?" I called out before reaching her. When she didn't answer, I figured it was because she couldn't hear. She was looking down at her phone.

"You didn't hear me ask what's wrong?" She jumped.

"No. Look at this." It was a message from Louise.

Please come see me tomorrow. I need to talk to you. After the message it was an old photo of River and Jasir.

"You ok?"

"Do you think I should go!"

"What harm would it do if you did go?" She shrugged.

"Then go see her. I'll go with you."

"I just don't want to relive old memories and—"

"And it'll be fine, trust me." She hugged me tight. Jasir ran over to get our attention.

"Mommy, look. It's the Power Rangers. Look. Look." He was pointing and jumping up and down.

"It's five of those colorful motherfuckers?" River popped me on the arm.

"What?"

"All the cartoons you watched, you never saw the Power Rangers." When River extended her arms to do the move, I walked away. Ain't no way in hell I was entertaining her shenanigans.

"What's up, nephew?" I had walked over to Deray and Arabia.

"Nothing. He greedy as hell."

"Damn he heavy." I complained taking him from Deray. Some of his boys came over with their kids too. River didn't mind because Arabia knew who they were.

"How you feeling?" I asked. My mother told me, she was expecting again.

"Same as before. Tired all the time and ready to eat as much as DJ." She kissed his cheek as I held him.

"Still didn't find Tricia?"

"No and the bitch had the nerve to take his daughter. Now he may have let her slide with the Huff shit because he was shot and not me, but taking his daughter was where she messed up." I understood because I'd feel the same.

"In a way I'm glad he's upset because when we have sex, the way his frustration shows makes me—"

"If you say anything else I'm making you leave." Arabia thought it was funny.

"I'm just saying, I know River gets you mad and like all men, you take it out on her, you know what."

"I'm not having this conversation with you."

"Whatever." She waved me off and took DJ. She wanted to take him in the bouncy house. Don't ask me why when it's mad older kids in there.

"Hey." I turned to see Mariah with Heaven in a snuggly. I only knew what it was because Arabia said Deray used it around the house when he had things to do and DJ wanted to be held.

"What's up." We hugged at her house but nothing changed as far as us speaking.

"I'm sorry for everything, Block. I didn't know that you

were really into her; especially since Melanie was still around." It was true.

When me and River first met, Melanie was my go to as far as fucking. Before making things official with River, I continued sleeping with Melanie and thought nothing of it. Shit, I had no feelings for either at the time so in my eyes, no harm, no foul.

Once River threw that good pussy on me, it was a wrap with Melanie. Unfortunately, she didn't take me seriously when I said it was over. Melanie was still showing up at places she knew I'd be at. She showed up at the bar a few times trying her hardest to take me home. Even as of lately, she was texting me nonstop from unknown numbers since I blocked her.

The last straw was recently when River was at the hospital this last time. Melanie saw me and started yelling out how we were never gonna be over and that I'm hers forever. People were looking at her crazy but that was her fault.

Long story short, two days ago, I paid her a visit. Onyx was with me and come to find out, the bitch was messing with one of the dudes that was cool with Huff. They were so busy fucking neither had any idea, I was there. It worked out for me because I ended both of their lives. Hers for not taking no for an answer, and his for not telling where Huff was hiding. Granted, he claimed not to know and that may have been true but too bad.

"Regardless if I were into her or not, that bullshit was uncalled for. Then, you were jealous because she not only had my time but Onyx's." She put her head down.

"You always been a bitch but never a jealous one."

"I know it's just—"

"It's just what? You fucked another nigga, kept that shit from your husband in hopes of using it to hurt him and he knew the whole time. You still wouldn't have mentioned it if y'all weren't going through shit." I had to bring that up to let her know that sneaky shit was gonna get her nowhere.

"He cheated on me a bunch of times and you knew." He chuckled.

"I ain't know shit because the nigga wasn't sloppy like you were. The bitches may have called you on the phone but you never caught him." She didn't say a word because she knew it was true.

I didn't ask what Onyx was doing because it wasn't my business. As long as he didn't lay hands on Mariah, we were cool. Once she found out about his infidelity, she stayed anyway. I refused to be one of those family members who went to war for her relationship and she went back to him.

"That man's brother attacked you in the hospital room and to this day, you still didn't mention it to your husband." Her eyes got big.

"Exactly. Out here tryna get people to see things from your point of view and still holding secrets."

"Block."

"Get the fuck out my face and don't apologize to me again." Walking away was the best thing right now. Mariah had no business coming to Jasir party talking about what went down. What if River heard her discussing Melanie, then I'd have to explain shit that was irrelevant since we weren't sleeping together at the time.

"You ok?" River grabbed my waist from behind.

"Yea. Why you ask that?" I pulled her in front of me.

"It's my responsibility to know where my son and man are at all times." I smiled.

"Mariah pissed you off."

"You can say that." I kissed the side of her neck.

"Well, I hope you're not too mad." She smirked.

"Why is that?"

"Jasir is staying at my parents' house which means it would only be me and you at the house. I may or may not have some freaky things in mind." I loved that she considered Maribel her mom now. She wanted a mother and thanks to Ernie returning, she had one.

"Can we go now?" She started laughing.

"We have all night." She put her hand in mine and the two of us walked around. By the time the party was over and the catering people cleaned up, it was after eleven. Needless to say, I locked up and let River do what she promised and I must say, she was slowly turning a nigga out. I ain't never leaving her.

Chapter Eleven

ARABIA

"Mariah, in my opinion, I think you should leave well enough alone." She stopped by with Heaven to see me.

"River thanked you for saving her and Jasir, you and Onyx are back together and life should be great for you. However, you're over here complaining about Block telling you to get the fuck out his face." I understood why he was mad when he told me the story.

Who goes to a kids birthday party and brings up a chick he used to mess with? Like he said, had River heard her it may have been some conflict between them. It had me second guessing if her apology to River was genuine.

"I'm just trying to get us to where we used to be."

"By bringing up Melanie and reminding him that River wasn't a chick you're used to seeing him with." No response.

"Let me ask you this." I put DJ in the playpen.

"Did you apologize to River in order to get Onyx back? Was it to get sympathy from him? What was your true reasoning for doing it?"

"To be honest, yes it was genuine. She did nothing for me to dislike her, besides that time in the salon."

"Oh, when you threatened to beat her ass if she used the wrong shampoo and conditioner." Mariah sucked her teeth.

When River and I became close, she broke down in detail what took place at the salon with Mariah. If I remembered correctly it was one of the times her and Onyx were going through it after Salina showed up at the reception. She took her anger out on River time and time again. The last straw was when Mariah disrespected her at Block's house and got beat up.

"Whatever. Look, I'm trying to be different now but no one wants to believe me." I stared at her for a few seconds before speaking.

"Then why keep bringing it up? If it's over, let it go. Stop trying to hurt River."

"I'm not."

"Mariah, bringing up women Block used to deal with at her son's party was disrespectful even if she didn't hear you." She had nothing to say as usual.

"If you don't get it together and Onyx thinks your apology was fake, he will leave for good next time." She claimed to understand but did she. It wasn't my just job to coddle Mariah when she knew better.

* * *

"Mmm, that's why I'm pregnant now." I whispered as Deray laid on the side of me. He had just finished making love to me and all I wanted to do was go to sleep.

"Fucking with me, you're gonna always be pregnant." He got off the bed and lifted me up.

"We have to be somewhere."

"Huh? It's after midnight." I whined as he brought me to shower with him.

"You're gonna want to be around for this." No idea what he spoke of, I stood in the shower allowing him to wash me up. If he wanted to leave the house this late, then he could wash me.

"Where are we going?" I asked, drying off.

"Out." Were the last words he said before putting on his clothes and leaving me alone in the room.

When the doorbell rang, I rushed to put my jeans on, grabbed the gun out the nightstand and hauled ass out the bedroom. This wasn't about to be another ambush.

"What the fuck?" Deray shouted seeing me come down the stairs with my gun pointed at the door. He had his hand on the knob shaking his head.

"Who is it?"

"My parents. Relax and put that damn gun away."

"You sure?" I stood there until he opened the door. His

daughter was asleep on his father's shoulders. I had a major problem with him bringing her out this late so he better have a damn good reason as to why. And when did he get in touch with Tricia to see her? Last I checked, he couldn't find her.

"It's the middle of the night, Deray. I didn't want the same thing to happen." He hugged me as his parents walked past us.

"There's bottles in the fridge if DJ wakes up." He didn't even wait for a response and closed the door.

"Deray, where are we going? Why are your parents here?"

"Stop asking questions and enjoy the ride." Sucking my teeth as he opened the passenger door, he smacked my ass. He closed the door, hopped in the driver's side, and drove off.

Wherever we were going, the roads were pitch black and bumpy. I know we're in Long Island but I've never seen this area. Pulling into a long driveway that was also dark, there was a small house with no lights on. You could see a pair of headlights coming from behind the house as we got closer.

"Don't ask no questions." Deray said parking next to the car. Shocked was an understatement for what I saw. Tricia was tied up in a chair crying. She wasn't beaten or bruised and her partner stood on the side smoking what appeared to be a blunt. I looked at Deray and he told me to stay put.

"Roll down your window." Shutting the car off, we sat there in silence. The chick finished smoking and walked over to her.

"Say what you need to say." Her partner yelled.

"I'm sorry, Deray and Arabia." Tricia was terrified watching the chick walk behind her. Outta nowhere, she yanked her head back, pulled a knife out and slit Tricia's throat from ear to ear. If I didn't know any better, I'd say she was trying to cut her head off because she kept going. One of Deray's boys had to pull her away.

"Ummm, what just happened?" Deray backed up, drove down that long driveway and onto the dark road. At first it was complete silence.

"When Tricia admitted to sending that nigga to my house to kill you, that's when I'd had enough. I wasn't aware she felt animosity toward you or was jealous of our relationship." I sat there listening to him tell the story.

"Her partner was cool as fuck and in the streets. I put her on my team and we became tight." He held my hand in his over the console. She thought it would be weird working with Tricia's ex, but Deray made it clear that he didn't date backwards and there was nothing to worry about.

"The day Tricia fucked me at my parents' house, I wasn't gonna say anything because she was in love with Tricia and it would hurt her. Shit, it would hurt anyone." I agreed because when he told me, I was.

"After admitting to wanting you dead, I called her partner up, told her the truth and said if she didn't handle her, I would." I gasped.

"To be honest, I'm glad she did it because the way I had her death planned was far worse than what she did." I was at a loss for words.

"Look." He pulled over at 7-11.

"At the end of the day, that nigga still set it up for both of us to be killed with her." I didn't disagree.

"Both of us are still here, we're married and expecting again. They didn't break us." Deray was saying the words but did he forget that they did when he faked his death.

"I'm not excusing what I did by not telling you the truth when it took place. However, I'll never do that again and if I did, you'd be the first to know." He leaned over to kiss me.

"You want something out the store."

"No." He stepped out the car and went inside.

I rested my head against the seat thinking about how Tricia, his ex, his baby mama's life was taken in front of me and him. Did he not care? Was he really that heartless when it came down to it?

"Here." Deray returned to the car with a cherry Slurpee and some skittles. They were my favorite.

"Why aren't you upset?"

"About what?" He closed the door.

"Tricia. She was your—" He cut me off.

"She was my ex, Arabia. I haven't had feelings for her in years." He pulled out the parking lot.

"I cared about her well being because she was my daughter's mother, but that all went out the window when she admitted tryna kill you." I didn't say a word.

"You're my wife, my other half and when there's a threat against you, it's against me as well." There was nothing left for me to say. My husband made up his mind and had no remorse for Tricia's death, so why should I.

Chapter Twelve

RIVER

"I'm not sure this was a good idea." I told Block when he parked in front of my mother's house. My body wasn't as weak anymore but due to the pregnancy, I shouldn't be stressing myself out either.

"If you don't wanna go in, don't but then you'll always wonder what she wanted." Blowing my breath because he was right, I finally got out.

"Why are they here?" I pointed to Onyx, his mother, Raymond, Chana, Maribel and my father.

"They're here for support." It was very weird seeing all of them show up for a conversation with Louise.

"You ok? Do you need anything? I'll be right next to you." Maribel said, hugging me as tight as she could.

"She'll be fine." My father pulled me away and stood in front of me.

"I know you're unaware of what's going on but just know it had to happen."

"Huh?" Leaving me confused, Chana knocked on the door.

It took a few minutes for Louise to answer and surprisingly she looked decent. Her hair was brushed back in a tight ponytail. Her clothes appeared to be ironed and clean, and the little signs of makeup were visible. Why was she dressed up? One by one everyone walked inside.

"Thank you for coming." She kissed my cheek which was another shocker. What the heck was going on?

Inside the house, the television was on, it smelled like food was cooking or had been cooked, and the place looked clean. Chana wasn't lying when she said Louise straightened up.

"Have a seat. Matter of fact, let's go in the basement to talk. It's more space for everyone." I shrugged and followed her with the rest of the family behind me.

"Wow!" I had my mouth opened seeing how clean it was as well. The washer and dryer were both on and the area that used to be full of clothes and trash, didn't exist.

"What in the hell?" I stared in the dark corner where a foot was peeking from underneath something. Louise lit a cigarette, pulled the string for another light to come on and there was Charlene lying there beat up. Blood was streaming down her face, bruises lined her naked body and one of her legs appeared to be crooked. Duct tape was on her mouth, yet it didn't seem as if she was trying to speak. She was staring at all of us out of the one eye that was barely opened.

"Yup, I've been beating her ass for a while now." My mother joked.

"What's going on?" Louise pointed to a chair for me to sit. There was another one across that she sat in.

"I want to tell you a short story and I need you to listen because it won't be repeated." I noticed Chana hop up to sit on the washer, Maribel and Onyx mom opened some folding chairs to sit, while my father stood behind me. Block, Onyx and Raymond were off to the side but close.

"When I was twelve years old, this bitch." Louise stood and kicked Charlene in the face.

"This bitch forced me to drink liquor and from what the videos showed, had me and my brother doing inappropriate things to one another." She took a few pulls of the cigarette and continued.

"Learning about the pregnancy confused me because before she showed me the video, I was a virgin. To be honest, I didn't even like boys."

"What?" She laughed.

"Yea, I had a little girlfriend in middle school. No one knew about us because she never came over. I'd go to her house, we'd watch movies, kiss and fondle each other. Ernie was the only one who knew all about it." I turned to see him shaking his head.

"The day Charlene forced me to drink was the same day, my father almost killed my mother. When he took her to the hospital, I was on the phone with my friend telling her how much she meant to me and couldn't wait to see her. That bitch heard me, snatched the phone out my hand and once she found out it was another girl, she ran in my parents room, found his gun and pointed it at me." My mother was becoming upset as she replayed the story.

"She told me, I had to sleep with a boy in order to knock the gayness out of me. When Ernie came to after our dad almost choked him to death, I was shaking my head no." My father cleared his throat.

"Charlene went in the kitchen to get liquor and had us drink cups of it. I'm not talking about little glasses. She made us use those red solo cups. Do you know how much liquor goes into one of those?"

"Why didn't you beat her ass?" Maribel chimed in.

"Charlene was older than me. I was a nonviolent person and didn't even kill bugs. There was no way I'd be able to fight her." My mother continued.

"Once we found out Ernie was my kids father, I fell into a state of depression. I stayed in my room day and night. My friend tried to contact me but my mind was gone. When Charlene started bringing boys over and making me sleep with them, my soul left my body. I was no longer Louise Thomas and just a human taking up space in this world."

"Damn." Onyx said.

"You alright? We can go." Block wiped my eyes as he squatted next to me.

"No. I'm ok." He kissed me and went back over to where he

stood.

"The day you two were born, I wanted to die. It was disgusting to have my brother's children; an abomination." Louise was now crying.

"You have no idea how many times I tried to kill you as a baby." Chana gasped along with Maribel and Mrs. Buggs.

"My mother walked in many times to pull the pillow off your face, or emptied bottles I made filled with poison of some sort. I was pissed when you didn't die after I forced those pills down your throat when you were twelve." I was damn near hysterical crying listening to her.

"Jasir was a casualty of war and I told you, if he died you would've killed yourself. I wouldn't have to look at you anymore." Chana was cursing my mother out but not me. She was explaining why she couldn't be a mother. As hard as it was to hear, it needed to be said.

"That's enough." Block snapped.

"Crazy thing about all of this was, in my eyes, you were never my child. It's the reason I stayed in my room all the time. You resembled Ernie and that sight repulsed me." She was telling the truth.

At a young age, I had to learn how to make my own food, and wash myself up. Louise didn't sign me up for extracurricular activities nor did she get me off the bus after school. She told the district she was handicapped so the bus would drop me off in front of the house. Louise had my entire life mapped out and it never included her in it.

"You heard enough. Let's go River." Block tried to take me

out but I refused.

"No. There's a reason she called me over here. Let her say it." I didn't mean to snap but she had something to say.

"You have always been smart." She moved over to where Charlene laid.

"After hearing about this bitch sexually assaulting you and Jasir, I had, had enough. You were my child and she had no right to touch you when she did so much to me all those years ago." Louise was shaking at this point.

"I got in touch with Chana, who reached out to Onyx in order for me to speak with his mother; my niece." We all turned to Mrs. Buggs.

"She came over and once we had a long talk, she called Charlene and told her to meet over here."

"What?" I yelled.

"Charlene didn't know this was my house and since my niece was a piece of shit to her son, Raymond years ago and couldn't let their father kill the bitch, I felt she owed us." Onyx and Raymond looked at their mother who was crying.

"She told me her story and in the end, I told her this had to happen." She lifted her head and mouthed the words, *"I'm sorry"* to Raymond. He waved her off.

"Oh, at first, she was very firm on not getting involved. That's until I kicked her down those same stairs." Louise pointed to the steps.

"Kicked her ass and let her know if she didn't do it, I was gonna kill her too." For my mother not to have been nonviolent back then she was damn sure showing her ass now.

"Wait a minute. Hold up." Raymond started pacing in the tight basement.

"How long has Charlene been here?" I wanted to know the answer to what Raymond asked.

"The day after she attacked Jasir and River." That was weeks ago.

"Is that why she looks unhealthy?" Chana questioned, jumping off the washer.

"Yup. The only reason it doesn't smell bad down here was because I made sure she had a bucket to piss and shit in. She was not gonna die before River saw her one last time. I wanted to make sure she didn't want to do what I will." Her statement made me very uncomfortable. Block noticed and made me stand and then sit on his lap. His arms around my body gave me a sense of comfort for the moment.

"Does anyone have anything to say to her?" Louise opened one of the cabinets overhead and pulled a gun out.

"Oh shit." Raymond blurted out what I was thinking.

"Any of you. I'm not asking again." No one said a word, not even Mrs. Buggs. She backed away, aimed the gun, and pulled the trigger.

BOOM! With one shot, Louise had Charlene's brain splattered against the wall. One by one, they each began to retreat upstairs. Mrs. Buggs cried but she didn't react the way I expected.

"River." Louise called out. Block was about to go upstairs but I squeezed his hand.

"This will be your last time seeing me."

106

"What? Why?" Not that I've spent any time with her but still. She grabbed my hands and held them in hers.

"For years, I wanted to die because the stain etched in my life having my brothers kids was a heavy burden." Now that I knew the truth, everything seemed clearer to me on why she was who she was.

"I understand."

"You are stronger than I thought and was able to get away from me before I killed you. Ever since then, all I've thought about was getting Charlene."

"She's gone now. She won't hurt anyone, anymore." I wiped the tears falling down her face.

"No. No she won't but the damage to me was already done. I was tainted and deflowered as my father would say." She started crying.

"I was a terrible, terrible mother to you." Now I was crying.

"But you didn't let that get in the way of being the perfect mother for Jasir. You and Ryan did an amazing job raising him."

"Why are you talking like that? I know it wasn't your fault now." Her voice was shaky. She backed away and smiled.

"The only way to rid myself of the pain, was to say what I needed to you and do this."

"NOOOOOOOOO!" Everything happened so fast, I couldn't stop her even if I tried. The way her body hit the floor when she pulled the trigger will forever be etched in my head. I rushed over to put my hand over the hole on her temple but it wasn't helping.

"What the hell happened?" I could hear voices but the only thing left to do was pray. Pray that she went to heaven and her demons were gone.

"River." I'm not even sure whose voice it was speaking to me.

"Just leave me alone." I had my mother's head on my lap.

"Let me talk to her." Chana asked everyone to leave us alone. They did but Block didn't move.

"She may not have said it but she loved you and Jasir, River." I turned to Chana.

"Each time you got hurt, she was there. She was texting me to find out the status and even had me come over to apologize for not being around." Chana smiled.

"All she did was talk about you and Jasir. How she used to watch you play with him and take him outside. She wanted to be that way with you too but the demons were eating her up. Charlene really damaged her and there was no way back."

"But."

"She had no idea how to be a mother, especially since her mom wasn't there for her either." I rested my head on her shoulder.

"I'm upset she had to take this route but it was the only way for her to be free." I didn't look at it the way Chana did but now that she said it, all of it made sense.

It was if Louise waited all her life to find Charlene and when she did, she made sure to kill her. Granted, I wish it happened before the sexual assault but we know now she'll never hurt anyone else.

"Damn, bro. You told us one body." Some guy had come down the stairs in a full hazmat outfit; even his face was covered with that helmet looking thing and a clear cover for the face.

"Excuse me." Chana had the guy follow her back upstairs. Block squatted next to me.

"Your mom told Onyx, Charlene would die today. That's why they were here but no one knew she planned on committing suicide. Shit, I definitely wouldn't have brought you for that." I heard footsteps coming down.

"It's time to go home." Wiping my face, he slid my body away from my mother, lifted me in his arms and carried me upstairs. Maribel and Chana were standing outside the bathroom door with gloves and towels. I looked at Block.

"You must be out your damn mind if you thought, I was letting you get in my new corvette full of blood." He made me laugh.

"I love you, Babe."

"I love you too." He kissed me and put me down to go shower. When I finished, he only had on a T-shirt. He must've thrown his other shirt away.

"What are they going to do with the bodies?"

"Well, Charlene will be burned. Your mother will go to the funeral home my boy owned. If you want a service we can have one, otherwise he's gonna bury her. We can get a tombstone ordered right away so you'll know where she is if you wanna visit." I nodded. He had everything worked out. All I could do at this point was cry and be happy she was free.

Chapter Thirteen

ONYX

"Laila, you should eat the broccoli, it's good for you." Mariah cut it up into little pieces for her. We were at dinner with her parents, and Raymond.

My mother declined to come because she knew my brother couldn't stand being around her. They were in close proximity when Louise killed Charlene but other than that, he stayed away from her. My mom felt he was being childish and like I told her before, he was the one who went through that and she didn't believe him. You can't take someone's feelings away from them.

"I don't have to do what you say." Laila snapped, shocking all of us.

"What you say?" I remained calm asking her. She had a tendency of getting upset and falling out on the ground. At times she was just like Salina. I loved my daughter but the older she gets, the worst her mouth got.

"My mom said not to listen to her and that she's a whore." The look on Mariah's face was of pure evil. In a way it's my fault for continuing to go back and forth with my ex, but on the other hand, Laila knew better than to speak like that.

"What's a whore?" Raymond asked while the rest of us sat there still tryna grasp the fact she said that.

"Someone who sleeps around."

"Oh, like your mother. The one who shared her bed with plenty of men." I shook my head at Raymond. He gave zero fucks how old a person was and would argue them down.

"She does not. I'm the only one who sleeps with her. You're a liar." She shouted.

"And your mama a ho." Mariah couldn't control her laughter. My brother was a clown and now that he met my wife, he wasn't about to let anyone come for her, not even me.

"Daddy, why is he saying that?" She whined.

"The same reason why you disrespected Mariah. What's that about?" She pouted with her arms folded.

"No need to question her. She's a child and saying what her mother told her to say." I could hear the aggravation in Mariah's voice.

"That's right." Laila chimed in.

"Onyx, you need to control her mouth because it's only gonna get worse." Mariah's mother said, wiping her hands with the napkin. Laila considered her as a grandmother too. She gave Laila a death stare amd she knew better than to talk back.

"Daddy, I don't want to come over anymore if she's there." Mariah slammed her fork down and Raymond was shaking his head.

"Yea, Daddy. Why you forcing her to go where she doesn't want to? Especially, when you'll be at our house more once I deliver." Salina started rubbing her belly.

"Mommy!" Laila jumped up to hug her.

"What you doing here?"

"Did you forget our daughter has that cricket phone in her book bag. I track wherever she goes." Salina had me purchase her a phone that only made calls to four people. Both of us, my mother and Mariah. We did have a tracking device placed on it as well in case she wondered off. Not that she did but you never know.

"And you decided to track her to a restaurant with her family?" Mariah's father asked.

"Technically, y'all aren't her family; well he is and that baby is, but not you three." If Mariah's father didn't stop my wife, I'm sure she would've bashed Salina's face in.

"I wanna go home with you, Mommy." Laila whined, aggravating the hell out of me.

"Why? Did she put her hands on you?"

"That's it. I had fucking enough." Mariah threw her napkin on the table and walked over to Salina.

"You can hate me all you want for taking the man you want but don't ever use Laila as a pawn to disrespect me or my family." Salina's eyes were real big.

"We don't even know if that baby belongs to my husband but if it does, guess what." Salina rolled her eyes.

"If that baby is his, you don't have to worry about me anymore because he'll be yours." I definitely didn't expect Mariah to say that. I thought we were on better terms.

"Oh shit." Raymond instigated.

"Really."

"Damn right really? I'm sick of you two and the games y'all play. I don't deserve that nor do I deserve to be disrespected by your spoiled ass daughter. Matter of fact, here." Mariah handed her Laila's bag.

"Take her and get the fuck on. Onyx you can go too."

"Mariah, honey. Don't let her get you upset." Her mom tried to calm her down.

"I'm sick of this shit with her. Me and Onyx could be doing fine and then she pops up and all his infidelities with her pop out. Now he has a fucking baby on the way with her. I just can't." She walked off leaving all of us at the table. Getting up, I noticed people staring and that didn't sit right with me. My wife was crying, my daughter was being rude and my ex didn't know when to stop.

"Let's go." Gripping Salina by the arm, I basically drug her out the restaurant. Laila was walking behind saying something that didn't make sense.

"Where's your car?"

"Let go of me." She attempted to break free but my grip was tight.

"There it is, Daddy." Laila pointed to her mother's car.

Taking the walk across the street with them, I had Laila get in the back seat.

"Why are you manhandling me? It's not my fault your wife a cry baby." I chuckled.

"I told you plenty of times to leave her alone and you didn't listen." Salina sucked her teeth.

"I'll be by to see you later." And with those last words, I walked around the car to speak with Laila.

"Bye, Daddy." She poked her lips out to kiss my cheek like always. I used my thumb and two fingers to squeeze her lips together.

"If you ever in your life, young or old disrespect Mariah again, I'm gonna beat your ass. Do you understand me?" She started crying as she shook her head yes.

"She is my wife, your stepmother and has never been mean to you. The next time you see her, apologies better fly out your mouth." I removed my fingers, kissed her cheek, and closed the door. Now I had to go and fix things with my wife.

Raymond sent me a text on the way in saying she left with her parents. I made him meet me outside.

"She mad as hell at you." He joked getting in the car.

"I'm dropping you off at the condo."

"Thank God! Don't nobody wanna hear you begging and all that moaning, if she lets your ass in the house." I ignored Raymond the entire way. He was right though, Mariah was mad and might give me a hard time.

Once I dropped him off, I drove home to deal with my marriage. Wondering if we would stay together this time, I smiled remembering all the good times we did have. Despite our past we managed to stick it out and then here comes Salina. She had to be dealt with because I'll be damned if I'm dealing with this for the rest of my life.

"Mariah." I locked the door and went upstairs. Looking in Heaven's room, she wasn't in her crib or basinet. Walking in my room, Mariah shocked me standing there completely naked with a smile on her face.

"Damn, you sexy as hell." She slowly walked toward me. I wasn't expecting this.

"Where's Heaven?"

"With my parents." She took one of my hands in hers and led me to the bed. Undressing me with a little help from myself, she pushed me back on the bed. My dick was hard as hell and ready to be inside.

"Oh shit." Her mouth covered my entire dick and right before I came she stopped, climbed on top and started to ride me. My hands were on her ass opening it as wide as possible to make her feel me as deep as possible.

"What you doing? Shit!" Her pussy was clenching down squeezing my dick. I was about to bust early.

"You love me, Onyx." She stood on her feet and went faster while she played with her breasts. The sight alone was making me harder if that's even possible.

"Hell yea."

"How much."

"A whole lottttt. Oh shittttt." Her pussy was getting wetter and I could feel her juices leaking.

"I'm about to cum, Baby. Tell me who you belong to." I don't know what Mariah did but my body started stiffening up and my toes were curling. Its happened before but the euphoric feeling was different than the other times.

"You, Mariah. Fuck! Ah shitttttt!" My body shook like it never did before. I watched her fall over tryna catch her breath.

"It's time." Was all she said before slowly getting out the bed. After catching my own breath, I went in the bathroom to shower with her.

"I'm already on it." Were the only words to leave my mouth. The two of us were finally on the same page when it came to Salina.

"Oh shit. Yes. Don't stop. Yes." Salina moaned out dramatically while she fucked some dude in her bed. The same bed my daughter claimed to occupy with her sometimes. That bothered me because why you have niggas in the house anyway that you're not married to.

After the shit she did the other day, my wife turned me the fuck out in the bedroom. Not only did she surprise me when I got home, she did some freaky ass shit in the shower that I ain't never had done to me. When we got married and even before, she knew I'd lay my life on the line for her and that hadn't changed.

Salina was a problem that needed to be taken care of sooner but my wife spared her. At the restaurant she had enough and who could blame her. All my ex did was harass her and Salina felt since we had a child together it would exempt her from my wrath. If she only knew the only person standing in the way of her demise was the exact person she hated.

"You done." I lifted a window to get the smell out. Clearly she never took care of her feminine problem.

"What the hell?" Salina covered her body while the guy tried to grab his jeans.

"Looking for this?" Walking over to where he laid to show him the gun he tried to grab, I had to laugh.

"Crazy how I was coming for you after leaving here. How does the saying go, *"I can kill two birds with one stone.* And that is true today, only it won't be with a stone." Salina rolled her eyes.

"What you want, Onyx? Can't you see I'm busy?"

POW! I let a shot off in dudes leg.

"What are you doing?" She had the nerve to ask. Dragging him off the bed, I started fucking him up.

"You put your hands on my wife, nigga. Then, you been hiding out with this bitch when my daughter not here." Salina gasped.

I had eyes on her house anytime Laila was here just in case. She stayed in too much shit for me not to. Come to find out, Sean's brother been here a few times and only got caught because Salina made him get groceries out the car. When the call came in, I told him to hold tight.

"Onyx, stop it. You're gonna kill him." Salina cried. I stopped hitting him. Dude could barely breathe.

"Bitch, you lucky my daughter wasn't here." I was mad as hell.

"We agreed the only nigga to come here was one you'd marry." Clearly she needed a reminder of what we discussed.

"You can't tell me who to have in my house." I ran up on her as she tried to get dressed.

"Bitch, do you pay a bill in here? Huh?" Complete silence.

"Exactly. Now you got Laila disrespecting Mariah for no fucking reason."

"Fuck that bitch. That's supposed to be me in that big ass mansion. Those are my clothes, my cars, that should've been me having all your kids and your last name." It was at that very moment I blamed myself for everything. Had I not played the back and forth games maybe she would've moved on. Maybe, just maybe we could've co-parented like River and Ryan.

"I did any and everything you asked. Pornos, threesomes, orgys, anal, I even fucked niggas you didn't fuck with just to make you see we belonged together." No idea why she said that last part. As she can see now, fucking dudes I'm not cool with got her nowhere.

"All you did was show me, you were down for whatever and I could never trust you. I mean what chick would really do all that and think a nigga wasn't gonna cheat or keep her as his one and only." She let the hurt show on her face.

"We belong together Onyx. Why can't you see that?"

"Nah, we don't. I belong with my wife and since you can't respect it, you gotta go." Salina tried to speak but the bullet pierced her skull too fast. I didn't even watch her body drop before turning to do the same with that nigga.

"I'm ready." Block walked in covering his nose with his shirt. The smell was disgusting. He walked in the house with me but stopped when we heard Salina moaning.

"You good?"

"I'm cool. I would've done it sooner but your cousin forbid it." We both started laughing and walked out when the cleaners came in. Once the bodies were removed, I watched the house go up in flames. It made sense for me to tell Laila her mother perished in a fire instead of by my hands.

Chapter Fourteen

BLOCK

Seeing Louise blow her brains out wasn't as bad for me, as it was River. Throughout the hurt and pain in her life, deep down she loved her mother and no one could take that away from her. Of course growing up she didn't understand why Louise had that much hate toward her but once it was all revealed, she had a better take on it.

That night, River asked me to run her a bath and I swear she stayed in there for four hours. Whenever the water got cold, I heard her adding more. When she got out, her skin was wrinkled and red from how hot she had it. Not thinking anything of it, we went to bed. The next day there were blisters on parts of her body and that shit scared me.

Rushing her to the hospital, the doctor confirmed our baby was ok, yet pulled me to the side and said she wasn't. He was able to point out signs of suicide. I told him to relax she wouldn't do that because of Jasir. It wasn't until he mentioned that anyone sitting in hot water for that amount of hours and not feeling the burn, was numb to the world and anything could happen.

Instead of taking River home, I asked if he could keep her overnight just for me to put some things in place. He did inform me that if River did anything crazy that he'd call security and have her placed on the crisis floor. I wanted to knock his head off but at the moment, I needed her to stay there.

I had Arabia reach out to people who knew therapists that could speak to her right away. My mother and Maribel both came over when I brought her home and have been there ever since. I'm hoping River gets better soon because I'm ready for them to go.

Chana was having a hard time dealing with seeing River like that. Her and Louise just met so it wasn't as painful for her but their father took it rather hard too.

Me and River were the only ones who saw it happen, however they all ran downstairs when the gun went off. Here it was that Ernie just found his sister and daughter, and now one was dead and the other was having a mental breakdown.

"You ok?" Maribel asked, sitting next to me at the island. I had Ryan keep Jasir at his house until we could figure out what was going on with River. She wasn't in a comatose state or anything like that, but she wasn't speaking to anyone.

"For the most part, yea. I just want her to be ok."

"Most people who witness a death like that or even worse

tend to go into shock. It didn't help that it was her mother." I agreed. The psychologist who came over reiterated the same scenario.

"How long does it last?"

"No one really knows. Every individual is different, therefore we can only hope for the best and that she'll be ok soon." She opened one of the water bottles sitting there.

"Why the fuck you sitting so close to my son?" My mother snapped walking in the kitchen. Those two go back and forth every time they get around one another. Crazy how aggravating my mother could be but her and River's family clicked right away.

"He will be my son in law so I can be close if I want. Why you in here anyway? You're supposed to be watching River." She always said me and River belonged together and needed to get married.

"I was until she asked for Block. I'm about to tell her, you were in here tryna sleep with him." Maribel threw the paper towels at her.

"I'll be back." Leaving them in there bickering, I headed upstairs. Opening the bedroom door, River was sitting with her knees up to her chest.

"Babe, I'm sorry." She apologized for no reason.

"For what?"

"Not being able to handle my mother's death and scaring you." I went to sit next to her.

"I'm not going to commit suicide because my son and the baby needs me."

"I need you." She turned her head toward me.

"Hell yea, I said it. You are the best thing that's ever happened to me. When you're hurting all I wanna do is fix it and I can't." She hugged me.

"Please don't leave me." River started crying.

"Why would I do that?" She pulled away and asked me to lay back so she could get on top of me.

"The doctor thought I was crazy and everybody tip toeing around me. Block, I need you too." Wrapping my arms around her body, she took a deep sigh.

"I'm not leaving you, ever." Her head lifted off my chest.

"I can't say I love you enough." That made me smile. The two of us stayed in the room until my mother barged in saying Maribel had to go. When I asked why, she said because she wouldn't make empanadas. River busted out laughing, which made me laugh.

"Let's go downstairs before they kill each other." We kissed for a few seconds and I made her get up because my dick was rising. I'm not sure she's ready to be intimate but if she was when everyone left, I would be waiting.

* * *

"What you doing here?" I had River sit next to me at the club. She knew about me coming out but not the real reason. I'm pissed that she showed up by herself; then again, ain't nobody fucking with her.

"I didn't want these chicks to think you were single or that you wanted a lap dance." She waved off two strippers who stopped in front of us.

"With all the freaky shit you do, I don't need none of that." Sliding my hands down her bare arms because the outfit was sleeveless, the person I've been waiting for just stepped in.

"How you get here?" I couldn't help but feel her up.

"Uber. I knew I'd be going home with you." She started to grind her lower half on my lap. Onyx whispered in my ear that Huff and his people went straight through security without being checked. That alone let me know shit was gonna get wild.

"River."

"Yea, babe."

"I need you to stay up here no matter what." She turned around.

"Come here." Lifting her off my lap, I took her behind the area we were in and up some steps to go inside the office.

This club was owned by an acquaintance who owed me money. To pay his debt, he informed me about Huff coming here incognito and told me I could do whatever. I definitely had a problem with his security not checking them at the door. Especially when he knew what we came for. It made me think he was in favor of the other guy and that alone would be brought up at a later time.

"What's going on and why are we in here? We having sex?" She jumped in my arms. River and I haven't been intimate since her breakdown.

"Later, listen." Putting her down, I made sure she was looking at me.

"Huff is here." She immediately started to panic.

"That's why I didn't ask you to come out with me." She began to pace.

"Does he know I'm here? What if he shoots me again? Block, my body won't sustain another shooting. Fuck! I shouldn't have listen to Chana and Arabia."

"Listen to them." I was confused.

"They told me to come dressed sexy and take you outside to fuck. You know, be spontaneous with it to make up for not giving you any. Why didn't I stay home?" I laughed.

"You're gonna be fine. Do you want to stay here in this office or go home?"

"Go home. I'll wait for you there." Hugging her tight, there was a knock at the door. Her eyes grew wide with fear. Opening the door, I sucked my teeth.

"What the fuck you want, Avery?"

"Avery?" River repeated.

"Why aren't you taking care of our baby? The test results were wrong so I had them done elsewhere." If I were a woman beater, I would've smacked the shit outta her for lying.

"How you get up here?" She folded her arms across her chest.

"I work here. Boss told me you were in his office so I thought you were waiting for me." I laughed hard as hell in her face. River moved in front of me.

"Sorry, Boo. That's me all day and before you attempt to talk shit; don't."

"Excuse me."

"I know exactly who you are Avery and my man, Jerome Winston only has one son and another on the way."

"You have kids?"

"You heard what she said." I definitely considered Jasir my son too, even though Ryan was in his life. He knew the difference and since Ryan nor River didn't object to me calling him that, it was what it was.

"Now, I suggest you go back downstairs to find a new baby daddy because this one is all mine." I walked out behind River grabbing myself. When she got a little hood, it turned me on.

"I can't wait to get you home." I forced her to turn around and threw my tongue down in her mouth.

"Sooooo, yall fucking in the hallway or what?" Raymond got on my nerves at times but he was right. Me and River had to wait until we got home to finish.

"Onyx told me to get her outta here and since we're cousins and not kissing ones, we figured you'd be ok with her coming home with me."

"Nigga, you better not drive her to fucking Rhode Island." He smirked.

"And if I do, you'll have to drive and get her." He joked, snatching River by the hand.

"I'll see you in a few. Be careful." She blew me a kiss on her way down the steps. Following behind them, I watched as they went out the back and hopped in his car. Once

Raymond pulled off, relief kicked in because she was outta harm's way.

"Let's go." I said, returning to our section.

Walking through the club women were damn near throwing themselves at us. Some had little to no clothes on while others were so tight they could barely move. The heights women went through to catch a baller was crazy.

"Ayeeee, what's up, Block? I ain't seen you in a minute." We were standing in front of the VIP area Huff had. The guy was a youngster who partied with us a few times. His mom used to make fish fries and give us ours for free for making sure he didn't get in no trouble.

Looking in Huff's section, there were a few niggas I've never seen before. He wasn't paying attention and his dumb ass had one of those hoodie face masks on that people wore to hide their identity. Funny how even with that on, I knew who he was.

"I'm chilling. Who you here with?"

"Shit, nobody. The flyer said it would be new strippers here and since I just got paid, why not?" He laughed.

"Tonight, ain't the night." I gave him a look and he hauled ass up outta there. I'm happy that even without saying the real reason, he knew what to do. Making my way into the section, his boys moved when they noticed it was me. Still not paying attention because he was tryna entertain some chick, I took a seat next to him.

"Women were always your downfall." Huff jumped at the sound of my voice. As loud as it was in here, there was no need to yell. He heard me perfectly fine being how close I sat next to him.

"What the—? Why y'all ain't say he was here?" I had to laugh at him tryna scold his team.

"I ain't fucking with Block. You see the niggas he got with him." Standing around was Onyx, and at least twenty other men from our team. My uncle Montell even sent a few to wait outside in case things got hectic.

"You know, had you took that L when Arabia left you, we wouldn't be here."

"Fuck you. She cheated on me an—"

"And you were cheating on her. The only difference was she married her man, while you still out here tryna fuck everything in sight."

"No, you mad I fucked your bitch." He thought it was funny.

"Aye, y'all. Block fell in love with a ho. A bitch who sold her pussy for a measly $300." Not one person cracked a smile.

"Pussy good tho, right." He boasted.

"So good you tried to kill her for not wanting to give you anymore, right." His ass shut right up.

"Since you think it's funny, tell your friends here how you can't go longer than six minutes, and I'm giving you an extra minute to be nice." River told me all they did was have sex in a missionary position and she always had to finish herself off. She was embarrassed when I asked her why, yet I understood she had to do what she had to.

"Or that, you was texting, calling and begging for the pussy.

The same pussy you was paying for. Between her and Arabia, your ass was hooked. Since my sister wasn't beat, you tried to revert back to my woman and well, let's just say there was never a comparison when it came to me." No response.

"What really pissed me off and the reason I'm here was the fact you terrorized the fuck outta both women. You beat up one a few times and almost killed the other." I stood up and stretched.

"How do you think I should take your life?" I nodded my head and a couple of the dudes with me, snatched Huff up and carried him outside. The individuals who were with him came out to see what was about to happen. Not one of them tried to stop the inevitable.

"Where's the truck?" I asked once we stepped outside.

"Coming down the street." Huff started to panic seeing the Mac truck approaching.

"Come on, Block. I'm sorry. Your sister was ok and River lived. Don't do this." Was he really begging and crying?

"You're one selfish nigga." I took the blunt from Onyx and took a few pulls.

"You knew I was slowly killing off your bloodline and not once did you think to come to me and say stop. Nah, you were too busy tryna fuck and thinking of ways to get at me." Huff never had a loyal team and I've told him countless times about it. Now the shit came back to bite him in the ass because not one nigga stepping up for him.

"How do you wanna die?" Onyx stopped the truck and had it back up.

"Come on. Let's talk about this."

POW! POW! I shot him in both legs making him fall to the ground. Nodding to Onyx, he moved out the way and all you heard was the truck speeding up.

"Oh shit." The closer it got, the more Huff tried to get out the street. Unfortunately, he couldn't move.

"This is for Arabia and River." When the truck hit Huff, you could see his body smash into the pavement.

"Damnnnnn, that nigga flat like a pancake." Someone yelled behind me. His entire body was run over. Even his head was just about flat.

"Anybody else wanna join?" It was only right to ask.

"Hell no." Some retreated back in the club and others left. Before leaving myself, I went in to find the owner. Security told me, he was in the office so I made my way there. The stares of those who must've found out about Huff didn't bother me. All it did was let them know not to fuck with me.

"Oh shit. Oh shit." I heard getting closer to the office door that was wide open.

"Just the person I'm looking for." Dude was sitting in a chair letting Avery ride him. I let off two shots. One went into Avery's back hitting him as well. And the next into his head. He should've never allowed those niggas in without being checked. He was responsible for his own death.

After staying to make sure no one spoke to the cops about the shootings, Montell had his team erase any and all security footage for tonight. The detectives were pissed because they had no leads.

"See you later." Onyx got into his car. Everyone else left a half hour ago but I had to stay for my own conscience.

"Hey, Baby. You ok?" River answered when I called.

"Yup and you better be ready to do all that freaky shit." I heard her laugh and turned around to see her standing there in the same outfit.

"I took an Uber back when you mentioned waiting for the cops to leave." She stood at the door letting me slide my hands up and down her legs.

"We never had sex with you driving." River got in and sat on my lap facing forward.

"What you tryna do?"

"Pull out and you'll see." Backing out the parking lot, River managed to get comfortable on my lap. She lifted that dress showing me that she wore no panties, unbuttoned my jeans and pulled my dick out.

"Sssss. Oh, how I missed you." She moaned after mounting herself.

"And he missed you too." All I can say is having sex while driving was an amazing experience but when it was time to cum, I had to pull over or we would've crashed for sure. River was the perfect woman for me and I wasn't letting her go.

Chapter Fifteen

RIVER

"She looked very pretty River." Maribel stood next to me at the gravesite. I did decide to have a small ceremony for my mother. Block paid the funeral home extra to hold the body until I was ready.

The day Louise took her life, I couldn't deal. She was the only mother I knew and despite the circumstances, I loved her. Then to hear Chana detail how much she loved me only hurt more because why couldn't my mother tell me. Why didn't she tell me what happened when she was a kid? So many questions plagued my thoughts but the only one I always wanted to know was, why she didn't love me.

"You think so. I'm not sure what her favorite color was and... and..." I started crying again.

"It doesn't matter. The service was beautiful besides Janetta tryna sing Eyes of the Sparrow. She sounded like a wounded cat." I was laughing and wiping my eyes.

"Block said she begged him to sing." Blocks mom couldn't sing for shit.

"Yea well, he should've told her no."

"What you over here talking to my daughter in law about?"

"I told her your ass can't sing and Heaven would've sounded better than you."

"Oh no you didn't. River did your mother tell you how she was sitting real close to Block in the kitchen. I saw her rubbing his leg and kissing on his neck too." I stared at Maribel. Block already told me how those two went at it over her saying that.

"Block too young for me but his daddy ain't." Maribel ran in the direction of Block's father almost breaking her ankle running in heels. I swear for those two to have just met, they've become close as heck.

"What they arguing about now?" Block rested his chin on my head.

"Evidently you're too young for Maribel but your dad not." We watched Maribel and Janetta play fighting against the limo. Block turned me to face him.

"This dress showing all those curves and the way that ass filling out, I'm not happy people can see it."

"Thankfully everyone knows this is your ass so it doesn't matter who saw it." I wrapped my arms around his neck.

"And besides, can't nobody do me like you and I don't even want them to try."

"Good answer." We kissed for a few seconds before I

walked back go the casket to say my final goodbye. I requested it not be placed in the ground until I left. Getting in the limo, I looked up at the sky and smiled. It was the perfect day for a funeral and I'm sure my mother had a part in that.

* * *

"Can I talk to you?" Mariah was walking toward me. I had a repast at the house with catered food. Between Maribel and Janetta, they would've argued over who was making what. To avoid it, Block insisted on having someone else make the food.

"Hell no. I need to be right here when you speak to my sister." Mariah rolled her eyes.

"Whatever." She pointed to the couch for me to sit.

"Look, I'm apologizing again because the original one may not have been genuine." Did she really admit that?

"I knew that shit was fake." Chana blurted out. Arabia walked in and took a seat next to me.

"Excuse me." I was confused but not too surprised. She blew her breath.

"I apologized in order to get my husband back. Then all of that stuff happened with your mom and Charlene. The way our family and yours came together for you only proved how childish I was in the beginning."

"You can say that again." Chana always spoke her mind.

"So, I'm saying it again. From the bottom of my heart, I apologize for my behavior. My entire family loves you and Jasir.

What happened to you in the past had nothing to do with me, I'm sorry."

"Mmm hmm. That sounded way better than the original. I still don't trust you though." Chana said making me laugh.

"Chana believe it or not, you're just like me."

"The lies you tell. I'd never treat my family the way you did whether I knew them or not."

"I respect that but I'm talking about the way you protect her. I'm the same with Arabia and the rest of my cousins."

"Anyway, River, I'm hungry and oh shit." Chana stopped mid-sentence and I didn't know why until Arabia slowly turned my head in the direction where Block was. He was on one knee and the whole family was watching.

"River—"

"Yes, Baby, yes." He didn't even get the chance to ask.

"I'm in love with you, River. Will you marry me?" I got down on one knee with him.

"I'll marry you right here, right now." He slid this huge diamond ring on my finger.

"I love you, Jerome Winston."

"You better. That ain't no cheap ring." I started laughing.

"That's big, Mommy." Jasir said, lifting my hand.

"It is, right." The diamond was a decent size and from the looks of it, I know it wasn't cheap. His house didn't even have cheap furniture, floors, appliances or whatever else he had in it. Block had top of the line everything.

"Can we eat now?" Janetta yelled out. Everyone congratulated us and to be honest, I could finally say I'm very happy with how my life was going. I had my son, my fiancé, and a new baby on the way. What else could a woman ask for?

"Let me talk to you real quick." Block took my hand and made me follow him upstairs.

"Everything ok?" I was nervous.

"Everything perfect. I just need to get a quickie because you look good as fuck in that dress." I laughed but gave my fiancé exactly what he asked for. By the time we finished, neither of us wanted to go back downstairs. When we did, half of our family were drunk and others were leaving or watching television. Life can't get no better than this.

Epilogue

Chana and **Ryan** were married the following year and welcomed a baby girl a few months later. Jasir still stayed between both houses and was ecstatic to be a big brother.

Mariah and Onyx decided to try out marriage counseling and it seemed to be working. They've learned to work on communicating with one another and parenting a sassy daughter, who still had her mother's ways. Laila did apologize to Mariah and to this day, she hadn't talked back since. It could be because Mariah finally broke down and gave her a whooping. Whatever the case, they didn't have any more problems out of her.

. . .

Raymond and his mother still don't speak but he did go to the family events now. He kept the house in Rhode Island but purchased one here as well now that he found a girlfriend. She was nice and had a sense of humor like him. We asked where they met and he said on, Only Fans. The guys had jokes for days. However, her only fans was for people who had feet fetishes. She never got naked.

Arabia and Deray raised his daughter as their own and was working on baby number three. She did finally start speaking to his mother but it would never be like before.

River and Block had a son and eleven months later, welcomed a baby girl. They did get married in between because he planned on keeping her pregnant until she couldn't have any more kids. River signed up for counseling as well to deal with her past. It helped her a lot because she was able to vent without someone to judging her.

The End....

From The Author

Thank You to all my readers and supporters for making this series a success. I love and appreciate you more than you know. Y'all are the reason I write. You are my motivation.

Now Available on Amazon

Bossed Up With A Billionaire: A BBW Love Affair

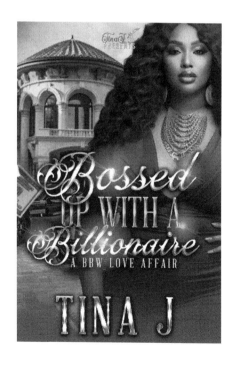

Sincerely Yours: Kamali & Alori

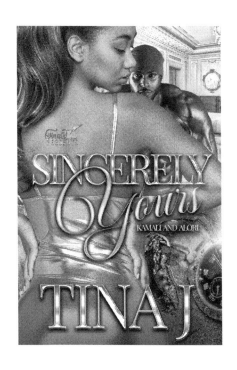

You Complete Me

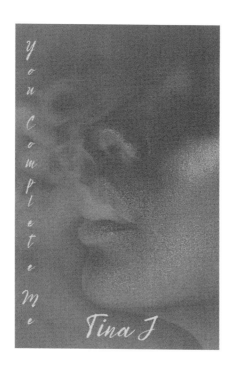

A'int No Savage Like The One I Got

Made in the USA
Monee, IL
09 September 2024

65388398R00096

Chapter One

JEROME "BLOCK" WINSTON

"You look beautiful cuz." I told my cousin Mariah, who was getting married today. We were very tight which is why I'm in the hotel room with her trying to ease her paranoia.

At first, my Uncle Trevor wasn't tryna hear his first born getting married; let alone having sex. My pops told me they had to sit at the house with him for hours in order to calm him down because he wanted to kill the dude. If my uncle only knew how much of a ho, Mariah was he wouldn't have reacted that way.

Well, I can't say she's a ho per se, but I can attest to her having mad dudes tryna fuck. Granted, she's only slept with two guys before this dude, Onyx but others would assume differently due to her always being seen with other niggas.

Anyway, Onyx isn't your local hustla, but he does get down and dirty. He's what the opps would consider a hit man, who takes out anyone and he gets paid very well for it. I know this because he and I often do them together which is how he met Mariah.

"Thank you. Do you think he's gonna feel the same?" She was always worried about what he'd think. Mariah is aware of his job occupation, yet she'd never seen him upset.

"Mariah." I took her hand in mine.

"Onyx worships the ground you walk on. Shit, you can meet him at the altar with a bonnet, slippers and a nightgown, and he'd still marry you." She smiled.

"What if women tempt him once we're married and—" I shushed her with my index finger.

"He doesn't see anyone but you cuz and best believe women will tempt him. However, you have something they don't."

"What?"

"His heart. Onyx is gone over you and the whole world knows he'll lose it if you ever left him." That nigga damn near went crazy the few times she did walk away.

"He's right, honey." My Aunt Maria said, placing the veil over her head. She married my Uncle Trevor before I was born.

"If by some chance a bitch does try him and he failed victim, don't forget you're license to kill a nigga." All of us a looked at my mother.

"Oh yea, and a bitch." She shrugged and started fixing the

back of Mariah's dress. My mother, Janetta Winston never got over my situation, therefore she stayed ready. I shook my head and took a trip down memory lane.

"Block, I'm sorry. It wasn't supposed to happen like this." My girlfriend Leslie, at the time said. I had been following her for the last couple of weeks due to her disappearing and sadly it led me to a situation I never thought I'd be in.

"What you mean, "It wasn't supposed to happen like this?" I watched her closely as she tried her best to put the remainder of her clothes on.

"I was trying something new for us and—" I cut her stupid ass off.

"You were trying something new by fucking two niggas and a bitch." I pointed to the other chick who hid her body with the sheet, and the two guys looking petrified in the corner. They had thrown their clothes on soon as the door flew off the hinges.

"No. Well... it was an orgy... I wanted to..." She continued to stutter as she tried to explain this bullshit.

"Girl, if you don't tell my son that you've been fucking each other for weeks, I'm gonna smack you myself." My mother barked.

We were having lunch when the private investigator sent me a location of where my fiancé was. Instead of going home, my mother insisted on accompanying me in case she had to get physical with a female.

"Block, I'm sorry. Linda is the woman who worked with me that I told you about." She pointed to the chick, who nodded as she

continued talking. Linda and I never met but they had conversations over the phone a lot.

"One night we went out after work and she had me try some drugs."

"WHAT?" I snapped.

"It was to ease my mind after finding out that woman possibly was carrying your child." I ran my hand over my head listening. Some bitch named Avery, I cheated on her with claimed I'm her kids' father but until it's born, I ain't staking claims on nobody.

"We started taking edibles and then the high would go away too fast. She introduced me to something stronger."

"Stronger? What was it, heroin, dope, crack, fentanyl, what?" My mother asked the question I was thinking but couldn't muster up the words to ask. Is it because in all honesty, I didn't wanna know?

"Heroin and small doses of fentanyl." Leslie admitted and put her head down in shame.

"Oh shit, son. Your bitch is a got damn crackhead." My mom picked her phone up and walked out.

"Block, if you hadn't cheated—" I stopped her before she could finish.

"You should've left me alone if you couldn't handle it. Instead, you stuck around and promised it wouldn't break us up." Leslie started crying.

"I know this is hard for you to hear, but imagine how hard it was when Robbie told us, he contracted HIV. We all got tested and it made sense to continue sleeping with one another since we

all had it." I was at a complete loss of words when Linda said it. She spoke in a non chalant tone too.

"What the fuck you just say?" Linda became scared once the tip of my gun touched her forehead.

"Leslie said she told you. I'm sorry for blurting it out." Her hands were up in the air.

"Which one of you motherfuckers is, Robbie?" Neither of the two men answer.

Pow! Pow!

Both of their bodies dropped. I gave zero fucks about anyone calling the police after hearing gunshots.

"Oh my goodness." Linda rushed over to the men.

Pow!

I let one off in the back of her head.

"Block, please don't do this." At this point, Leslie had already used the bathroom on herself and was begging me not to kill her.

"I may have taken you back since you did the same for me." I had the gun pointed at her.

"But you caught that shit and continued fucking me." Disgust was written all over my face.

"Block, I made you wear condoms because you cheated on me." Did she really try and come up with an excuse?

"I don't give a fuck! It could've broke."

Pow! I shot her in the leg and watched her body fall to the ground.

"Block, pleaseeeeee." She cried.

"The way I see it is, you're gonna die anyway, but save a space for your parents because if I have it, they'll be joining you."

5

"Block wait!" She put her hand up at the same time I put a bullet in between her eyes. Staring down at Leslie had me shed a tear because I really did love her. I guess her love for me wasn't the same.

She brought up my cheating but it only happened once after a bachelor party. If she wanted to get me back; ok fine, but she kept doing it.

"You ok, son." I felt my mom's hand on my shoulder bringing me back to reality. Everyone was staring at me as if I were crazy.

"I'm good. Let's get you married, cuz."

"Can y'all give us a minute?" Mariah had everyone step out the room.

"Block it's ok to feel a certain way right now. You were going to marry her."

"Are you telepathic because how do you be knowing what's going on in my head?" We both laughed.

"Because I'm your bestie and we have superpowers." She made me laugh. Me, her and my sister were the closest outta all of the family and some of the cousins hated it.

"I love you, cuz." Mariah hugged me and backed away.

"There's a good woman out there for you but it damn sure ain't Avery." My family hated that bitch.

Ever since she claimed I'm the father, she'd speak to anyone from my family she saw. Well not my mother or Mariah because my cousin beat her up twice already, and ma dukes said not to ever speak even if she did have my kid.

"Is everything ok in here?" Onyx's mother came inside after knocking on the door.

"I should've known you two were having y'all famous cousin talk." Miss Dorothy said making us both laugh. She kissed my cheek and told me to go calm my friend down. Onyx thinks Mariah's having cold feet and didn't wanna marry him.

"Miss Dorothy, I hope you made that banana pudding and upside-down pineapple cake."

"Boy hush, you know the food is catered." I gave her a look and she pursed her lips up.

"Fine. I put it at the dessert table, now go." She shooed me away from her.

"Love you too, Miss Dorothy." She showed me out the door. That woman knew she could cook her ass off. It's the exact reason everyone called her up when we having something just to be sure she's the one making the food.

"Is she ready?" My Uncle Trevor asked on my way out.

"Yup." I left out the hotel and headed over to the church. At least I'll be able to get drunk and eat some good ass food.

"What the fuck you want now?" I barked at Avery, who was calling me nonstop.

I fucked her six months ago and it was the worst mistake of my life. Leslie was the love of my life and we had been together since middle school. Most people would say a hood or street nigga can't stay faithful but it wasn't the truth. I've never cheated on her until that day and I'm still boggled about how it happened.

I drank a lot, yet always knew what was going on around me. That particular night, all I remember was watching strippers, smoking, and drinking. When I woke up the next day still inside the club with my dick hanging out and cum all over it, I knew shit was about to get bad.

Telling Leslie hurt me to see her cry but I'm a stand up dude for the most part. There was no way I could hold that in because bitches like Avery were looking for ballers so I already knew once she saw Leslie, she would let it be known we slept together.

Unfortunately, my fuck up resulted in an unwanted pregnancy. The crazy part was that this happened six months ago and she was exactly six months. I'm not saying it wasn't possibly but it's suspect as fuck for sure.

"Block, why are you treating me bad? I'm not the one who cheated on his woman." I blew my breath listening to her whine about my behavior. In a way she wasn't lying about it being my fault. However, I'm still on the ropes that someone drugged me there. The toxicology report came back fine but there was something fishy.

"I'm not gonna ask again what you want."

"Fine. Can you drop me off some money to get a crib?" I disconnected the call immediately. Avery was a bad ass stripper and made hella money at the club. When her stomach began to show, my sister Arabia allowed her to work at her restaurant as a hostess. She may not have been making that stripper money but she was paid well on the strength that the baby may possibly be mine.

Pulling in the lot at the church, my phone rang over and over. I ignored it and went to check on Onyx. That nigga ain't got it all either and will burn it down if my cousin don't show up.

Chapter Two

MARIAH WINSTON

"My son is going to cry." Ms. Buggs said, taking a few photos.

"I hope so." I told her being completely honest. It wasn't that Onyx didn't think I was beautiful, it was more or less the drama we went through over the last four years to get here.

The fake pregnancies from his ex, the women calling my phone all hours of the night saying he was with them, when he was next to me. The chicks who claimed he stopped paying their bills and so forth. The theatrics took forever to stop and it was only done because I gave Onyx an ultimatum. It was me or them but not both. I didn't consider it one but some of his family did; especially his grandmother.

Me and that woman could not get along for shit and I could

care less. She had Miss Buggs at the age of thirteen so they basically grew up together. His mom did indeed have him at the same age; it's like the cycle repeated itself. Unfortunately, his grandmother Charlene never grew up and looked at Onyx like her homeboy and someone to always give her money. The woman doesn't work and won't because she felt as if her grandson should be the breadwinner.

I blamed him for her actions. He's been in the streets since he was a pre-teen and graduated from selling drugs to doing hits on politicians, and a lot of other big-time people. I'm not a fan of his work, but it's his business and I don't stick my nose where it didn't belong.

"Is she ready yet?" Charlene burst through the door with a small flask most likely full of liquor. She's a drinker for sure which is what the family seemed to blame her outburst on but not me.

However, her ass ain't never drunk when she tries to come for me, and I say try because I don't back down regardless of how old she is. I'm taught to respect my elder, but elders need to show respect as well.

"Weren't you supposed to be checked into rehab for your fake drinking problem?" I spoke sarcastically still applying a little lip gloss.

"No the fuck you didn't." I turned to face her.

"Yea, I did. See, this is my wedding day so if you're here to pop shit, turn the fuck around and get out."

"Bitch, I know—"

"Bitch?" I went to remove my veil and caught myself.

"You know what? I'm not going to let you ruin my wedding but best believe this bitch." I pointed to myself.

"This bitch will rock your ass to sleep after my reception so don't disappear, okay." I lifted my dress to keep the bottom from dragging and left her standing there.

"What's wrong?" My mother Maria could always read my facial expressions even when I didn't want her to.

"Nothing. Charlene on her bullshit again." My mom tried to go inside the room but I caught her by the bicep.

"Daddy is downstairs waiting and if I'm a second late, he'll come up." I stared at my mother who had a look of hate on her face. She despised that woman too.

"It's my wedding day." I smiled to keep from going back in the room to lash out myself.

"Mariah."

"I know, mom. I just want to meet my husband at the altar." She placed her hand in mine and walked on the elevator with me.

"Are you excited?"

"I am." She patted my hand.

"That's all that matters for now." Before I could ask what she meant, the elevator doors opened and there stood my father, my Uncle Monty and Uncle Travis.

My Aunt Janetta was outside talking to one of my cousins, my siblings and the bridal party were in the lobby. I loved my family to death. We are always there for one another.

* * *

"I now pronounce you, Mr. and Mrs. Buggs." The pastor said. Onyx held me close and kissed me gently but not enough to get me aroused.

"I can't wait to get you in the limo." I laughed as we walked through the people taking pictures and giving out a million hugs. One person became visible which made me excuse myself in order to catch her. Onyx was busy speaking to the guys in my family and paid me no mind.

"Hi, Salina." The woman turned around with a smirk on her face.

"I just had to see if he really went through with it." Her response didn't catch me off guard. She's a bitch and it's what a scorned ex would say.

"It's the exact reason I didn't pound your face in when I walked down the aisle." I offered phony grin.

"Excuse me."

"Congratulations, Mariah. You looked beautiful." A woman said making her way past us. I thanked her and directed my attention back to this chick.

"You heard me. Your stupid ass stuck out like a sore thumb with this red hair, bright orange dress, tacky ass gold shoes and clown looking makeup."

"Tacky?" She worried about me saying tacky and not the fact she resembled a circus clown. The blush was red as hell on her cheeks and she must've been cold in that sleeveless dress because her nose was red. The lipstick wore off but the lip liner showed and lastly, one of her eyebrows was cut higher than the other. How you talking shit at someone's wedding and look a mess?

"Onyx may not have recognized you because some of his family dress in those weird type of outfits too but a woman always knows when a hater comes around." He had a few cousins who loved wearing bright color hair and clothes. It's not to say he didn't recognize his ex but he may not have been paying attention.

"I'm not gonna ask why you're here because you gave me the reason. I'm gonna give you time to leave." I lifted my dress to walk away.

"Do you think it's ok for me to attend the reception?" Salina thought it was funny. I turned around.

"Absolutely. I would love for you to attend." I smiled and turned to join my husband at the limo.

"Oh, but don't get upset when, Onyx sees you and what happened last time, happens again. Byeeeee!" I dragged the word out on purpose.

Salina can play as if she was hood all she wanted but the last time she tried to be funny, Onyx had one of his cousins put her in the hospital for a couple of weeks. So, if she wanted to continue playing this game, who am I to tell my husband to leave her alone.

"Fucking bitch." I said out loud walking toward Onyx.

"I saw that heffa. You want me to beat her ass real quick." My cousin Arabia, who is Block's sister asked getting ready to take her earrings off.

She and I were born the same month and two days apart.

14

People often mistook us for sisters, and not because we looked alike but because we were one in the same. Our personalities, our attitudes, the way we dressed, as well as knocking a bitch out if she got outta line was exactly the same.

"What's wrong?" Onyx lifted my head when I got closer. Arabia walked off when Block called her over.

"Nothing. I'm just happy to be, Mrs. Buggs." Wrapping my arms around his neck, he stared in my eyes for a moment and then searched the crowd.

"Get in." His tone was full of authority, yet he didn't show any anger. Once the driver pulled off, he raised the partition.

"I'm gonna handle that." Without responding, he had me sit on his lap. The petticoat to flare my dress out got in the way so I took it off.

"I fucked up bad in the past but I promise, you are the only woman I've ever wanted to rock my last name." He placed a gentle kiss on my lips. A few minutes later the driver parked, got out and Onyx made sure to give me what I needed to relax before going in the reception. When we finished, I said a prayer that our foundation would never be broken.

"Ok, cuz. Onyx about to come out here and snatch you up." Arabia said as the two of us twerked to one of the rap songs playing. I spotted my husband standing in the corner talking with his eyes trained on me. Mouthing the words, *I love you* made him smile.

Onyx was so damn sexy to me and he knew it because I've always told him. He had that chocolate skin with deep waves in his hair. His goatee wasn't too long but long enough to tickle my clit any time he went down. He wasn't a big guy but he did lift weights in order to stay fit for his occupation.

Unfortunately, those bitches in the streets told him as well, which caused him to cheat. Little did he know, I got my lick in as well and never said a word. A woman doesn't have to mention if she cheated or not, just knowing it myself always made me smile.

"He'll be alright. Great! Here come this bitch." Arabia started putting her hair up after pointing to Charlene coming our way.

"Relax, Mariah. Relax." I told myself taking deep breaths. Wedding or not, I'll slide this bitch if she talks slick.

"Congratulations, granddaughter in law." She tried to hug me and Arabia stood in front of us.

"We don't like you so move the fuck on." She folded her arms.

"I wasn't talking to you."

"And? It's my cousins wedding and so far you managed to piss half the guests off with your shenanigans." People were complaining that she was falling all over the place, cursing at them and drinking more than she should.

"What?"

"Look at you barely standing with two drinks in your hand." My eyes connected with Block, who was on his way in our direction.

16

"Anyway, I'm here to say, I'm happy for you and glad he didn't marry, Salina." Was this bitch being smart?

"Whatever." I chimed in.

"Oh, you didn't know he proposed and she turned him down." She snickered before taking another sip of whatever was in her glass.

"Yea, I think it was last year after y'all broke up. He claimed, you were a bitch and he missed her. Why you think she showed up to the wedding?" My anger was brewing. I could hear Arabia telling me not to listen to her but it was too late. Charlene knew how to get under my skin.

"He told her about your marriage and Salina wanted to see if he went through with it. I mean, you did leave him a few times for sleeping with not only her, but others."

"A'ight, Charlene. You had too much to drink. Let's get you home." Block moved her away.

"Have a good honeymoon." She yelled. Block guided her toward the door.

"Ignore her stupid ass. Everyone knows, Onyx didn't want anyone but you." Tears streamed down my face because it was at this exact moment, I knew Charlene was right. Onyx had gone back and forth from me and Salina, and then to others. He had a kid with his ex before me, and I always trusted him to get his daughter with no problem. What if he was sleeping with her? What if he only married me because she wanted no parts of him?

"Mariah, don't you dare let her ruin your wedding day with her bullshit." Arabia rushed to wipe my eyes. Out of my peripheral, I could see Onyx heading this way and asked Arabia to take me out. I didn't want anyone to know how upset Charlene made me.

"Why is she crying?" Onyx spun me around at the door and hugged me tight.

"That's between y'all. I'll be inside." Arabia wasn't afraid of Onyx but she didn't like to get in couples problems.

"Did you ask me to marry you because, Salina turned you down?" When he pulled on his goatee, I knew then it was true.

"I'll tell you what happened later."

"Maybe you should tell me now since everybody think they can show up and ruin my day." Salina was standing at the door using her two hands to peek inside.

"THIS WAS MY FUCKING DAY ONYX!" I screamed, punching him in the chest." He grabbed my wrists.

"Get the fuck off me." I snatched away.

"Mariah. Mariah." I heard him yell. I went outside to the limo and told the driver to take me home. Fuck this marriage!

Chapter Three

ONYX BUGGS

"Why the fuck you here?" I gripped Salina up by her bicep and drug her down the stairs and to the car. Why wasn't I surprised to see my grandmother sitting in the front seat passed out. Those two stayed in touch after we broke up and literally ran off any chick, I tried to be with before my wife. Mariah didn't back down from any of their antics and stayed ten toes down for me, which was why she became the wife.

I'm not ashamed to admit I took her through a lot and caused major heartache. The baby scares, bitches calling her all hours of the nights, the videos and photos of me with women. None of us having sex but they left nothing to the imagination either. However, Mariah showed absolutely no weakness and those ho's were mad, including this one.

"Charlene asked me to pick her up." I threw her body against the car.

"Y'all both messy as fuck." I opened the door to check the pulse on my grandmothers neck. She was known to get pissy drunk.

In this case, I wanted to know if she really was because why did she tell Mariah that shit. Granted, it was true but I'm not sure if the time frame was correct to what she revealed. Slamming the door shut, my grandmothers eyes shot open. Just like I thought, her ass was faking.

"I'll deal with you later." I walked over to Salina rushing to get in the driver seat. I snatched her by the hair, gripped it tight enough to make her eyes go into a slit and forced her to look at me.

"I don't know what fucking game you're playing but I'm telling you right now, I'll slice your throat if you continue bothering, Mariah."

"Ok, Onyx. I'm sorry." She tried her hardest to remove my hands from her hair.

"She is my wife and no one will come before her, except my daughter. Are we clear?" She nodded. I released her hair and shook my hand to remove the patch that came loose from me gripping it. She got in the car quickly and pulled off, damn near crashing into park cars.

Blowing my breath, I called Block on the phone and asked him to give me a ride. Mariah's phone showed she was on her way home and if she wasn't, I'll be able to find her with the tracker.

"What happened?" He questioned, pulling his Maserati truck around the building.

Block and I have been friends for the last ten years. We met doing a hit for the same guy that included two kingpins from Jamaica. Once we completed the task, we stayed in touch and now he was like my brother.

Me and Mariah met two years after we did, but I was with Salina and she was pregnant with my daughter. I've tried countless times to make it work with my ex but she was too jealous and needy. Everywhere I went she wanted to be up my ass. Any woman who spoke, Salina accused me of sleeping with her. The entire relationship was a disaster and I stayed around for as long as I could.

Mariah and I ran into one another after Salina had the baby, we linked up and been together ever since. I loved everything about her from the way she giggled over dumb shit, to her putting my ass to sleep after sex. There was nothing I wouldn't do for Mariah, even lay my life on the line for her. That's why her leaving our wedding bothered the fuck outta me because she never let a woman throw her off her square.

"Charlene and Salina happened."

"Yea, I had to take Charlene out because she was talking shit to, Mariah. When did Salina show up?" He pulled off.

"Man, I don't even know. One minute, Mariah's on the dance floor, and the next she's crying and leaving." I rested my head against the seat. I swore to never make my wife cry again, yet someone else was doing it on my behalf.

Parking in front of my house, we said our goodbyes. I asked

him to tell everyone at the reception we snuck out to go on our honeymoon so no one would assume otherwise.

Walking in the house, I could hear doors slamming and what sounded like her on the phone. Making my way up the steps after locking the door, I found her in the bedroom wearing only the white panty set from under the wedding dress. We never got the chance to wash up so I could see the juices from us having sex soiled in her panties.

Snatching her up from behind, I walked in the shower to start it. Mariah started punching me in the back and kicking as she begged to be put down. Once the water reached a warm temperature, I placed her on her feet, ripped the panties off and unhooked the bra.

"Get in." She stood there with her arms folded showing how mad she was.

"A'ight then." Removing my own clothes, I stepped in and lifted her body to join. The water from the shower head wet both of us up. Her hair started to loosen from the bun due to the steam so I reached behind to remove the pins, letting her hair flow to the middle of her back. Mariah took very good care of herself.

Staring down at her number eight shape, I bit down on my lip as my hands roamed her body. Her C cup breast began to harden with each kiss I placed along her shoulder.

"You looked beautiful today and still do." She rolled her eyes and leaned against the shower with her hands behind her back.

"I don't give a fuck about that bitch and you know it."

"Onyx, she—" I quieted her by crashing my lips on hers. Once she returned the kiss, and wrapped her arms around my neck, I lifted her legs in the crook of my arms, inserted myself slowly and stared into her eyes.

"Ssssss." She moaned.

"You are my better half, Mariah. The only woman I would ever marry." I was hoping that me admitting that, she wouldn't be angry any longer.

"But—"

"But we'll discuss that irrelevant shit later. Right now, all I wanna do is make love to my wife. Can I do that?" She blushed hearing me call her, my wife.

"Yes." For the rest of the evening, me and my wife were the nastiest we've ever been in the bedroom to one another. I can honestly say, there were no mistakes made when I chose her as my forever.

"Hurry up, babe. We're gonna miss our flight." Mariah called out to me in the bathroom. We were supposed to leave last night after the reception, but once all that shit went down; we stayed home and booked an early flight this morning.

I wanted to take the family jet for privacy but she decided to take commercial in order to gloat to strangers about us going on our honeymoon. Women loved to show off.

Our bags were in the car since last night. All we had to do

was get dressed. She was telling me to hurry up and her ass was standing at the bottom of the steps completely naked.

"Sooooo, we rebooking another flight." I lifted her in my arms once I got downstairs.

"No, silly. I wanted to know if you see a difference in me yet." Checking over her body nothing seemed to be different.

"Are you pregnant?" I guessed it because like I said, nothing stood out to me.

"Yes. Baby, I'm five weeks." I let her down and stared at her.

"How tho? I can't have any more kids." The doctor told me after my daughter, I needed surgery on one of my testicles because it ruptured.

"Say what now?" She saw my face changing and backed away.

"You fucked someone else?" I don't even know why that question came out.

WHAP! She smacked the fuck outta me.

Pushing her against the wall, I held her hands above her head.

"I know all about your got damn surgery. I also know it's possible to have more kids as long as no more damage was done." I felt like shit because the doctor did tell me that and every year since I've gone to see him, he always said there wasn't anything wrong with me. Again, I'm not even sure why those words came out.

"Did you forget that bitch made me lose our first kid? Are you saying that child wasn't yours either?" She kneed me in the dick and stormed upstairs.

When me and Mariah first got together it took her four months to have sex with me. Three months later, she popped up pregnant and unfortunately miscarried after the fourth month. She blamed me because my ex taunted and stressed her out with lies the entire time. Never mind the fact other women found out about her and started to antagonize her too.

For years she refused to get off birth control. She told me almost a year ago she wanted a baby and would get off so we could start a family. Now here I was accusing her of sleeping with another man when I know it wasn't possible since I'm aware of her every move. I ran up the steps to find her and I'm sad to say she was balled up in a fetal position on the bed crying hysterically.

"Mariah, I'm sorry."

"This has been the worst twenty four hours of my life." I was offended like a motherfucker but why? Salina showed up at our wedding and reception. My grandmother didn't make it any better by spewing those lies and here I am, questioning the paternity.

"What?"

"The wedding was perfect but your bitch showed up there. Then, she showed up at the reception with your hateful ass grandmother. Lastly, you accused me of sleeping with another man over a pregnancy we both been working hard to have." I sat down on the bed with my head in my hands.

"You caught me off guard and—" There really wasn't an excuse.

"Just go, Onyx."

"What?"

"I'm not going on a honeymoon; you can't fuck the hurt outta me and to be honest, I don't want you anywhere around me right now. You let your family and arrogance ruin what was supposed to be the best day of my life." Those words stung and I had nothing to say.

"Lock the door on your way out and do what you do best."

"Mariah." I moved closer. She almost fell off the bed trying to get away from me.

"I don't wanna lose this baby, Onyx. Please leave me alone." With nothing to say, all I could do was respect her wishes and leave. Yes this was our home but she was right, another miscarriage would most likely break her and I never wanted that for her.

Packing some clothes to leave, I kissed her on the cheek, and locked the door behind me. I drove to the condo we owned, went inside and waited until sleep found me. How could I allow the one person in my life that I loved feel so much pain?

Chapter Four

RIVER THOMAS

"Mami, make sure you wash her hair good, ok. She pay a lotta money." Marissa said, pointing to some woman walking over to the sink. Her accent was very heavy at times but I could understand her for the most part.

I was a shampoo and cleaning girl at the Doobie shop in Newark, NJ, located on Central Ave. This place had a lot of clientele and stayed busy on the weekends. On a good day, I could make thirty five dollars in tips from the ladies. Some may assume that's not a lot but for me only shampooing hair, that's good because they don't have to tip.

Anyway, the woman made her way to where the sink was. As she sat, the scent of her perfume lingered and I could tell it was expensive, just like the Gucci purse with the outfit and sneakers to match. This was the first time I've seen her in here but clearly she's a regular if Marissa knew her.

"You ready?" I asked because she was occupied with her phone and hadn't sat properly in the chair yet. I draped the apron around to keep her from getting wet.

"Yea, give me a second." She typed away angrily on her phone and turned it off. After placing it on her purse, she made herself comfortable in the chair.

"I'm ready." I turned the water on to make sure it reached the right temperature, and right before she laid her head back, she stopped.

"I'll beat your ass in here if you put any chemicals in my hair besides the regular." Who the hell was she speaking to?

"Ummm, ok but don't snap at me." She sat up.

"What you say?"

"I said, don't snap at me. There's a way to speak to people." I waited for her to respond while still feeling the water.

"How long you been working here?"

"Ma'am, I'm just trying to wash your hair. Marissa already gave me directions on what shampoo and conditioner to use." It's obvious this chick was having a bad day.

"That's not what I asked." I put my hands up and called Marissa to the back.

"Look, I don't want no problems. I'm here to work and go home." Once Marissa came to where we were, she already knew something was up.

"Your little employee here thinks it's ok to disrespect customers." This bitch just told a bold face lie.

"Who, River? She barely speaks. I'm surprised she said anything." I stood there waiting to hear her response. Marissa was right, I minded my business at work and left. I've learned so much about women and their men by listening to them in here, I could probably start a gossip column.

"I told her not to use a certain shampoo and she snapped." Nothing surprised me with people these days but to lie for no reason was an ultimate low.

"I'm not calling you a liar but are you sure. River never speaks." I'm glad she had my back.

"Either you get her away from me or I'll take my business elsewhere." Marissa was struggling with what to do.

"It's ok, Marissa. She was the last person anyway. I'll go in the room and wait until everyone leaves." Marissa nodded. I understood the whole be nice to customers thing but that woman was miserable. She took her anger out on me for no reason, so the best thing for me to do was walk away. I'm no fighter, but no woman will put her hands on me either. That chick was ready to fight and I need this job.

Rolling my eyes at the woman, I went into the small room we take a break in. It's tight but I've spent many of nights here to sleep when there was nowhere else to go. The last time Marissa caught me by coming in early. She wasn't mad and told me, I should've let her know so she could help me.

Three hours later the shop was closed and the only people left were me and Marissa, who was counting up the money. Placing the headphones in my ear that I got from Five & Below, I got to work.

By the time I finished, sweeping, mopping, cleaning out the sinks, wiping down the dryers and sanitizing everything it was after ten.

Grabbing the envelope Marissa left with my weekly pay in it, I turned the lights off and locked up. It was almost Christmas and the weather was brick cold. Rushing to my basement apartment that was ten minutes away, I almost broke my ankle going down the stairs from the black ice.

Opening the door, I hurried to shut it and turned the heat on. Waiting on government assistance for my utility bills was like waiting for them to give me food stamps. The state did finally offer me $120 a month on stamps, and I do have free medical insurance. That's the least they could do for what they put me through.

This apartment was literally five hundred square feet, if that. When you walked in that was the kitchen area. It held a small stove, refrigerator, one counter space and two cabinets. The bathroom was small as well with only a shower, toilet and the sink had no cabinet underneath. The living room was the biggest space which was also my bedroom so full size bed was fine where it was.

Rushing to get in the shower before my company came, I hid the envelope from Marissa and went to shower. Using the pear body wash I got from Target with a gift card from someone as a tip, I lathered the soap up and scrubbed off the day. When I finished, I dried off, threw on some shorts, a tank top and waited for my company.

* * *

"Who is that?" I cracked the door for Brandon, after looking out the peep hole and seeing someone with him. He was someone I dealt with when money was needed.

"That's nobody. He was in the car so I told him to come in." Brandon tried to push the door open.

"Ugh, not." He blew his breath as if he were aggravated. I don't know what he thought this was. He must be outta his mind if he assumed it was ok for another man to enter my place. Especially, one that I didn't even know.

"Damn, you ready for me?" Brandon closed the door and I reached behind him to lock it. He started removing his clothes like usual and soon as I turned the light off, he turned into an animal and not in a good way.

Brandon had an ok size dick but he could never last longer than ten minutes. I'm not saying men had to last all night but at least make sure the woman got hers too. He would finish, dress and leave, making me grab my bullet to finish myself off.

"Here." I passed him the brand new box of condoms, took my shorts off and laid on the bed. There was no four-play between us and his kissing was downright disgusting and sloppy. I hated when he tried to stick his tongue in my mouth. Unfortunately, kissing was part of the deal between us. Some say kissing brings on emotions, however, not when the person can't do it correctly. Then again, what may not be good for me, may be good for someone else.

"Damn you feel good." My legs were on his shoulders as he

pumped quickly. I'll admit he had me wet down below but I knew better than to get into it. because he would finish before me.

"Go, daddy. You're doing good." I yelled, feeling like the chick from waiting to exhale stroking his ego knowing he wasn't doing a damn thing for me.

"Yea, River. I'm about to cum." A few seconds later it was over.

"Whew! I needed that." He pulled out, and went in the bathroom to take the condom off.

"Oh shit." He shouted, making me jump up.

"What's wrong?" He called me inside. I had to stand at the door because only one person could fit in there.

"The condom broke." He lifted it off his dick showing the hole.

"What the hell?" I pulled him out and rushed to sit on the toilet. I'm not sure why when I know damn well trying to push his sperm out wasn't going to work.

"Here." I looked up to see him handing me three hundred dollars.

"If you want more money my boy outside. I'm sure he'll love to dig in that pussy." Hopping off the toilet, I pushed him toward the door. He was really crazy to think that I would sleep with another man in the same night, or at all for money. I'm not a prostitute but I'm also not going to turn away funds.

"I don't even want to do this with you." He stopped after opening the door.

"You can make a lotta money selling your pussy to more

people. Just make sure I still gotta spot." I slammed the door in his face and cried. Why was my life this bad and why did I result in selling my coochie for a lousy three hundred dollars? Maybe I was a prostitute but I can't be if it's only one person. Women fuck for money all the time to get purses and other stuff. No one considers them a ho, why should I.

I locked the door, put the chair under the doorknob, and went to shower. The money he gave was for me to save but I'm damn sure getting a Plan B pill in the morning. Ain't no way I could bring another child in this world.

Chapter Five

ARABIA WINSTON

"Hola, mamacita." I spoke to Marissa at the doobie shop. She was the only one I trusted to do my hair.

"Hey, honey. Go to the sink so I can wash your hair." Putting my sunglasses in my purse, I searched for the chick, Mariah said was talking shit a couple of days ago. It shocked me to hear about it because Marissa don't allow drama in her shop.

When I saw who it was, it really surprised me, to know River was the person Mariah accused. I figured it was her from the description my cousin gave. The oversized clothes and glasses was a dead giveaway.

River Thomas went to school with me, and even then, people would consider her a mute because she never spoke. The rumor going around was that she got pregnant by a neighbor and her mom was crazy. Mariah went to a private school so she had no clue who she was.

"Hey." I spoke to River when she emerged from the back. She turned around looking for the person I was speaking to.

"I'm talking to you, River. You don't remember me?" She shook her head no.

"We were in the same gym and chemistry class in high school. The teacher paired us up a few times on projects." River was smart as hell and got straight A's for as long as I could remember.

We happened to be in the same class all throughout the four years but those two were the ones we had to be in close proximity, where the others we could sit wherever. We've only been out of school for a few years so she should remember me.

"Arabia?" She questioned in a confused tone.

"I know, I know." I laughed at her trying to figure out it were really me.

In high school, I was a tiny girl and hadn't developed physically until the middle of junior year. It was if I had a growth spurt.

"I gained a little weight." Patting my thighs with my hands she laughed. I weighed maybe 110 pounds soaking wet in high school. Now I was 155 full of ass and muscle. Never had any surgeries and made sure to eat healthy and take care of myself.

"How are you?" She shrugged, standing there holding her own hands. That was another thing, she would stand there even after a conversation was finished until you walked away or someone told her to move.

"Ok, Arabia. Let's get this hair washed." Marissa laid me back and started the process.

"How long has, River worked here." I asked when she walked away and it was just the two of us.

"Oh no. Don't tell me, she was being rude." She poured the shampoo in my hair.

"Nothing like that. We went to school together. That was my first time seeing her in a long time."

"She started last year but you usually came on her days off." It explained why we never ran into one another.

"I feel sorry for her because she doesn't bother anyone and has been trying to get her kid back home with her." As Marissa ran down a tad bit of her business, I closed my eyes. Her hands were working like magic as she scrubbed my hair.

"Marissa, someone is here for you." River spoke softly.

"River, finish Miss Winston hair, put her in rollers and under the dryer. Set it for a half hour please." River did what she asked and pointed in the direction of where to sit. Coming out the back, it looked as if the cable company was here.

When the door sounded off again, it was Block. He stopped by to give me cash for my hair. I forgot to go to the ATM and these salons charge three percent for using a credit card. It didn't matter how much money I had, a bitch was always looking for a cheaper deal. Block asked Marissa where I was.

"Here." He handed me money and sat next to me.

"What's up?" I lifted the dryer a little to hear what he had to say. Block started asking me about Avery working at the restaurant. None of us could stand her but on the strength of her possibly carrying my niece or nephew, I played nice with her.

"Are you special or something?" Looking up to see who he was speaking to, River stood there star struck.

"Leave her alone."

"Tell her to leave then. Standing over here looking like Velma from Scooby Doo." I couldn't hold the laugh in. River had on some circular glasses with a turtleneck shirt, a long skirt that almost touched the floor, some dingy converses and her hair was in a bob like style but not maintained. You could see her hair growing in from the back.

"Ummm, I was just going to say, you have blood on your sleeve." Block and I focused on his shirt and sure enough there was specks of blood.

"Fuck! I knew chopping his hand off with no hazmat suit would leave a mess." River stood there with no facial expression. Most people would gasp or even run away but not her.

"You ok?" I asked while Block tucked his sleeve under.

"I'm sorry. Can you get up so another customer can sit there?" We both glanced around the salon and no one was here. After me, Marissa was closing. Why would she even ask that?

"Get the fuck out my face." River was aggravated but didn't say a word walking away. She almost fell over one of the salon seats looking back at Block.

"She's nice, don't do that."

"Fuck her. What's up with you and Huff because you're in New York an awful lot." I swallowed hard, pulled the dryer all the way down and leaned back. Block lifted it up and stared.

"I don't wanna know if you're cheating because Huff is my boy. Just make sure the nigga treating you right and he don't come for Huff?" I nodded.

We spoke for a few more minutes about other stuff and he left. It gave me time to think about what needed to be done when it came to Huff and Deray.

Huff has been around my family for years as a kid. Him and Block were very close and three years ago, we got drunk, had sex and had been a couple ever since. I cared for him and at one point, I was in love but over the last year, he wasn't what I wanted any longer. His sex was sloppy, he had money but somehow stayed broke and he really thought I didn't know about the chicks he was sleeping with. It didn't matter to me because I was doing my own thing too.

Deray Smith was the man, I wanted. We met at a club in New York and linked up the next day for lunch. He was like a breath of fresh air to me and honestly, he had his head on his shoulders and wanted to get out of the drug life; where Huff planned on being in the game until he died.

Anyway, Deray and I finally crossed the line by having sex and once we did, he became very territorial. He no longer wanted Huff around me, nor did he want me to stay alone in Jersey. Granted, I stayed in the Palisades which wasn't far from Long Island. I met his family, his close friends and even his kids mother, who turned out to be cool as hell. She was into women now so there was no threat in my eyes when it came to them being around one another at family functions. Now I'm in a bind trying to figure out who was the best fit for me.

"Hey, you ok?" River asked, removing the dryer lid.

"Yea. What's up?"

"Marissa said she would be back in twenty minutes but I'm not sure. Would you like me to take the rollers out?" Hesitating because I'm only used to Marissa doing my hair, I agreed.

"Ok. I don't have a station so you can have a seat at, Marissa's." She went to turn the Open card over to Closed, locked the door and headed to me.

"I'm sorry about earlier with the guy. He was very handsome and the words got stuck when I tried to say, "Hi." I smiled at her in the mirror as she removed the rollers.

"It's ok. Block was my brother and women do that all the time." He was four years older than me and graduated, when we finished eighth grade. She wouldn't know who he was since we weren't friends.

"I bet."

"Do you have a man?" She scoffed up a laugh.

"I'm just trying to get my son home." So it was true about her being pregnant in high school.

She must've been taken out when her stomach started to show because she didn't attend, prom, the senior trips or graduation. I only remembered a few teachers discussing how messed up her life was and her mother made no attempts to help. Not trying to pry, I asked a question around it.

"Oh, is he still at day care?" It was almost six. River turned the flat iron on, used some clips to hold my hair up and parted a small piece in the back.

"It might be a little hot." She didn't burn me and continued.

"No. My mother did something foul and the state took him from me. He lives with his father, who keeps begging me to take him back."

"Oh."

"Trust me, I want my son. That's my whole heart but after what my mother did, they're making me get my own place and as you can see, this was the only job to hire me." She removed one of the clips to part more of my hair to flat iron.

"Did you contact social services?" She sucked her teeth.

"The social worker put me on the Section 8 and Housing list. She also said it's no telling when they'll call me." She shrugged.

"Yea, I heard it's a long wait." There are thousands of people trying to get help.

"It's been two years since my son has lived with me." I could hear her voice crack.

"Why can't you stay with your son's father?"

"He stays with his mom to help with the bills. Its definitely more than enough room and they did offer, but my pride wouldn't let me." His mom brought a house two years after graduation and right before the drama with my mother. The social worker had no problem placing him with them due to the space and the fact it wasn't next door. The same day they took my son. My mother had the nerve to kick me out as if it was my fault what happened.

"I get it."

"Yea, in order for him not to go into foster care, he took custody of him." As she told me some of her story my heart went out to her.

By the time Marissa returned, River had finished my hair, wrapped it and did my eyebrows. Marissa had an area to have that done as well.

"River, you did a great job." Marissa praised her as did I.

"Thanks. I could never afford to get my hair done so I watched tutorials and mastered it. The same with doing eyebrows." She admitted, picking up the broom. I wondered why her hair wasn't done. Then again, after hearing parts of her story, I wouldn't do mine either.

"Here you go." I tried to hand her a twenty dollar tip and she refused. Marissa had gone to the back room grab her things.

"Being able to talk to someone was enough of a tip for me. Thank you." She smiled and closed my hand with the twenty dollars in it.

"I'm not a hairstylist but if ever, Marissa isn't here, I'll do it for you." She hugged me quick and tight before walking off to where Marissa was. She did a great job that's for sure. I went to my car, drove home, packed a bag and headed out.

"What you gonna do when I get your sexy ass pregnant?" Deray had my hands over my head staring down at me while he slid inside my tunnel slow.

"Whatever you want me to do. Why do you feel so good."

"Open your eyes." I did what he said and fell even deeper in love seeing him smiling down.

"You been fucking him?" He pulled out and rammed himself back in.

"No. He hasn't been by since me and you started sleeping together. Fuck, I'm about to cum." My body was in an arch as he continued.

"Who you belong to, Arabia?" He did it again.

"You. Oh gawdddd, I'm yours baby." My hands were freed. I wrapped them around his neck and pulled him in for a kiss.

"Derayyyyy, I love you."

"I love you too." He lifted one of my legs and drilled into me faster. Our skins were smacking and the moans between us became louder.

"Shit, this pussy fire." I felt his fingertips squeezing my ass and let go. He followed behind and left his dick inside. The two of us laid there in silence.

KNOCK! KNOCK! Someone was at the door.

"I'll be right back." He kissed the top of my shoulder and turned my face to kiss his lips. Watching him throw on his shorts, I smiled seeing the hickeys on his neck. It wasn't done on purpose but he didn't stop me from sucking either. After a few minutes, I heard popping noises. I quickly dialed Block praying he would answer. As the phone rang, I sent him a message.

"You better have a good damn reason to be calling me while I'm in some pussy." One thing about my brother was he would never let my calls go unanswered regardless of what he was doing.

"I sent you an address. Get here fast." With no questions asked, the phone disconnected.

Jumping out the bed, I rushed to throw on one of Deray's t-shirts, grabbed the gun he kept under his mattress and tiptoed to the door. Checking the clip, I could hear voices but none of them were familiar.

"We about to take everything from this nigga." Someone yelled from downstairs. Clearly it was a robbery and since I'm not sure what happened to Deray, I put my big girl panties on and went to check on him.

From what I saw, there were four men standing around talking at the bottom of the stairs. Still not being able to see Deray, I tried my hardest to lean over the banister. That's when I saw someone dragging him into another room by his legs.

"Let me check upstairs." Backing away from the banister, I waited in the corner for whoever the guy was to get all the way up and pulled the trigger. His body dropped.

"What the fuck?" Two other guys rushed up the stairs. Wasting no time, I put a bullet in both of them as well. It was one person left and he had yet to come up, which meant he either left or was waiting for me.

Stepping out the shadows, I walked over to the guys who were now on the ground bleeding to death if not dead. None of them looked familiar which led me to believe these were people he didn't know.

"I don't know. That bitch must be here because I heard

gunshots upstairs." The last person was on the phone thinking he was whispering but I could hear everything.

If anyone knew who I was, they were well aware of my shooting skills. My dad prepared me at a young age to stay ready for anything. He would take me and Block to the shooting range when we were barely teenagers; he was older but I was eleven at the time.

Feeling the steel in your hands gave you a sense of power and I'm glad to have gone with them every time. Even now, I go to the range a few times a month just to brush up on my skills and work with the new guns.

"Nah, he not dead but he will be. Possum shot him in the stomach." My heart broke hearing Deray was hit and possibly dying; time was of the essence to get to him. I refused to waste any more time, made my way down the steps, and stood directly behind the idiot. He was so busy on the phone, he never paid attention to me coming down.

POW! I shot him in the back to make sure that even though he may live, he'll be paralyzed. Deray will wanna know who sent him. Removing the phone out his hand, I lifted it to my ear.

"Whoever you are, I will find you and when I do, you better pray I take it easy on your family." The beeping nose alerted me that the person hung up. Rushing to find Deray, he was in the living room taking slow breaths. I ran in the downstairs bathroom to grab a towel. Placing it against his stomach, I called 911 and was surprised when the woman told me someone made the call and they were a minute away. Block must've done it when we hung up.

"You're gonna be fine, baby." I kissed his lips.

"I love you, Arabia." He struggled to say.

"I love you, too. Baby, stay awake ok. The ambulance is pulling in the driveway." I wasn't sure if they were but I wanted him to think positive. Shortly after, Deray was being rushed away by the paramedics. Cops were now asking questions, pictures were being taken of the crime scene and all I could do was cry.

"I don't give a fuck about no crime scene. Where the hell is my daughter?" My mom's voice echoed through the noise.

"Mommy." I hopped up from the table and ran to the door. Her, my dad, Block, and Onyx were there. I know they had to come from Jersey, but it felt like it took them forever to get here.

"Let's get you dressed and we'll discuss everything else later." I nodded. She walked behind me up the stairs because I was only in a T-shirt. How did this happen?

Chapter Six

BLOCK

Seeing my sister in such disarray was fucking with me. There were dried up tears on her face, blood splattered on the shirt and her skin, and most of all, I could see the hurt and pain etched on her face. Even though Arabia never said it, I knew she was in love with the guy from New York.

In my eyes, her and Huff were just messing around and not really into one another. I'm sure Arabia knew about him cheating because everyone knew. It's most likely the reason my sister felt no remorse for doing her.

Unfortunately, whoever sent those niggas for her friend will have to see me. Regardless of who they were really there for, my sister's life was in danger and somebody was gonna pay. Once she got dressed, we headed to the hospital.

"Hey, honey. Are you ok?" An older woman rushed inside

the emergency room panicking. There was a man, two other guys, two women and a kid asleep in the stroller as well. I'm not sure where they stayed but it had been three hours since we arrived and they're just now getting here.

"I'm ok. Miss Smith, those are my parents, and my two brothers." Onyx may have only been around the last ten years but the two of us were closer than the niggas I grew up with, including Huff.

"Hello." She spoke and walked over to my mother.

"Why you walking up on me like that?" If it was one thing Janetta Winston hated, it was someone invading her space.

"Don't worry, I'm only here to hug you. Arabia explained to me about you not wanting anyone close."

"What I tell you about telling my business, Arabia?" They started laughing.

"Have they said anything yet?" Some chick asked my sister. She had red eyes and the woman next to her had to be a stud because she was dressed like me.

"No. He was shot in the stomach. The paramedics said if he was hit anywhere else they wouldn't know until later. Do you know anyone named, Possum?" Arabia questioned them the same way she questioned us.

"No, why?" His father responded.

"The guy on the phone said, Possum was the one who shot him." With a name like that he should've shot himself. Arabia finished relaying what took place to them. Me and Onyx stepped outside only to be joined by Deray's two brothers. We learned the younger one was in high school getting ready for college and the other one, did all the tech stuff for Deray.

"I don't understand how this happened. Deray had cameras everywhere, and to my knowledge he wasn't beefing with anyone."

"What the fuck you tryna say?" I became defensive thinking he was accusing Arabia of setting him up.

"What do you mean?" When he asked that, I knew he wasn't street. Any hood nigga would know what I was insinuating. His pops walked out to join the conversation.

"Listen, Deray was in love with your sister. He had plans to marry her in the next year so before you think we're making assumptions about, Arabia, we're not."

"Then what you mean, you don't understand." I asked his brother again.

"Deray has never been in trouble with the law, never been to jail, made a lot of money over the years and not once did anyone try to take his life. Someone must've been watching him or your sister. Didn't she say they were going to kill her too?" His father made a lot of sense, but who would follow them and for what is the question.

"Noooooo!" We heard a scream come from inside and ran in. Doctors were standing there trying to hold Arabia up. All the women had tears in their eyes.

"What happened?" His brother asked and by the looks of things I'd say he didn't survive.

"He didn't make it." My mom answered hugging his mom. The whole scene was sad and fucked up.

"Nah, my brother too strong to die from a gunshot to the stomach." The younger brother yelled breaking down.

"Evidently, the bullet exploded in his stomach and he was hit twice in the side. The person must've only shot in the torso area in order to get him close like that." My pops relayed the information from the doctor.

We sat there while, his parents and brothers went to the back. When they returned, something was different. The doctor said no one else was allowed in to say their goodbyes. Arabia was devastated and hurt hearing those words, but on their way out his parents said she didn't need to see him like that.

Once they left, we drove back to Deray's house, let Arabia grab what she wanted as far as memories and left. Onyx drove her car home because she was in no state to get behind the wheel.

Huff called my phone on the way back. We were supposed to meet for a shipment later that was going overseas to a new distributor. I wasn't too trusting of it and had my doubts. I told him we had to reschedule and I'd speak to him later. He asked if I was good but how do you explain that his girl was mourning over the other man she loved. The entire situation was crazy.

"Aye, you." I all but yelled at the weird looking girl at Walgreens. She never turned around and continued walking. Getting aggravated, I made my way to the aisle she went down and swung her around. Her bifocal glasses fell and so did the items in her hand.

"What the—?" Shorty became mute all of a sudden when she saw it was me. This was the same chick from the hair salon that Arabia told me to leave alone.

After my sister left the salon that day, she called asking if I'm still messing with the chick, Dana, who worked at the Section 8 office. When I told her on occasion, Arabia asked if I could get Dana to push this chick name to the top of the list. At first, I said no because Dana was a pain in the ass. Her sex was decent but she wanted a damn relationship and I didn't.

Anyway, I had to go meet up with Dana, dick her down real quick and lie about who the chick really was to me. I claimed she was a cousin that had issues with her mother and lived in a shelter. Not knowing any of her business, that's what Arabia told me to go with.

She supposedly got in contact with her or was, and I wanted to make sure before cutting Dana's annoying ass back off.

"I know I'm sexy but can you speak?" She rolled her eyes and started picking her things off the floor.

"Did some bitch named, Dana call you?" She nodded but still didn't talk.

"Aye, I need you to stop acting like a mute and use your words." She put her glasses back on and I'm telling you, she could probably see the future with how thick they were.

"That was very rude of you to say." Some woman walking by had the nerve to add her two cents.

"What's rude was you minding someone else's business.

Now take you and your Depends up to the counter and fuck off." The River chick busted out laughing.

"Hmph."

"Exactly. Hmph, minding somebody business with those big ass diapers in your hand. You probably got a pissy one on now." River walked away trying her hardest not to laugh. Following behind, I found her in the aspirin aisle.

"Why are you following me?"

"Oh, she does speak and ain't nobody following your dusty ass." She shook her head. Why she wore these big and dingy looking clothes was beyond me.

"I just wanna know did a bitch call to offer you housing." She remained quiet for a moment.

"Who told you about that?"

"You don't need to worry about that. I just need to know so I can block her stalking ass." River shifted her weight to one side.

"Yes she did, two days ago but I haven't found a place yet." At least Dana did her part.

"Did she offer you two bedrooms?"

"No. Because it's only me right now—" I cut her off.

"I told that bitch when my dick was stabbing her throat to get you a two bedroom. See, this what I mean when I say bitches don't listen." I contacted Dana in front of her.

"Hey, sexy. I'm playing with myself thinking of you." Even her voice annoyed me. River covered her mouth with her free hand laughing.

"Didn't I tell you to get my cousin a two bedroom." I barked waiting for her to respond.

"I tried but until she gets custody of her son, they will only offer her a one bedroom. Shit, after what her mother did, I'd be surprised if the state will give him back." River's eyes started to tear up hearing what Dana said.

"A'ight. Just make sure when she gets her son, the two bedroom becomes available."

"Ok, baby. You coming by tonight? If you do, I can probably get your cousin in an apartment sooner than later. I know a lot of landlords looking for tenants." Blowing my breath, I agreed. Arabia would kill me if I left this chick hanging.

"You owe me." I hung up and put the phone in my pocket.

"Umm, unless you want me to wax your eyebrows or cut your hair, I don't have anything to offer." She shrugged and headed to the register.

"My sister told me, you did her hair because the stylist was out. Her man passed away and she won't leave my parents' house to get it done for the funeral."

"Oh no. She was very excited to see him that day." River placed her couple of items on the counter. The cashier stared at me more than she did ringing the stuff up. I put the two packs of condoms down and the soda I grabbed.

"Magnum? I bet you rearrange bitches insides, don't you." River turned her face up when the ratchet cashier asked. That shit was a turnoff. Who the fuck says something like that?

"How old are you?" I handed her my card to pay for both of our things.

"Twenty two."

"Twenty two, huh. My dick would put you in the hospital and your mouth, wouldn't be able to suck half my shit." River started placing her things in one of those reusable bags. Jersey really made it where plastic bags can no longer be used. It was annoying as hell buying reusable ones every time you went to the store.

"Matter of fact, my dick too good for you. I wouldn't waste a nut on a chick who thinks rolling her tongue and talking nasty turned a nigga on. Not only that, that booger hanging out your nose has been shaking every time you breathe in and out. Those little ass titties not even suckable and I bet the pussy stink too from those coochie cutting jeans you're wearing tryna catch a nigga." The girl was damn near in tears but that's what the fuck she get.

"Before you go home, make sure to grab some Monistat 7 and Summer's Eve wipes. Stinking ass bitch." I felt a hand to my back. River was pushing me out the store.

"What's the address?" She headed toward a blue van with new temp tags. Once she opened the door, I knew it was hers.

"Wait a minute. I know you didn't buy this Scooby Doo van." Walking around it, I laughed hard as hell. It was the same make and model and the only difference was it didn't say Mystery Machine on it.

"First of all, this was donated to me from the church." She had her hands on her hips.

"Well, donate that shit back." I opened the side door and it was nothing, no seats, just metal.

"Oh shit. Where's the rest of the van?" She hopped in the driver's seat.

"Whatever."

Boom! Boom! Was the sound when the engine started. Black smoke came out for a second.

"Yo, this van needs to be taken out to the field and shot. The fuck is a church donating this to anyone for." She maneuvered her way to the back and slammed the side door. Once she got back in the driver's seat, I opened the door.

"You really shouldn't look like Velma and drive a Scooby Doo van. People may look for Scooby and Shaggy." I was cracking myself up. River had on another long skirt, a turtleneck with a long old school looking jacket, those same dirty converses and an old crossbody purse. If I didn't know any better, I'd think she was homeless.

"You think because you're handsome, drive a Maserati truck, dress nice and smell good, that you can put people down?" She shut the driver's side door.

"I can say what I want." I didn't care about her getting upset.

"You have no idea what I've gone through in the past."

"Honestly, I don't give a fuck and here's the address. The funeral is Saturday. Be there by seven in the morning to get her ready, or I'll come snatch you the fuck up and drag you there." I headed to my truck.

"The hair products will be there so you don't need to bring anything." She rolled her eyes.

"Oh, make sure the exhaust is clean before coming. My

54

mother might shoot you if she think that's a bomb in front of her house." I sat in the driver's seat and sparked a blunt. Feeling her eyes on me, I turned to see River staring with googly eyes. Rolling down my window I waited for her to do the same.

"Get your weird ass outta here before I call the tow company to come get that shit." She backed up quickly and called herself speeding out the parking lot. All River did was leave everyone coughing from the damn fumes.

I left to go speak with my pops about this damn funeral or should I say memorial, since his family cremated him.

Chapter Seven

RIVER

I had to pull off from Block because he was so damn handsome, he had the power to make me drop my drawers in the Walgreens parking lot. The way he smelled, smiled and his swag alone had me wanting to ride him in the front seat of his truck. Who am I fooling? That man would never give me the time of day and if he did, he'd probably dog me out.

I didn't appreciate him talking about my new van that was donated by the church. Marissa knew some of my situation and told me to attend services with her on Sundays. Unfortunately, the entire service was in Spanish but I followed along with the translator on my Boost phone. I had to download the app and use earphones because them speaking at the same time confused me.

Nonetheless, the congregation prayed for me a lot. They often brought food packages to my house, gave me clothes that I couldn't fit which was why they were always baggy. I only had the money from working with Marissa and the basement was under her house. In no way am I complaining after all the benches I've slept on and shelters I was in.

When they took my son, I was placed on the psych ward. They claimed due to the severity of how bad I hurt the female cop for assisting in taking him, I needed to be evaluated.

To this day, my mother never apologized, and for the last two years my son was only allowed to see me twice a month per the courts. Thankfully, his father brought him by every Friday night and I wouldn't drop him off until Monday mornings before work.

Marissa would let me bring him in on Saturdays since it was the busiest day. All the ladies loved him and we made sure he was safe at all times.

Parking in front of my place, I grabbed the two magazines and chips from Walgreens. Brandon was coming over and as much as I didn't want him to, that three hundred dollars would come in handy now that the Section 8 voucher came in.

Over the last two months he would stop by two times a week. Sleeping with him, I made $4800 and while it may not be a lot for some, it's more than enough for me. I still remember when he brought up the proposition.

"Yo! What's good with you?" Some guy approached me at the food store. He was handsome to say the least, but why was he stopping me.

"How can I help you?" Not trying to stop, he jumped in front of me.

"You got a man?"

"No." Moving around him, I went to the self-checkout. When I made it outside, he was nowhere to be found. I prepared myself for the long walk home. Not even five minutes later, a Mercedes truck pulled up next to me. It was the same guy from the store.

"You need a ride?"

"No thank you." I kept walking until he got out his ride and ran up on me. He was persistent as hell.

"Let me give you a ride. You look like you need it." He pointed to my dingy sneakers. I'm not sure why he thought that was a giveaway. I've walked miles every day.

"What do you want?"

"Just to make your day easier." It felt like this was a trap but being my feet were tired from standing at the salon all day, a ride ain't so bad.

He tried to make conversation but I wasn't interested in anything he had to say. When we got in front of my place, he put his hand on my lap and asked if I wanted to make extra money. Taking offense to what he said, I hopped out. Hearing him behind me, I stopped because he wasn't coming inside.

"It seemed like you needed money and I'm tryna offer it for a good time here and there." It didn't take me long to say no. As I put the key inside the door, he ran over with a piece of paper.

"Call me if you change your mind." It took me a month to finally reach out and that's because my son was coming over and my food stamps were gone.

Long story short; he came over, we fucked for less than ten minutes and he left three hundred dollars. Now we're two months in and his ass still only offering the same amount. I thought about giving him head but he's not my man and doesn't do it for me. It wasn't worth it, especially if he would probably only give me the same three hundred dollars.

KNOCK! KNOCK! The sound brought me back to reality. I opened the door for Brandon, did what needed to be done, showered and went to bed. This will be all over soon.

"Who the fuck are you and why is that piece of shit van parked in front of my house?" The older woman said a mouth full upon opening the door. I hadn't even gotten the chance to knock yet.

"I'm here for, Arabia." I whispered. It wasn't that I'm mute like most people assumed, I just preferred not to speak. When you don't, no one can put you in any drama and most people leave you alone thinking you're crazy.

For some reason Block didn't feel the need to stop speaking to me. Between him and Arabia it felt good to converse with someone besides myself and social workers. I had absolutely no friends or family, well there was my mother but that's another story.

"Who you here for? It can't be my son since you're dressed like a monk." I swear the whole family must be ignorant.

"Umm, I'm gonna go." Block didn't pay me any money to

come here for his mother to insult me. Therefore, if Arabia needed her hair done, they could go to the shop.

Walking to my van, I heard music blasting coming down the street. The vehicle stopped directly in front of mine blocking me from leaving. I had to fan myself when Block emerged.

This man has on an all black suit with shiny black shoes and shades. There was a small chain tucked inside his shirt and those dimples on his cheek made me want to dip my fingers in them by how deep they were.

"You done already." He took me out the fantasy when he spoke.

"Yea so, your mom wasn't very inviting and—." He grabbed me by the sweater and basically drug me to the front door. Turning the doorknob, he forced me inside. The house was nothing less than beautiful and a bitch was scared to move.

"Ma!" He yelled, pulling me by the wrist.

"What?" She came to the top of the stairs wearing a robe.

"Did Arabia shower yet?"

"Yea but she went back to bed. Who the fuck is she?" His mother pointed to me as if someone else was standing here.

"Don't start. I had her come do, Arabia's hair. Now what room did you put all the stuff in?" She told him the one closer to the downstairs bathroom. When he pushed me inside, the room held a bedroom set, and a bathroom that held everything needed to do her hair.

"This is nice." I ran my hand over the marble countertop.

"Don't steal nothing." I swung around too quick and almost fell had he not caught me.

"For a dirty chick, you smell good." I pushed him away from me.

"River? What are you doing here?" I turned to see Arabia walking in with her hair all over the place. There were bags under her eyes, she appeared to be lethargic and all she had on was pajamas.

"Your brother forced me here because he mentioned having sex with some woman to give me housing. Talking about I owe him." I wasn't going to lie about my reasoning for being somewhere I've never been.

"Shit, you do. I may add another, *"I owe you"* on your ass." He put up fake quotes.

"Dana's pussy was dry as fuck that night; felt like I was sliding my dick up and down sandpaper from wood class." I stuck my finger down my throat to pretend I was gagging.

"Listen here, Daria."

"Daria?"

"You know that ugly chick on Beavis & Butthead." I swear he must watch cartoons all day. He called me two names of characters already.

"I thought you said I looked like, Velma."

"Have you seen, Daria? They're damn near twins. Both ugly as hell, big ass glasses—" He was having a field day insulting me.

"Alright you two. Damn, if I didn't know any better I would say y'all wanted each other." Arabia said taking a seat in the chair someone placed in the bathroom before I arrived.

"I wouldn't fuck her with a dildo. Then again—"

"Goodbye." When he went to leave, he stopped and stared

at me for a second. Walking back to where I stood, he removed my glasses.

"Excuse you."

"Just wanted to make sure you wasn't cock eyed too." I snatched my glasses back and started to work on Arabia's hair. It took a little longer than expected because I had to rewash it.

"Arabia, the limo is here. You ready?" Her mother yelled outside the room. I was almost done with her eyebrows.

"There. Now you're ready." She stared in the mirror and burst into tears.

"I'm sorry. You don't like it?" I was rushing to clean up in case her family decided to kill me for her hair not coming out the way she wanted.

"No. It's fine. I'm crying because I'm pregnant and the baby's father was murdered." It was at this very moment, I knew she needed her mom. Not seeing anyone in the bedroom, I went into the bathroom to try and calm her down. When it didn't work, I started to ask about other things.

"Did he know?" She shook her head no.

"It was going to be a surprise for Christmas." She wiped her face, thanked me and told everyone she would be ready soon.

After cleaning and making sure everything was unplugged, I stepped out to quite a bit of people talking. I'm aware of their parents and the brother, but the woman who tried to get me in trouble at the salon was here too. Were they related? Not trying to converse with anyone, I walked quickly to the door.

"Aye!" I halted for a second, but kept going when his cologne lingered in my nose. There was no need for us to be that close to one another now that I've done what he requested.

"Don't start that truck until I walk away." I offered a fake smile and got in.

"What now? Your favor was done and I did her eyebrows." He stood outside my truck peeling off money.

"Oh, I don't need that. You did enough by as you say, *"fucking bitches for my housing."* I started cackling and he jerked me out the truck. His hands gripped my collar and I was standing on my tippy toes looking crazy.

"That shit not funny. The bitch really had my dick hurting." I could smell the weed on his breath from how close we were.

"How do you know your dick wasn't dry and it was you making her hurt?" He let go of my shirt to stare. Once his hand went to the top of my van and he stared down at me, I became shy, uncomfortable and most of all turned on.

"Let me know when you move into your apartment." He backed away smirking.

"For what?"

"Ima need to come over and fuck that goofiness outta you. Make you know what it's like to stalk this dick." He grabbed himself.

"You're so full of yourself." I hopped back in the van, closing the door and locking it. I started it with him standing there and thankfully the black smoke didn't come out. He probably would've really killed me if I messed up his suit.

"And just so you know, my pussy's not for sale anymore." I gave him the finger.

"Ayo, what the fuck you just say?" I heard him yell and tried to speed off. Unfortunately, the van only went five miles an hour when you first drove it. As long as I got away, I didn't care.

Looking over for my purse, I noticed the money on the floor. He had to have thrown it in when I wasn't paying attention. Picking it all up at the red light, I quickly counted it.

"$1000!" As much as I needed that, it would have to be returned. No man will ever say he gave me anything.

Chapter Eight

ARABIA

S tanding in the mirror smoothing out my dress, tears flowed down my cheeks. Who knew I would be burying the man I was in love with? We weren't even supposed to last as long as we did. It literally was a one night stand that never ended.

"You ok?" Mariah closed the door behind her. She met Deray and thought we belonged together as well. Our chemistry was out of this world. They say everyone had a soulmate, and I truly believed he was mine.

"I just want to get through today." She hugged me.

"Ugh, why was the bitch from the hair salon here?" I pointed to my hair. She knew Marissa didn't make house calls. I'm very appreciative that Block found River to come do it for me. Granted those two carried on like old friends and not anyone who recently met. I could also tell she had a crush on him just by the way she stared whenever he was around.

"I thought she got fired." Mariah was a bitch and to think she wanted River fired, aggravated me.

"You ready?" My dad interrupted whatever nonsense Mariah was about to say. He reached out for my hand, walked out the room and down the steps with me. Everyone spoke and soon after, we all got in the cars. Mariah rode with me because Block told me, her and Onyx still weren't speaking.

On the drive to Long Island, I took in the scenery. The trees, houses and open land was so beautiful to me. Deray would come pick me up and we'd just drive with no destination in mind. I'm gonna miss him so much.

"Damn, girl. He knew a lotta people." The church was beyond packed and the limo could barely get down the street. In the short amount of time we knew one another, Deray was loved by many. No matter where he went, people always showed love. Unfortunately, someone had it out for him.

"Let's get this over with." I snapped, when the limo pulled up in front of the church.

"Arabia." My dad called out.

"You're upset and mourning but don't you dare go in that church with an attitude." I looked at him.

"His parents and daughter are in there too. All of you are hurting so you need to be respectful." I nodded. My father was right. Of course I'm angry at what took place but my attitude had to be pushed to the side, at least until the funeral was over.

The door opened and Block, Onyx and some of my other

male cousins were standing there. They were all strapped as they should be. We didn't know these people and if someone popped off no one wanted to be unprepared. Mariah grabbed my hand and my mom took the other.

Walking in felt crazy because there were a lot of people. Deray would've been happy seeing everyone showed up for him. When we got to the front, I ran my hand over the photos placed on cardboard. His parents had him cremated, therefore this was more of a memorial service than anything. It was another reason I didn't want to be here. I never got to say goodbye or see his body, and if I'm being honest, there was resentment. Why wouldn't they allow me to see him? Why cremate him before the funeral? As much as I wanted to bombard them with the questions, I remained quiet.

"Hey, honey." His mom stood to hug me. The usher's escorted my family to the set of pews reserved for them. She had me sit in between her and Tricia. His daughter, Amani crawled out her mother's arms and into mine. Deray had her over all the time and I loved her like she was my own.

During the funeral, different people went to the podium to speak. One chick in particular stood up claiming to be his one and only. His mother was mad as hell, but I wasn't. If he had other women, I couldn't be mad being Huff was my man. Well, after me and Deray slept together, I stayed away. So even though neither of us officially said it was over, in my mind we were.

It was the reason I stayed with Deray every night either at my house or his. During the day we worked, texted one another and even had lunchtime sex on FaceTime but at night, it was me and him.

When the chick stepped down, she rolled her eyes at me which in my eyes said, she made the story up. Why would you be mad at me if he was yours, and how did she know who I was?

Once the funeral was over, we headed over to the repast and that too was packed. There was a ton of food and drinks. Not trying to stay long because I know when the liquor kicks anything can occur, I asked for a plate to go. My family was at a table grabbing up their food to go as well.

"Are you ok?" Tricia asked. Amani was asleep on her shoulder.

"For the most part. I miss him a lot." She smiled.

"He loved you, Arabia."

"You think so." He told me all the time but it was good to hear that he mentioned it to his family; his baby mother at that.

"You're all he spoke of. He couldn't wait for y'all to have a kid." She hugged me.

"Everything isn't what it seem." She whispered in my ear before pulling away.

"Huh?"

"I'll be in touch." Tricia walked off leaving me confused. What did she mean by that? I headed over to tell my family it was time to go. Some men were outside arguing and we didn't need any problems. It was too many of them.

After getting in the car, I stared out the window the whole ride home. Mariah tried to talk but I wasn't in the mood. Right now I had to figure out if I'm keeping the baby, and if I did, how would I be able to tell him or her about their father being murdered.

* * *

"Where you been? I haven't seen you in almost two weeks?" Huff barged in my home uninvited. Closing the door behind him, I went into my living room to sit on the couch and finish a movie I was watching.

"Where you been?" He popped the top of a soda bottle and drank it down quickly. Who told him to go in my damn kitchen, better yet my refrigerator?

"Why, Huff?" If he felt like I was missing for that long why didn't he come searching for me sooner?

"What you mean why? You're my woman." I started laughing.

"Since when?"

"Don't play games, Arabia." He put the empty bottle on the coffee table and made his way to me. I turned the volume down on the television and focused my attention on him. Huff was always a handsome man, yet he could never fully satisfy me enough to fall in love. Yes, we had love for each other but not the kinda love me and Deray shared.

I wanted to be under him every second of the day. The way he held me, kissed me, and told me how much he loved me was enough to make any woman fall in love. I've always told him, I believed he was my soulmate and he said the same to me.

"Huff, we haven't had sex in months, you haven't been over here in months and weren't you just in some chick face at the club two nights ago?" He was surprised to hear what someone told me. Huff was a playboy and that was ok as long as the chicks didn't approach me with no nonsense.

"You know those bitches don't mean nothing to me." I laughed. All men say the same thing when their so called main chick called them out.

"Huff, even though neither of us said it, we've been over. There was no me and you." He snapped.

"You better not be fucking no one else." Once his hand went to my throat, I went in defense mode. My feet were kicking him in the stomach while my fingers were digging in his eyes. Never in my life had a man put his hands on me.

"Bitch!"

WHAP! The slap to my face caused my nose to bleed instantly. Not wasting anytime trying to stop it, I picked up a glass statue off my table and bashed him over the head with it. I collected them whenever I visited another country during vacation.

"Nigga, are you crazy putting your hands on me?" He was moaning and holding his head.

"Get the fuck out my house." He refused to move and rolled on his back crying like a kid about how bad his head was hurting. I walked in the kitchen to grab some paper towels for my nose.

"I'm sorry, Arabia. You're the only woman I love and now

you don't want to be with me." How did I even lay down with this punk?

"Get out my house!" I wasn't playing no games with Huff. Once he put his hands on me, there was no way I could respect him. Slowly getting off the floor, he put his hand on the coffee table to balance himself.

"My bad, Arabia. I'll be back when we both calm down." Was he serious right now? Not bothering to answer, I followed him to the door and slammed it. He better hope I don't mention this to Block because Huff would never see another light of day.

Chapter Nine

MARIAH

"Honey, you're letting my mother win." Ms. Buggs said, rubbing the side of my arm. I stopped by her house to talk. Onyx had been staying here, and at the condo we owned. I missed him like crazy.

"I'm trying to be respectful by not putting my hands on her but she's making it extremely hard. Then, to invite Salina to the wedding and reception was low." I'm not sure if she invited her to the wedding but the bitch called Salina to pick her up.

"You don't care about that." I looked at her.

"No, Mariah. You're happy Salina and my mother witnessed my son make you his wife. You're upset, Charlene told you about Onyx asking Salina to marry her prior to you." I hated that she could read me like my mother. Everything coming out her mouth was true.

"You never allowed Onyx to tell you the truth, and then you were even more upset when he asked if the kid was his." I sucked my teeth. He wasn't supposed to tell her everything.

"We all know my son had that testicular surgery, just like we all know the doctor said it's a possibility he may or may not have more kids." I tried to speak but she cut me off.

"I admit it was a shock to him, but did it ever dawn on you to ask him why he questioned it." Where was she going with this? ·

"But why would he? I've never slept with anyone else." She pursed her lips up before standing to walk to the sink.

No one knew about the guy, I messed around with; did they? I never even told Arabia about him and she's my best friend. If anyone says they're an open book and will tell their friend everything, that's a lie. No one tells every single thing they do. It's the exact reason when people die, some families are surprised after hearing about the person committing a crime.

"Why did you make that face?"

"I'm just going to say this and stay out of it." She walked back over to me at the table.

"My son, your husband loves you to death so I suggest, no I recommend you tell him whatever you've done in the past since y'all have been together before someone else does." She kissed my cheek. I was about to respond but her mother stepped in.

"Well, if it isn't the chick who didn't go on her honeymoon." Charlene strolled in with a cigarette hanging out her mouth. Who told her that?

"If it isn't the old woman who wants to fuck her grandson."

Onyx's mother gasped. I saw the messages Charlene sent Onyx a few times telling him how handsome he was, and if she were younger, and not related she would've snatched him up.

One of the messages even told him Salina allowed her to watch a video of them having sex. What grandmother watched her grandson have sex with anyone?

"Whatever. You're always saying outrageous stuff." She attempted to start another conversation with Ms. Buggs but I refused to let it go.

"Oh, so when me and Onyx first got together and you stayed the night, you weren't standing in the hall listening to us have sex?" She dropped something by the door and when Onyx checked, she was picking it up. The room she stayed in happened to be downstairs so there was no need for her to even be up there.

"Or how about the time, we were having sex in the pool. When I looked up you were watching." She had a surprised look on her face.

"I never said anything because Onyx warned you that very night not to stop by because he planned a romantic evening for me. Let's not even discuss you walking in on him in the shower not knowing I was there." Once again she had stayed the night at his place. She had no idea I came over and even had the nerve to wear a silk robe with nothing underneath.

"Thankfully, I snatched your stupid as up by the hair before he saw you because he would've killed you." His mother was at a loss for words.

"So, before you waltz your trifling ass up in here talking

shit, don't. That's my husband and what we go through will never be your business." She looked at me and then, Ms. Buggs, who now had tears in her eyes.

"You're going to let her speak to me like that?" I gathered my things to leave.

"Don't worry, I'm leaving but remember this." I stopped on the side of her.

"All the tricks you and Salina have up your sleeve will be the reason my husband takes your life." I looked her up and down.

"Problems or not, Onyx don't play about me." I shoulder checked her so hard she fell onto the kitchen table.

"Mariah." His mom ran after me.

"No disrespect, Ms. Buggs but I don't give a fuck if that bitch broke a hip. Keep her away from me."

"You need to tell my son what you just told me." The fear on her face had me worried.

"What?" She looked back for Charlene.

"Onyx needs to know what she did. Please make sure you tell him." She was practically begging me to mention it but why.

"Why can't you?"

"There's a reason and right now, I can't reveal anything. Please promise to tell him." She was about to cry again. I made the promise but who knew when I'd speak to him.

It was going on three weeks and neither of us reached out to the other. Granted, I saw his sexy ass at the funeral but no words were spoken. Maybe I should stop being stubborn and make him come home; then again, the questioning about our child was still looming in my head. I'll speak to him one day, just not today. I needed to go home and sleep. This baby had me extremely tired.

"I knew that bitch was trifling." My mother slammed the glass down she just washed. After leaving Ms. Buggs house, I came here to talk.

Maria Winston never held her tongue, and a few times her and Charlene almost came to blows because she tried to sleep with my father. My dad was handsome to say the least and whenever we went out women would stare. As far as I know, he never stepped out on my mother and if he did; they kept it away from me. It was a good thing too because he made sure to show me how a woman should be treating by the way he treated my mother.

The entire time Onyx and I have been together, he always treated me with respect. Unfortunately, he allowed women to slide in and almost destroy everything we built. What baffled me the most was his grandmother wanting all of his attention. It's as if no one should come before her; not even his mother. It made me believe Salina must've allowed her to do whatever, which is why they're so close.

"His mom wanted me to tell, Onyx." She stared at me.

"How do I tell him, his grandmother wanted to have sex with him? It even sounds disgusting saying it." She dried her hands off and came to sit with me at the table. Lucky for me, she made dinner and since there was more than enough, I ate too.

"First of all, stop being stubborn and go get your husband." I tried to speak but she cut me off.

"I don't want to hear about how upset you were because he asked, whose kid it was." Me and my mom were close so when I told her what Onyx said, she never took a side.

Actually, she told me to wait on marriage because we weren't ready. They say your mother always knows and while I may have not wanted to hear it then, she was right. For us to have so much going on the day of our wedding said a lot.

"Fine. I'll go get him." I caught an attitude. My mother placed her hand on top of mine.

"Get the marriage annulled."

"What?" She cupped her other hand and placed it under my chin, forcing me to look at her.

"You're a grown woman acting like a child right now. If this will be the way you act throughout the marriage, then it's best to end it now."

"I don't want to get it annulled." Tears began to pool in the corners of my eyes.

"Then grow up and deal with your problems in house. There's no reason everyone knows what's going on. I mean, his grandmother couldn't wait to talk about y'all not having a honeymoon, but whose fault was that." I didn't say anything.

"Exactly, yours. You made your husband leave, you didn't celebrate your marriage, and you let the world know problems existed from the start." Laying my head on the table, I felt her rubbing my back.

"In the future, any arguments you have never throw him out the house if you want to keep your business private. Especially, when women are praying on y'all downfall." I heard her walking out the kitchen. Keeping my head down for a few more minutes, I finally got the strength to move. Making my way to the door, I heard giggling and looked up to see my parents feeling each other up. That's what me and Onyx used to do all the time.

"Bye." I kissed both of them on the cheek and went about my business. Finding my husband was never a problem; getting him to forgive me and move on was another. That man could hold a grudge for a long time.

Chapter Ten

ONYX

Staring at Mariah in front of me wearing nothing but heels had my dick hard as fuck. We've never had an issue in the sex department so of course I'd be turned on. However, I'm a man before anything and we need to discuss what took place almost a month ago. Moving her out the way, I grabbed a robe to wrap around her body.

"Let me guess, you fucked another bitch." Shaking my head, I went downstairs to grab a drink. Mariah was talking shit as she followed, only aggravating the hell outta me.

When she showed up at the condo, I had every intention of having sex with my wife. I was horny and ready to stay in it all night afterwards. Unfortunately, I know until we speak on what took place it will come back up and I'm not tryna deal with the same situation over and over. My wife thinks I'm a street nigga who don't care about shit but she was wrong.

All the times Mariah was hurt from the different women approaching her, had me just as upset. Salina pretty much allowed me to do whatever I wanted in our relationship, as long as the drama didn't come to her. Mariah wasn't having it and each time I fucked up, it put a strain on our relationship. Now I'm tryna deal with this head on and all she wanna do is fuck and move on. I'm nowhere near perfect but I wanna be for her.

"Onyx, I'm sorry. It's just the shit with your grandmother and Salina annoyed me. I feel like you just allow them to come for me." I poured another shot of Patron as she plopped down on the couch. Her hands were covering her face as she spoke but the tears were clear as day.

Making my way to where she sat, I made myself comfortable on the seat across from her. Circling my cup as if I'm stirring it, I couldn't help but smile. My wife was beautiful in all aspects, but her attitude went from zero to hundred quick. I'm not saying it shouldn't in certain situations, however she needed to work on not blowing up.

"First of all, I would never allow them or any woman to come for you. Any woman that popped off to you, were no longer heard from, were they?" I took a sip of my drink staring at her. She lifted her head.

"As far as, Salina goes, I asked if you wanted me to get rid of her, and what did you say."

"She's your daughter's mother, Onyx." I used my elbows to lean on my knees still staring and holding my glass.

"What did you say?"

"No." She whispered.

"Exactly. As far as my grandmother, there was a reason she hadn't taking a dirt nap yet." I took a sip as she stared, confused by my words.

"I'll never be ok with them harassing you, but you need to let me know when shit going on." Mariah wanted to deal with them in her own way but when it affected our relationship, that's where it was my job to handle it.

When I confronted my grandmother about the things she said at the wedding, she did that fake crying. Even had the nerve to claim how much she adored my wife. Everything she said was a lie and again, soon as the word comes down, she will reap what she sowed in her past as well. No one was exempt from my wrath when fucking with my family. That was a hard lesson I had to learn from my pops.

"Daddy, you can't hurt her." I was nine years old watching my father about to kill my aunt. She was bleeding profusely and if I didn't know any better, I would've assumed she was dead had it not been for her begging him to stop. He wasn't hitting my aunt, but the knife wounds were more than enough to show me this wasn't going to end well.

"Tell your nephew why you're in this position." She was trying to wrap something around her legs to stop the blood from gushing out. The gashes were so deep you could see the white meat.

"No, I'm not telling him that." My dad walked over and chopped one of her hands off with a machete. Where did he get that?

"Daddy, no." *At my young age, this was something I should've never witnessed. Turning around to leave, my dad called out to me.*

"Onyx." He made me face him.

"You're going to grow up one day having to make difficult decisions." I nodded wiping my eyes. I loved my aunt and here he was torturing her.

"Never allow anyone, not even a family member to get away with things you'd never allow a stranger to." He shot my aunt in the head in front of me. That was one of the many murders I witnessed before becoming a killer myself. Over the years, my kill game was on point and I had no plans of ever stopping.

At the time, I had no idea what he spoke of. That's until my mother told me why it happened years later. To this day, I never went to therapy over seeing her and others murdered. Now that I think about it, no one filed a missing person's report and he wasn't arrested for killing her.

"Onyx, I just want to be happy." Mariah broke me outta my thoughts. I placed the glass on the coffee table and moved to where she sat.

"Marriage is going to be hard. But what I'm not gonna do is stay around for anyone who wasn't sure about getting married in the first place." She had a surprised expression. Her mom told me about the concerns Mariah had before the marriage. It aggravated me that she didn't talk to me about it, yet I respected her mother's opinion. I had a talk with Mariah and asked her repeatedly if she was sure about being married. Once she said yes, there wasn't anything else to discuss. Now we're here tryna stay together and we haven't been married a full thirty days.

"If you wanna get this annulled and go your separate way, let me know. I'll have the lawyer draw up the paperwork." I was in love with Mariah but I'm not one of those men who will force her to stay in an unhappy marriage. I stood to get another drink.

"I wanna stay married." A grin crept across my face because I didn't want her to go.

"Don't put your hands on me again." And with that, I poured another drink and left her sitting right there while I went upstairs.

* * *

"Yesss, Onyx. Don't stop, baby." Mariah moaned as I pulled out her wet pussy and rammed myself back in. We've been stuck in the Bahamas for the last week making up and sightseeing. This wasn't our honeymoon spot but it did fine for now.

"Fuck me back," I smacked her ass to make it jiggle and put my hands behind my head as she threw it back. My wife was turning into a certified freak every time we had sex. Like now, she wanted me to stick some butt plugs in her ass at the same time. We ain't never did no shit like that. She picked up quite a few sex toys since we've been out here and I must admit, they were worth it.

"FUCKKKKK! Onyx, I'm about to cum." Squeezing her ass cheeks harder after inserting them, I went faster and seconds later we both succumbed to one of the strongest orgasms ever. My body stiffened up so bad, I swore it was me having a stroke. She fell face forward and started snoring instantly.

"Shit, we gotta use those more often." I spoke out loud. Falling back on the bed with my hand over my face, I set the alarm for three hours because we were having a candlelight dinner she set up on our last night here.

It seemed as if we only slept five minutes before the music from my phone went off to wake us up. Rolling over, I hit the snooze button and pulled Mariah closer. She snuggled under me and once again the damn alarm sounded.

"We may as well get up." Mariah turned over.

"You sure we gotta go to dinner?" She laughed and slid her hand into my boxers. Pulling her hand away was hard, yet had to be done or we wouldn't go anywhere. I kissed her on the forehead and both of us struggled to get up.

By the time we made it to the dinner, we were thirty minutes late. None of that mattered when I saw the set up. The entire restaurant was closed, with red balloons spread out. Some had the words, *I love you* and others had, *Congratulations*. What caught my eye the most was Mariah pointing to a cake. Walking over to the table, a smile graced my face.

There was a huge sonogram picture made into the cake with the due date circled. It had to be a screenshot she sent for them to put on it. The words, *I'm sorry* was on one side of the photo and the words, *We love you* were on the other. Mariah handed me a small gift bag to open.

"You really went all out for this honeymoon?" I removed the handcuffs and a sex coupon book.

"I love you with all my heart, Onyx and I promise to try and not blow up again. I also want you to know we had issues in the past but I would never, ever have a child with anyone else." Before I could address her last statement, a waitress brought out an unopened bottle of red wine and a bottle of Patron. She opened both of them for us and poured them in one of the glasses off the table.

"To us, baby." Mariah took a sip.

"To us, ma. And just so you know, Ima tear that ass up when we get back to the room." She blushed as I gulped down the drink. The waitress had us sit while she took our orders.

Glancing around the room at the DJ, the decorations, the cake, other gifts she had for me on another table, all I could do was smile. My wife went all out for me over here so it's only right to make sure she arrived home with just as much, if not more. Hopefully, we can stay this happy.

Chapter Eleven

MARIAH

"Damn, girl. What's up with you walking?" Arabia questioned as we walked through the mall. We were both pregnant and decided, why not go look at baby items. Our mothers instilled in us not to purchase anything until we were six months, due to superstitions.

At first, I told my mom to relax but after reading up on women's stories who claimed they miscarried once they brought stuff too early, I agreed. I'm not sure I could take another loss anyway. That was a day, I try to forget but every now and then it haunted me.

"Nothing. Me and Onyx did a lotta freaky shit over in the Bahamas." As I told her a little about it, she had me cracking up by telling me the wild shit her and Deray did. For a moment; she shed a few tears but was able to get herself together. I'm sure that's going to happen a lot, even more when the baby arrived.

"Hey, there's River." She pointed to the other side of the hall.

"River." Arabia called out making me suck my teeth. I really had no reason to dislike the woman. She caught me on a bad day and she should be happy, I didn't tell Marissa to fire her. It wouldn't be the first time I've done that.

"Why the fuck she acting like she doesn't hear you?" The chick had a sweater with a hoodie connected covering her head. The jeans had holes in them and not sure if they're the fashion type or ones she put in them. Those converses were so run down, I'm surprised the sole wasn't coming off.

"Probably because your mean ass walking with me." We crossed in between the kiosks for Arabia to speak.

"River? What the hell?" She turned and the woman had a black eye and busted lip.

"Oh, hey." She tried to walk off but nosy ass Arabia had to inquire about the injuries.

"Are you ok? Did someone jump you?" My cousin was very concerned and I didn't know why. She barely knew the chick and here she was asking about her face.

"No. I'm fine. It was nice seeing you again." Once again, nosy Arabia stopped her from leaving.

"Did you move into your new place?"

"Next week. Please, I have to go before he finds me." And with that, the woman River started speed walking outta there.

"He?" Both of us questioned, staring at her dip in and out

of people. The two of us went on about our business but there was a tad bit of uneasiness regarding River. Who was she running from and did a man really do that?

"What do you want for dinner?" I asked Arabia coming out of the mall. It was after six and we didn't want anything from the food court or any of the surrounding food places.

"You wanna do Chinese? We haven't had that in a while." My cousin loved eating from there. I always told her, she was gonna turn into a fortune cookie.

"I guess. Let me see if, Onyx wants something." Picking up the phone to call him, I had to take a deep breath. This bitch walking toward me had a grin on her face which meant she was about to start. Keeping the phone in my hand in hopes Onyx answered, she stopped in front of me.

"What's up, ma?" Instead of answering, I let him listen. She wouldn't know because the Air Pod was in my ear. I hated to be the bitch to call my man but I promised, I'd let him handle it.

"You told, Onyx that I was sending videos of us having sex?" Salina had the nerve to question me.

"Yes, I told my husband exactly what you did because at the time we were on our honeymoon fucking the shit outta each other, and he wanted to know why my phone kept going off." She turned her face up.

"Honeymoon? Tuh! You didn't even have one from what I was told." She was very confident in her statement.

"I'm gonna kill that bitch." Onyx was still listening on the other end.

"You are so desperate for him that you'll say anything. Did

it ever occur to you that I'm the one woman, he won't let go?"

"Yea right. Onyx for everybody and I would assume you know that since he cheated on you, what—?" The bitch started counting on her fingers.

"A million times." I laughed.

"And after a million times who did he come home to? Who did he give his last name and another baby to?" I rubbed my stomach. Her facial expression changed to sad.

"And lastly, whose child will grow up without her real mother because she can't move the fuck on?"

"BOOM! She got you there, Salina." Arabia made a joke.

"Well... Onyx wouldn't kill me because whose pussy would he fall into when y'all break up or as one would put it, have a fallen out?" She swear Onyx wanted her and in a way, I blamed him for doing exactly what she said; running back to her.

"That's right, fall into. Your pussy so deep, ten dicks can fit in there at once." My husband told me at the end of them having sex, she was wide open.

"Get in the car, Mariah." Onyx voice was playing in my ear. As much as I wanted to entertain Salina, I did what he requested. This was going to turn ugly so it was best to move on.

"That's right, bitch. Keep it moving. Onyx will always be mine." She yelled heading into the mall.

"Don't even think about responding." There he was again being my voice of reason. Me and Arabia placed our things in the truck and left. Onyx said he would speak to me at home before disconnecting the call.

"Think about the baby, Mariah." I didn't say anything.

"Any other time, I would've said, fuck it but we're both carrying children right now. Her time will come." Arabia's right. I will see her again and next time, Onyx won't be on the phone.

* * *

"Hey, where's the chick who shampooed hair?" I asked Marissa. She was standing at the counter ringing someone up.

I'm not sure why, but ever since we saw her beat up at the mall, it made me wonder if she was ok. I also wanted to know who did that to her; Arabia did too. She was supposed to be here but Deray's mom asked her to stop by. Something was very weird about that family but my cousin wanted to be around them and I can't blame her.

Being around when he was shot took a lot out of her and she kept blaming herself for not getting out the bed when he answered the door. We all told her know one could've known that would happen and she may have been killed as well.

"She knows not to do your hair. I'll be right there." Marissa pointed where I should go. Instead of engaging in more conversation about River in front of customers, I headed to the back.

"Oh, excuse me." Someone bumped into me from the side. River looked terrified and aggravated to see me. The black eye was now yellow and her busted lip was nonexistent. Her clothes were still too big and those damn sneakers had to go.

"You're fine." Taking a seat by the sink, I felt her staring.

"What?" She jumped. Damn, this woman had some serious issues if she's jumping at the sound of my voice.

"Did Arabia come too?" She whispered loud enough for me to hear.

"No. She had something to do." I put the phone in my purse and stared at her. She wasn't bad looking if you can get past the bifocals, big clothes and matted up hair. How the hell wasn't her hair done and she worked in a salon?

"Who whooped your ass?" She sucked her teeth. I didn't mean for it to come out that way.

"My bad. Who put their hands on you?"

"You wouldn't know him." She walked off when Marissa stepped in. Well, I can tell Arabia, I tried to get it outta her. There wasn't much to be done if she didn't wanna tell the person's name.

After sitting in the shop for a couple of hours, I drove home in hopes to arrive before Onyx.

Ever since we made up on our honeymoon, the two of us were like teenagers. He would pick me up from work, take me to lunch and on a few occasions we'd have sex in the car. I've gone to his office and done the same thing. I'm not saying we never did this but it felt even better now that we were on good terms.

I pulled in and saw his grandmother standing there. When I got out the car, she walked over to me.

"Why are you here?"

"Look, we got off on a bad start and now that I know my grandson loves you, can we start over." I had to take a double look behind me to see if her statement was directed to me. For years she's hated me and now out the blue she wanted to be friends.

"Mariah."

"Don't say my name and the only reason you're here was because my husband told you he was gonna fuck you up if you said anything disrespectful to me again." She rolled her eyes.

"No need to be fake or phony because I don't like you either." Hitting the alarm on my car, I walked past her.

"Mariah, he will cheat again." And there goes her pettiness. She couldn't wait.

"Whether he does or not, it won't be with you now will it." She gasped as if I offended her perverted ass.

"If you return to my house again, I'll put a bullet in between your eyes and tell the cops an intruder trespassed." Charlene was at a loss for words.

"I'm the wrong bitch to play with." I stepped in my house and slammed the door behind me.

A few hours later, Onyx came home and found me upstairs watching a movie. Without so much as a hello, he pulled my legs to the edge of the bed, undid his jeans so his dick could be unleashed and fucked the shit outta me. When I asked him what that was about, his only words were, *"It was about time I put my foot down with his grandmother."* All that did was tell me he watched us on the camera.

At least I know he had my back and for that, the two of us engaged in more nasty sex for the rest of the night.

Chapter Twelve

RIVER

When the Mariah chick walked out the salon, I was able to breathe a sigh of relief. I'm not scared of her or anyone for that matter, however, I try and mind my business whenever possible. I also didn't want her popping shit and make me lose my job. She was that type of woman that tore others down to make herself look good. Well, that's what she appeared to be in my eyes. I was shocked that she asked who whooped my ass. What did she care for?

Anyway, Brandon stopped by my place unexpected the night before I ran into Arabia and Mariah at the mall. We had sex, he handed off his normal three hundred dollars and then he started asking why wouldn't I allow his friend to have sex with me. I'm no idiot not to assume he doesn't consider me a whore, however it's still my body and I have the right not to share.

Brandon got angry and started calling me all types of bitch's. The reason he got real angry was because I asked why he wanted his friend to sleep with me so bad, and if he wanted to join. He accused me of calling him gay and began throwing punches. I'm not sure what he thought it was. I started punching him the face and wherever else I could. When I thought he was done because he was outta breath, I lifted my foot and kicked him in the dick.

Somehow he was able to swing and punched me so hard in the face, I fell. My eye felt like it was closing and now blood drained from my lip. The door flew open and I'm assuming the guy he wanted me to sleep with, stood there staring. He had a few words with Brandon and then carried him out.

That day in the mall, I saw him walk in one of the stores and headed in the opposite direction in hopes he wouldn't see me.

Running into Arabia and Mariah had me feeling some kinda way. They looked and smelled expensive, and here I was portraying a homeless person. Well, I can't say I'm without a place to stay but as usual, people only saw my attire. The way Mariah had her face turned up made me embarrassed and the best thing to do was get away. How ironic was it that she stopped by the salon inquiring about me? I'm glad Marissa had me do other things because the look of disgust on her face was one I could do without.

"Here." My son's father, Ryan tossed Jasir's bag at me.

Ryan used to be my neighbor growing up and we were very close. At one point in our life, we told one another everything and said we'd always be around for the other. He was my first sexual experience and vice versa. We did any and everything on one another even if it were only once, just to try it out. We turned one another out in my opinion.

Unfortunately, like all teenage boys, Ryan hit puberty and you couldn't tell him shit. His crater face was now clear of zits and the girls loved it. They started gassing his head up and telling him how handsome he was. Meanwhile, the two of us were still besties and having sex.

One night after he came home from one of the parties, he asked me to come over. The party must've been left unattended by adults because he was drunk. Ryan brought some little bottles of liquor from the party and we drank together.

Long story short, we were real nasty that night and had unprotected sex which we never do. My mother was a piece of shit and his mom worked all the time so it was easy for us to have sex without anyone catching us.

Neither of us had any stability in our lives when it came to our parents. He's been back and forth to his fathers and my mother rarely spoke to me. I'm not even sure if she knew what I looked like since she stayed locked away in her room.

When I found out about the pregnancy, me and Ryan went to the abortion clinic together. Because neither of us were of age, I couldn't get one without an adult present. His mother said she wasn't going and that's what we get for being fast. My mother called me all types of names and said to deal with it on my own.

I had to get home schooled for the remainder of my senior year because my body was so tiny the baby kept me in a lot of pain. There was no prom, senior trip, graduation, or anything for me. At first there was a lot of regret but once my son was born, it all went out the window. He became my everything.

The guidance counselor and a few teachers stopped by with baby clothes, a car seat, play pen, bottles and other items a baby would need.

Throughout my high school years, they were my support system and often asked me to live with them. My mother refused to sign over her parental rights, therefore I was stuck and once my child was born the invitation wasn't asked again.

A year later, I found out the reason my mother wouldn't allow me to live with them. Come to find out she was receiving a check from the state for me and then added my son.

Evidently, she was leaving the house whenever renewal came and when I wasn't home. I was able to get a job but it didn't last long because my mother did something to Jasir and they took him from me. Some would say, that's when I lost it because I haven't been right since.

"River. You ok?" Ryan yelled, making me jump.

"I'm good. Where's Jasir?" Throwing the book bag on my back, I fixed the straps to make them tighter.

"In the bathroom." I heard his little feet running on the wooden floors. His momma's house was perfect and it was stable for him. I don't know what I'd do if he was placed in foster care.

"Mommy!" He jumped in my arms and gave me the biggest hug ever.

"Hey. Guess what?" I put him on my hip.

"What?"

"I have a surprise for you." Ryan stood there listening to us speak.

"Really! Is it candy?"

"No and you shouldn't be eating that. You're going to get bad teeth." I never wanted my son to be one who had those silver caps.

"Daddy, gives me candy when he's on the game." I looked up at him. He shrugged.

"Any news on when you can take him?" I rolled my eyes. It wasn't that he didn't love Jasir; its more or less because he felt my son belonged with me.

"That's my surprise."

"What? Can I live with you again?" I sat Jasir down on the front porch.

"Hey, River." His mom hugged me on her way in the house. She appeared to be exhausted from work and I can't blame her. She worked the day shift and came home to help care for Jasir, so Ryan can work his night shift. I appreciated the hell out of her too because it's her house and she didn't have to let Jasir stay here.

"Grandma, mommy has a surprise." I took him in the house because no one needed to be in our business.

"What's the surprise, mommy?" Jasir rushed to sit on my lap when we went in the living room. Ms. Rogers and Ryan were standing there waiting too.

"Mommy got housing and I'm moving to a new place next week." A huge smile came over my face because of how happy he was.

"Really? Will I have my own room?"

"Yes." Clearly Block fucked the hell outta the woman because after he called her in Walgreens that day, she reached out saying there was a two bedroom voucher available. I don't even care how she did it.

"That's great, River. Are they helping you with furniture and other stuff?" Ms. Rogers walked over to hug me.

"Honestly, I'm leaving the bed where I'm staying now and buying air mattresses until I get something."

"You know I have the table set and brand new living room set my mom had before she passed away in storage."

"Yea but that's your mom's. I can't accept that." She put both hands on my face.

"You are an amazing mom to my grandson. After the things you've dealt with, y'all deserve the best." I started crying.

"Thank you so much."

"I'm happy for you, River. Now that little nigga can sleep in his own bed instead of kicking me in the back all night." I busted out laughing. They had a room for my son here but he never slept in it.

"Don't come for my baby." I kissed all over Jasir's face.

"Thank you for being his father when I couldn't be his mother."

"River, you've always been his mother. Yes, you went through some shit but there was never a day that went by that I thought any less of you." He hugged me tight. This was the best friend I missed. We talked about Jasir all the time but our friendship dwindled after a while. It was my own fault for shutting him and everyone else out.

"If you want, me and Tom will bring the furniture when you're ready." I nodded, wiping my eyes.

"Thank you and do you mind buying him a Paw Patrol comforter set?"

"What for? His ass gonna be in your bed." That made me laugh because he was right.

"I know but when he played in his room at least he'll have the theme." I stayed a little longer talking and left. Jasir wanted to get lunch at the diner. Ryan handed me $500 to start purchasing things for the bathroom, as well as making me get the comforter set. He was never stingy with money but I refused to ask for any when he was the one who had our son.

"Look, mommy." He pointed to what appeared to be a monster truck in the parking lot of the diner. We were waiting on the check from the waitress.

"Wow! That is a big truck." It was a F-150 with tires that seemed too big for it. The exterior color was black but from the window being down you could see the interior was cream. Not seeing who hopped out because the truck pulled up at the door blocking the view of my van, we continued admiring it.

"What up?" A deep voice made me turn my head and I immediately became embarrassed. Block stood there shining bright like a diamond with all that jewelry showing. His clothes were neat and the fade made me think he just returned from the barber shop.

"Hey, are you driving that monster truck?" Jasir asked making Block smile and my panties instantly became moist. What the hell was he doing to me?

"That's my truck, little man."

"It is?" He was so excited when Block said yes.

"Yo, you got a kid?" I stood up and accepted the bill from the waitress.

"Jasir is my son, and you better not say he looks like Scrappy Doo." I thought he was gonna bust a gut by how hard he laughed.

"Actually, he's handsome and let me find out shorty got style."

"His dad dressed him today and for your information, my son will always have style." I placed the money on the table and told Jasir to come on.

"His momma should take lessons because—" I cut him off.

"Don't you dare put me down in front of him." He folded his arms. One thing I didn't play was anyone disrespecting me in front of my son.

"Why would he put you down, mommy? You're already

standing." I snickered a little and tickled him on the way out. Hoping that was the last of Block, we went to my van. I put Jasir in the front and buckled him in the booster seat. Until I had money to get seats in the back, this was how it had to be. I did push the seat as far back as possible. When I went to get in the driver's seat, Jasir's door opened and his seatbelt was being taken off by Block.

"What are you doing?" Hopping back out the van, I walked around it.

"Shorty, wanted to see my truck so that's what I'm gonna let him do. You got a problem?" Jasir had his hand intertwined with Block's as they walked toward his truck.

"Fine but it's only because he would be mad if I said no." Following behind, I watched Block put him in the front seat and explain what every gadget was. Ryan was a damn good father and it didn't hurt that he was showing him how to respect people. Jasir would say, *thank you, no Sir, you're welcome* and whatever else required a respectful response.

"Mr. Jerome gave me twenty dollars to buy candy." He jumped out the truck and ran up to show me the money.

"Did you tell, Mr. Jerome we don't eat candy? It's bad for your teeth."

"What kid don't eat candy? Let me find out you a hater."

"A hater?" He moved closer to where I was.

"You're a hater because you can't afford candy; at least not the good kind." He whispered.

"You mother—" Block quieted me with his finger and I wanted to bite it off. Jasir went back to the truck.

"Don't get no ideas. My dick too good and juicy for you to suck on it." His voice irritated me.

"Why because you dress nice and smell good."

"Exactly." He shrugged.

"I'll have you know there were men I've met that dressed nice, had money and nice cars and their dick was either small or had a sweaty stench." We weren't speaking loud and Jasir was in his own world playing with the money.

"Those niggas weren't really clean then, now were they?" Why did he find comedy in everything I said?

"And besides, I can tell by all these clothes you wear, the pussy stink." I was so offended, my words were caught in my throat.

"You're always covered up; how can your body breathe?" He continued.

"You probably don't have a matching panty set, and ain't no nigga fucked you well enough to make you stalk the dick." I have never in my life had anyone speak to me with such vulgar; yet I was intrigued and turned on.

"Mr. Jerome, when I get my own room can you come by and play video games with me? My dad works at night so he won't be able to all the time." Block stared at me. Kids will ask the most random person the craziest things.

"Alright, Jasir. I think, Mr. Jerome wants to go home." I lifted him from the front seat and walked to our van. After buckling him in, I closed the door and headed to the driver's side.

"Aye!"

"What?" Opening the front door, I put one foot on the step to get in the van.

"Let me know when he gets his new room."

"I most certainly will not."

"My homie asked me to come over. Stop being a hater." I gave him the finger and slammed the door. Block was a pain in my ass and he knew it.

Once we got to my place, Jasir showered, we watched movies and he fell asleep. The whole time, all I could think about was moving into a new place and finally having some sort of normalcy.

Not that Marissa helping me wasn't appreciated, but hitting rock bottom and finally being able to pull myself up slowly, was a task in its own. Thankfully, Ryan and his mom loved me and my son enough to stay by our side.

Over the next few days, me and Jasir went to Target to get the regular items needed for a new place. When I dropped him off, he hugged me tight and I promised to pick him up Friday after work. Ryan asked me for the new address and said him and Tom would be there early Saturday morning. He didn't have to worry about that, me and Jasir were staying the night in our new place.

Chapter Thirteen

ARABIA

"He's with you all the time." Tricia said, rubbing my arm. Today was my first prenatal appointment and Deray's mom and his baby mother wanted to be here. I'm not used to anyone seeing me like this. These breakdowns came out of nowhere and usually no one was around.

As far as Deray's mom and baby mother being with me, don't ask me why but if they're going to be in my life, I guess there's really no harm in sharing these moments with them.

"I need him here physically, not spiritually." His mom smiled.

"Me too, honey. Me too." The doctor stepped in and introduced herself to them. I wanted my mother to come as well but she refused. Janetta had what she called a sixth sense, an intuition about things and people. She said and I quote, those bitches are suspect as hell. I don't trust them so be careful. Of course it made me laugh because she really believed in all that superstition stuff.

Anyway, she stopped by everyday now checking on me which was shocking. My mother loved her kids but she didn't know how to love us if that made sense. Some kids had that undeniable, and indescribable love from their parents but not us. Our father, Travis tried his hardest to be what she couldn't but it wasn't the same.

Don't get me wrong, she was down for us no matter what but we never really heard, *I love you* or received hugs on a daily basis. She didn't pack us snacks for school nor did she sleep in the room with us if we had a bad dream. She'd make us go in the room and turn on cartoons. When we tried to discuss it the next day, she would be too busy.

My grandmother was a mean old lady too, and I remembered how she used to instill in us that love wasn't real and didn't mean anything. Her famous line was, *"That's why men cheat and women go crazy.* It didn't make sense to me but it did to her. My therapist said someone hurt my grandmother years ago and she bestowed that pain on my mother, which trickled down to us.

The doctor walked in, turned the machine on and inserted the tube to do the ultrasound. It was a tad bit uncomfortable but it was for a good reason.

"There is the baby." She pointed to a spot on the screen. It wasn't too big but at twelve weeks, I couldn't expect to see a full grown baby either. How crazy was it that me and Mariah were a month apart?

"Can we see what she's having?" The gynecologist tapped away and a few minutes later pulled the tube out.

"Arabia can find out next month what the baby is. Right now, it's too early." She shut the machine off and asked them to excuse her while she performed another exam. Once they closed the door, she did the breast check and asked a few questions.

"How are you feeling?" She helped me up and had me go behind the screen to get dressed.

"I'm ok. I miss him a lot." Every time anyone asked about Deray, my eyes would get watery. My doctor knew what happened because after the funeral there was a little bleeding so I rushed to the emergency room. They contacted her and when she arrived at the hospital, we talked about it.

"Those memories will be etched in your head forever. Just make sure to love your baby endlessly." I moved the curtain out the way after getting dressed.

"Excuse me." I was slightly offended by her comment.

"Arabia, you're going to be a new mom, who unfortunately will have to raise this baby alone. You will go through a lot of emotions; angry, sad, and most of all hurt. Depression and Post-partum can possibly kick in. You're going to need a strong support system around you was all I meant."

"Oh. Yea, I guess."

"You may hear that from others as well. Be prepared for anything but also be careful because all trimesters of pregnancy are important."

"I know."

"I'm serious. Some will assume only the first few months or the last three months are and forget about the middle. Treat every day critical and that doesn't mean stay in the bed all day or never leave the house. Again, it just meant to remind you about being careful, especially if the baby was the last of him." She hugged me and escorted me to the front. Glancing around the waiting room, I noticed Tricia and Deray's mom had left.

"Bye, Miss Winston." The young secretary waved. She was always super nice to me.

"Arabia." I heard and turned to see River coming in my direction. I know times were hard for her but damn her clothes are always three times to big on her.

"Did you get out that van?" I pointed to an old school vehicle.

"Yes that's my, Scooby Doo van as your brother called it." I laughed.

"Anyway, how's the baby? Do you mind?" She asked about rubbing my belly.

"I don't mind and he or she is doing great. What are you doing here? You expecting?" She fell into a fit of laughter.

"Heck no. My social worker said in order for me to get custody of my son, I had to be healthy."

"And she sent you to the gynecologist?"

"Oh, no. I'm here for my yearly checkup. I did all my blood-work and the physical yesterday. You know they had to make sure I'm not an alcoholic or drug user." She rolled her eyes after saying it.

"That's great news. Block mentioned your housing coming through." She let a grin creep on her face at the mention of his name.

"You like my brother?"

"What? No. I mean he's cute.... But no..." She was so flustered, she started stuttering.

"It's ok. To be honest, I think you left an impression on him at some point." My brother mentioned running into her a few times and the day she stopped by to do my hair, the two of them went at it like a couple. Once he brought up her getting a housing voucher, he started talking about stopping by to make sure the apartment was livable. He never does that. Matter of fact, he had never shown interest in anyone that wasn't some IG model.

"Yea, well he damn sure left one on my son." She began telling me what took place at the diner and that solidified exactly what I thought. Block was feeling her and it was a matter of time before he made his move. I hope she's ready because Block had bitches for days and they stayed ready to fight for him to stay in their life.

The main one she'd have to worry about was, Melanie. They've been sleeping around for the past six months. Ever since he had to take his ex's life, he hadn't settled down. She seemed nice on the outside but Melanie was bat shit crazy too.

I had to step to her a few times because she would key Block's whip or go by his house tryna fight. At the end of the day, he was a man and I would never allow him to put his hands on her or any woman. Now if they attacked him with something, I can't control what he did.

"Why don't you come by, tonight? I'll order some take out and we can watch a movie." River didn't have any friends and since I'm positive Block will come for her, I may as well get to know her better. We were only acquainted at school so this would be different.

"I'll stop by but I won't stay long. I'm moving into my new place soon. I want to make sure the apartment I'm in was cleaned and spotless before moving out." I understood that.

"Ok. Do you remember my address?" She told me no, so I gave it to her again. The two of us parted ways. I hopped in my car and drove to see Mariah. She was bored and wanted company. Maybe I'll invite her over to watch a movie, then again, maybe not. She wasn't feeling River and I think it was mutual. Mariah wouldn't be uncomfortable but River would.

"Why is the Mystery Machine pulling up in front of your house?" I shook my head at my mother. She was a piece of work and couldn't be speaking of anyone other than River. Block must've told her about the van.

"Ma, I invited someone over as a girls day. Don't start."

"Well, why am I here?"

"You popped up and said you didn't feel like driving home." I shrugged, reminding her of what she said.

"Don't bother her." I headed to the door and opened it before she could knock or ring the doorbell.

"Hey, River." She handed me a bottle of champagne and told me to open it after the baby arrived.

"The food just got here and I'm warning you now, my mom is here?" She froze. One thing I learned about River was she only spoke to me and Block. Anyone else, she didn't want to be around. In some instance, I could understand, especially the way Mariah and some of my family acted toward her.

"She's harmless unless you fuck with her kids." I wasn't lying. Janetta talked a lot of mess but won't bother you.

"Do you have any other clothes?" My mother was rude as fuck though. River had on some baggy jeans that had a belt so tight around the waist, one would think she was choking her stomach. The shirt was just as baggy and her hair was pulled back into a mini ponytail. I say mini because the bob hairstyle grew out and there was enough to put it up.

"MA!" I yelled.

"It's ok, Arabia. Yes, I have other clothes but they're just as big as these." River took a seat on the couch.

"These clothes were donated to me from the church, just like the van. I'm sorry if my attire doesn't fit your liking but this was all I could get. One day, I'll be able to wear name brand clothes but until then, I'm more than comfortable in these. And besides, I don't have to worry about coochie cutters or exposing my body for attention." River shrugged.

"Hmph. All you had to say was you were poor."

"Ok. That's enough. Ma, either you're going to be

respectful to River or you have to go." My mother stared at me, then River, then back at me.

"Fine, I'll go because I can't sit here staring into those fishbowl glasses. They're making me dizzy. I swear one of her eyes swam to the other side." Out of nowhere, River busted out laughing, which made both of us laugh.

"River, I'm sorry about her."

"Don't apologize. That one was funny." I had her get up to follow me in the kitchen. She sat at the island as I took the shrimp scampi out the bag, along with a salad.

"Hold on. I have to wash my hands."

"Thank goodness for that. We wouldn't want your hands to get wet and dirt fall off." My mother was not stopping with her ignorance.

"Ma, I swear if you say one more rude thing, I'm gonna have daddy pick you up." The only person my mother didn't play with was my dad. He was never abusive toward her that I know of but when he laid down he law, she'd listen.

"It's ok, Arabia. I respect the fact she doesn't hold her tongue like most. I'm used to people talking about me when I leave. At least, I'm aware of how she really feels." River grabbed a paper towel to dry her hands.

"That's right, Arabia. She can respect it. Now where's my food." My mom arrived right before I ordered and made me get her something too.

For the next few hours, the three of us watched movies and shared a few laughs. Of course my mother made her slick comments the entire time, but River appeared to be amused by them.

Around seven, River told us she was leaving to pick her son up. He was staying the night and they were moving in the morning. I couldn't help but be happy for her.

"Next time you come over, where some contacts so I don't think fish are stuck in those frames."

"And if I do come over again, make sure you're not here and we won't have that problem."

"Ok, PigPen. Let me find out." I laughed at the two of them go back and forth all the way to her van.

"On your way to solve the next mystery, be sure to pick up some seats for the back." My mom got in her own car as well. If River stayed around like I think she will, those two will get along just fine. Closing the door, I locked up and went upstairs to shower.

Getting in the bed, I replayed some of the videos me and Deray had. We really would've been good together.

Chapter Fourteen

BLOCK

S taring at this motherfucker walking around the club pretending like he didn't put hands on my sister, had me mad as fuck. I only found out because Mariah asked my sister why her nose looked crooked, and under her eyes were yellow. That alone let me know Arabia held in what took place because the bruises were already clearing up. When Mariah told me what Arabia said, I had to calm myself down.

One thing I didn't fuck with was any man putting hands on a woman. It's the exact reason those two came to my defense with stupid ass Melanie or any other woman who tried to get physical. Now if a chick hit me with a bat or tried to run me over with her car, my reaction would be on them.

"Hey, babe." I removed Avery's hands from my shoulder.

"When the fuck you due? This pregnancy lasting forever."

Her stomach was poking out a lot but I wasn't lying. It felt as if she had been pregnant more than nine months. Two months ago, she was due in two months, now here we are and she got her pregnant ass in the club.

"Umm, next week. I sent you a text."

"Oh, I ain't get that shit. My number been changed since you decided to blow my shit up with fake labor pains. Move." I pushed her out the way but not too hard. It's a possibility the baby may be mine so she was lucky.

Making my way over to the VIP where Huff was getting a lap dance, someone caught my eye. Melanie had the most evilest expression as she stared at Avery. I nodded my head to, Tory who always had my back as well. He knew about crazy as Melanie and went to escort her out the club for me. I'm not in love with her, however if things get crazy I don't want her in here.

"You know shit won't be the same after this." Onyx said, walking behind me smoking. He asked me to wait for him before approaching Huff.

"Ask me if I give a fuck?" We counted with our eyes the amount of people inside VIP. None of them could fuck with me or Onyx. The count was to figure out how many we had to take on at once.

Huff wasn't big time like myself, but he did run with his own team for the most part. He loved fucking strippers, ho's, and I would indulge here and there but he was addicted. Allegedly he slowed down once him and Arabia became a couple. Somehow his addiction got the best of him because he was back at it.

"Bounce." I barked at the half naked stripper on Huff's lap. She was grinding on him as if they were fucking.

"I don't have to go nowhere." The chick got smart. I lifted her up by the hair and tossed her in the other direction. Huff rushed to put his dick away.

"Nigga, why the fuck you out here raw dogging bitches and you with Arabia?" He hopped up.

"My bad, bro. She broke up with me and I was horny." This nigga tried to give me a pound.

"She should've left your ass since you put your hands on her." The fear on his face showed instantly. He already knew what it was. My fist connected with his jaw and I saw firsthand that shit break. Blood started gushing out right away.

"Oh shit." I heard behind me. Huff cupped his hand to try and catch the blood. My fist kept connected with his face over and over. I was tryna kill that motherfucker and probably would've had no one stopped me.

"A'ight. Let's go." Onyx and Tory pushed me out the section as Huff appeared to be dead on the floor. Not one person said a word as we walked down the stairs and out the club.

"Umm, Block." I heard Avery's annoying ass voice.

"What the fuck you want?"

"I think my water broke." Looking at her pants there wasn't anything wet.

"How you don't know if it broke?" Onyx and Tory were shaking their heads.

"Can you take me to the hospital?" I looked at her for a moment before speaking.

"Hell no! You won't be getting blood and gush all over my ride." I sent for an ambulance because my family would talk shit if I put her in an Uber.

"Block!" Avery yelled.

"What? I'll follow the ambulance when they get here." She bent over holding her stomach. No one was saying anything to Avery as has stood there in pain.

"You can't take me?" I walked over to her.

"Avery don't pretend as if I wanted this baby that I'm still unsure is mine. Call me all the names you want but the fact remained that you brought this on yourself being sneaky."

"Block, I—" She started stuttering.

"I have yet to prove you had something put in my drink, but my gut has never been wrong." Lifted her head to make sure she saw how the seriousness on my face, I said one last thing to her. I could hear the sirens from the police behind me.

"If I ever find out that you did something to my drink that night, I'm gonna fucking kill you." Onyx pulled me away because they were bringing Huff out and he didn't want me to swing on him again.

The shit with Avery still had me at a loss for words. Never in my life have I been a cheater and the night me and her had sex, was a mystery. She can play as if I'm stupid all she wanted but I will find out the truth if it was the last thing I did.

"Block, you really fucked him up." Some guy who was friends with Huff said walking out the club.

"Remember that when you or any of y'all motherfuckers try to retaliate. My bullets don't have a name for you or your family, and my hands are deadly. Don't fucking play with me." The guy put his hands up in surrender.

"Let's go." Onyx was cracking up. I hopped in my ride, waited for them to place Avery on a stretcher and followed behind. Half of me wanted to be happy becoming a father. The other half didn't want this kid and prayed it wasn't mine.

I'm all for a woman having the right to keep a child but the bitch can't be mad if the nigga don't wanna be bothered. Just like a man should've worn a condom, the bitch should've never let a man go in raw. They both at fault and if that were the case, then they both should be able to choose what to do.

"That baby ain't yours." My mother spoke loud enough for everyone to hear.

We were sitting in the room with Avery after the delivery. I stood off to the side watching her give birth in case the child was mine. I'll be able to say I saw her being born. Not once did I hold Avery's hand or tell her to push. Again, this was an unplanned and unwanted pregnancy so I'm doing the bare minimum.

She was in labor for ten hours getting on my damn nerves with all the whining and crying. I swear the nurses took their time coming in the room when she rang the bell because she irked their nerves too. It was always, *"Oh I'm in pain, can you give me something strong,* blah, blah, blah. Regardless of how many times they told her no, she'd call them right back in the room.

Anyway, her mother and sister Leah arrived not too long ago talking shit. I had to stop ma dukes from smacking Leah, who assumed she could say what she wanted. When my mother walked up on her, the bitch threatened to contact the police.

"Why you say that?" I'm not gonna correct her. The old saying had always been, your mom or grandmother would know if a child was yours or not.

"The kid darker than the bottom of my shoe and it's bald headed." We heard one of them suck their teeth.

"Ma, really?"

"Hell yea really. You and Arabia had a lotta hair. That little girl got a tiny piece sticking up like Alfalfa on The Little Rascals." I couldn't help but laugh at this point. She was saying anything.

"Watch this." She made her way to the crib and pushed it over to me.

"Look, the baby is cute cuz it's a baby but no hair and she don't resemble no one in the family, not even your father's side of the family and they some ugly motherfuckers." The baby stirred in her sleep. I pushed her back to Avery.

"And you don't have no connection to the baby." I shook my head.

"How much longer before the test results return?" I asked

the doctor when he walked in to check on her. It's only been three hours since the delivery and I refused to leave. I wasn't taking the chance of her getting the results changed, especially when she still a suspect in drugging me.

"It can take a few hours."

"A few hours? It's been longer than that." Avery rolled her eyes when my mother spoke. Instead of listening to her argue with the doctor, I went out the room. There was a nurse coming in my direction with paperwork in her hand. It could be a coincidence because the nurses station is across from Avery's room.

"Hi, I'm here to drop off results." The nurse wasn't loud, yet she wasn't quiet either.

"Aye! Bring me those results." The woman turned around and smirked. The way she licked her lips and switched toward me, gave me every inclination she wanted to fuck.

"He is the potential father and the mother is in the room he's standing in front of." The secretary yelled out the information. She also let her now it was ok to give me the paperwork.

"Here's your envelope." She handed it to me but wouldn't let go.

"Bitch, do I look like I'm tryna play games?" Her hand released it.

"Owww." She sucked her finger after getting a paper cut.

"That's what your dumb ass gets." Ripping the envelope open, all my eyes focused on were the results. It read, *"The alleged father is excluded as the biological father of the tested child.* Walking in the room, it appeared my mom was about to yoke Avery's sister up.

"Let's go, ma."

"Block, where you going? The birth certificate papers—" Avery said. I walked over to the bed, pushed her mother out the way and mushed the paper in Avery's face.

"You played games the entire pregnancy and that baby ain't even mine." Her sister gasped.

"No, she is yours." I pulled the paper back, pointed to the section, and waited for her to respond.

"The test wasn't done correctly."

"We're in a hospital where they do this constantly. How you figure outta all the tests they perform, they found your name and did it wrong?" Complete silence.

"I lost my fucking girl behind your bullshit and come to find out, the kid not even mine." Leslie wasn't perfect and maybe if Avery never lied, we would've still been together and she wouldn't have had threesomes and orgys. What am I saying, my ex was indulging in sex acts with her friend and it could've happened before anything went down between me and Avery. I guess we'll never know at this point because she damn sure not coming back.

"Block."

"My sister gave you a job on the strength that was my kid. Women didn't whoop your ass for running your mouth due to me shutting it down." I was becoming more and more angry thinking about the lies.

"Well, you're not pregnant now." Before I could grab my

mother, she punched Avery in the mouth. Blood rushed out instantly from the force she used. My mother was no joke when it came to fighting and she heavy handed.

"That's for lying and you two." She pointed to Leah and her mother.

"Say one word and I'm gonna whoop your ass like it's never been done before." Both of them nodded. Thankfully, the doctor stepped out because I would hate to find him after work and take his life.

"Let's go." I pushed my mother toward the door and took one last look at the kid.

"I feel sorry for you little girl." Walking out, I breathe a sigh of relief. Having to deal with Avery for the rest of my life due to having a kid would've been hard.

Chapter Fifteen

RIVER

"I'm ready, Mommy." Jasir came out the bathroom with toothpaste dripping down his mouth.

Today was the day for us to move into our new place and I couldn't tell who was more excited; me or him. Here it was five in the morning, and we were dressed and ready to go.

The only thing coming with me from here was the 46 inch TV Marissa gifted me yesterday as a surprise for my new place, my clothes, and toiletries. Everything else was going in the trash.

I had my leggings on with a T-shirt, a pair of black van looking sneakers I picked up from Target and my hair was brushed in a ponytail. My hair was growing a lot now that I allowed Marissa to do it. She started getting new shampoo products in and would give me some to use.

As another gift she put my hair in a doobie. I took it down and had a shoulder length ponytail for today.

Jasir wanted to wear moving clothes too, so he had on a pair of sweatpants and a T-shirt as well. Ryan packed him some black adidas to match and gave him a snap back hat too. Jasir was very spoiled and I'm happy because I wasn't able to do it.

Most young couples end up having a turmoil relationship. Me and Ryan had our disputes here and there but we never argued in front of Jasir, and we never allowed him to see us with someone else. Well, I haven't been with anyone except Brandon and that was for money. If Ryan had someone, he never mentioned her either.

Anyway, I had him go in the bathroom to wash his face, took one last glance around the place and smiled. This was a safe haven for me when there wasn't anywhere else to go. I appreciated Marissa very much and hope one day I'll be able to repay her.

KNOCK! KNOCK! Me and Jasir froze. I wasn't expecting anyone and I'm the type of person who never wanted uninvited guests to show up unannounced.

"River, open up.

"Daddy." Jasir ran to the door. Ryan and Tom stood there dressed in sweat outfits.

"What are y'all doing here? I thought we were meeting at the house. Hey, Tom." I gave both of them a hug.

"My mom wanted us to check and make sure you didn't need help." A smile came over my face as he mentioned her. She was a saving grace too when it came to Jasir.

"It's early, though."

"I knew, Jasir would be up. He was too excited last night over the phone." We shared a laugh.

"All I have is the TV, the two totes of clothes and that duffle bag with my feminine stuff in it." They picked up the few items and walked up the outside stairs. A bitch may have been poor but I've always been very clean with my hygiene.

"Let me give, Marissa the key and I'll be ready." Jasir followed me to the front of the house. I knocked lightly since it was still very early.

"Hey, honey. Is everything ok?" Marissa opened the door asking with her coffee in hand.

"Yes. I wanted to hand you the key." She took it with her free hand and held mine in hers.

"I'm so happy for you and I'm going to pray every day that things get better for you."

"Marissa, I'll still be at work." I never quit and the place was literally only a few streets over. The woman Dana hooked me up with a landlord she said had multiple properties and they were close by.

The one he offered me was in a four family house with a private entrance. The backyard was big and there was a small parking lot on the side. The apartment was very spacious and now that I'm on Section 8, I didn't have to worry about being put out anymore. Granted, I can be but I'll still have my housing voucher which is more than enough security for me right now.

"I know but you'll be alone and—" She started to tear up.

"Aww, don't cry. My mommy will still see you." Jasir hugged her around the waist.

After hugging and saying our goodbyes, I told her I'll be at work Monday and she offered to follow me home so she could come see the place. I took one more look at my old apartment, said a quick prayer and pulled off. God blessed me in more ways than one and I did not plan on taking any of it for granted.

* * *

"Is this it, mommy?" We pulled in one of the spots. Ryan and Tom took us to the diner for breakfast before coming here. Jasir had cereal but he wanted pancakes too. He could really eat for a tiny kid.

"This is it. Are you ready?" He removed his seatbelt quick. Ryan pulled the U-Haul behind my van.

"Jasir, wait. We have to grab these bags." I opened the side door and pointed to a small bag with his toys in it. I grabbed a few and closed the door back. The neighborhood appeared to be in a good spot but you never know.

"Which door, Mommy?" There were two entrances in the front, and one on each side.

I had the entire downstairs and the landlord had an alarm system on the property in general to cover the outside area. I purchased a Ring doorbell for my door once you walked in the hallway area to have my own sense of security.

"That one over there." I gestured with my head because my

hands were full. I put the bags down, put the key in and immediately started crying.

There were balloons all over, as well as the furniture his mom gave me. Peeking in the kitchen from where I stood was a big basket wrapped in cellophane. A card sat in front of it along with a bottle of champagne. We heard footsteps and Mrs. Rogers walked out the bathroom.

"When did y'all do all this, and how did you get in?"

"Funny thing." His mom dried her hands off with a paper towel I'm assuming she found in the bathroom.

"Me and your landlord have been a thing for the last few years." Ryan sucked his teeth. He was a mommas boy and didn't want to hear about her and any man.

"What?"

"I knew about all the properties he owned but he never had any openings. The day he mentioned having one, I brought your name up and he said, you were going to be his new tenant." I gasped.

"I told him not to tell you so it would be a surprise."

"So y'all knew about it?"

"We did and pretended to be surprised. Do you like it?" I gave her the biggest hug and Jasir was right behind me doing the same. I'm not sure he understood why but he did it anyway.

"You deserve this, River." She pulled back to look at me.

"Do not let what happened in the past with your mother define your future." I wiped my eyes.

"Had you not been stubborn and stayed with us—" I cut her off.

She always told, no begged me to stay with them when I first became homeless. However, my pride wouldn't let me. Then, I couldn't take care of my son financially or any way, and that alone did something to me mentally. I've always heard about women doing things to their kids when they were in bad situations and I didn't want that for Jasir. As much as it hurt me to leave him with Ryan and his mom, I knew in my heart it was for the best. People can judge all they want but until they're in my shoes, they'll never know.

"I will always be grateful and thankful for you and Ryan." We hugged again before Ryan told us to get it together with all the crying.

"Mommy, come look." Jasir yelled from one of the bedrooms. Going to where his voice came from, I stopped short at the room door.

"You didn't." I stared at the twin size kids bedroom set with Paw Patrol curtains, a comforter set, rug, toys and a flat screen on the wall with an entertainment center underneath. A toy box, and since the closet door was open, I could see clothes hanging up and a few shoe boxes.

"Jasir deserved his own space and I know it would take time to get him a bed." Ryan walked over to me.

"He's our son, River. What you can't do, I will. Now enjoy the moment." We embraced once another as well.

"Uncle Tom, can you get off my bed? You're too big." Jasir tried his hardest to push him off.

"River." His mom called out. I left the three of them in there acting crazy.

"Everything ok?" Ms. Rogers was sitting at the kitchen table she gave me. It was beautiful too.

"I know you have a job and I also know the pay isn't that well, being a shampoo girl." I sat there listening.

"My job put up a hiring sign so I filled out an application for you."

"Ms. Rogers, I don't know anything about doing security." She was the head security at the hospital for the last twenty years. When the state offered me housing, I received childcare as well for when Jasir was placed back with me. My food stamps would go higher as well.

"You don't have to and I worked it out where you'll only do part time. That way you can pick Jasir up from school. If you want more hours on the weekends, let me know and I'll put you on the schedule." All I could do was cry.

"Now, as far as that van. We gotta do something about that." I instantly started laughing.

"I love that van." She got up from the table.

"It's cute but my grandbaby resembled a cave kid in it when y'all pulled up." She shook her head as she stared out the window.

"A cave kid?" She told me it was something she made it up.

"It's better than somebody saying it's the *Mystery Machine and that I look like Velma from Scooby Doo.*" I repeated what Block always called me. For a moment Ms. Rogers stared.

"What's wrong?"

"Now that you say it, you and Velma do look alike. The

thick glasses and your usual attire." She joked making us both laugh.

For the rest of the day, they all stayed over helping me unpack and put away the things I did buy. Brandon was no longer in my life but the little money I made off him, helped out a lot.

Ms. Rogers drove me down to Rent-A-Center and put a bedroom set for me under her credit. I offered to pay the monthly fee but she refused, saying it was a housewarming gift. It would be delivered in a week because it was out of a catalog and she did not worry about a price.

Once we got home, Ryan had already fed Jasir, bathed him and got him ready for bed. I locked up when they left, showered and went to sleep in my son's bed next to him. I forgot to pick up an air mattress so we'll get one tomorrow at the store.

I admit a few tears fell down my face again because I never thought I'd be here. Now that I am, I'm making sure not to ever mess up.

Chapter Sixteen

ONYX

"What are you gonna do about, Huff?" I questioned Block, who was staring down at one of Huff's boys laid out on the ground, courtesy of him.

Evidently, this guy was upset that Block beat his friend up at the club and embarrassed him. He decided to take it upon himself to retaliate by approaching us at the bowling alley. We went faithfully on Thursdays and everyone knew that. He asked Block to come outside and had him walk to the side of the building. I'm assuming when he got his ass whooped, he didn't want anyone to see it. People tried to follow but knowing my boy, it wouldn't be a sight anyone needed to see.

I give it to him though, he did get a few punches in, and that's because Block played a game with him. Talking about if you knock me out, I'll let you live. Everyone inside the alley told the dude not to do it but you know some niggas don't know how to back down. He wanted to prove something and unfortunately, all he proved was that his mother would have to pick out a black dress for his services. Sadly, he was no match for Block.

"Until I find out if he came on his own or Huff sent him, I'll keep my ears to the streets." He stomped the dude one last time in the face before our team came and scooped him up off the ground.

"That nigga got a death wish." I said, smoking on our way to my truck. He caught a ride with me.

"He definitely on some other shit. I'll find out what made him come for me because he always been a bitch. I'm sure he mentioned something to someone" The two of us hopped in my truck.

On the drive to take him home, we discussed an upcoming hit we had to do as a team. It was taking place in Connecticut in a few days. The only reason we're doing it together was because four people had to be taken out at once. Granted, it may be two seconds apart but it would be done at the same time.

Block was the one person I'd do anything of this magnitude with. He was my brother from another, mother and nothing would change that. I reminisced on how we linked up.

"Where you from?" This dude asked, as we put our guns up. We had just did a hit on two Kingpins. We weren't worried about anyone catching us because the sniper guns used, allowed us to shoot from damn near another town away.

"Jersey but ma dukes moved me and my brother to Rhode Island as teenagers to get away from some family shit." Not tryna tell too much of my business, I switched the subject.

"How long you been doing this?"

"For the last five years," He shrugged, grabbing his bag.

"Damn. I only been at this shit for a year."

"How old are you?" I felt a tad bit offended when he asked my age.

"Twenty, why?"

"How did you get into it so young?" We headed down the stairs of the building still conversing.

"I've seen a lot of murders in my young age so at the age of eighteen, I stayed at the gun range learning how to shoot every weapon the place had. Then, I started going to gun shows and purchasing a lotta high tech shit just for fun." He opened the door that led outside.

"One day, I was leaving the range and someone approached me about a guy named, Montell that wanted to speak with me regarding a job." At the time, I had no idea who Montell was, or that he was a notorious man who had people killed for even the smallest incidents.

One time he had me take out a politician for not voting for his cousin who ran for a Councilman. But when he signed me up to take out his pops for cheating on his mother, I knew then, he gave zero fucks about anyone.

"Anyway, we met up, he explained to me what the job entailed, and how much money was at stake. Once he mentioned bonuses, and offered the mansion we stayed in at the time, I was

down for whatever." My pops didn't raise no dummy. I knew before signing on for anything to make sure the deed to the mansion was in my name and he paid me a bonus up front.

My mother wasn't happy and refused to move in the place at first. Renovations were done to her liking and she finally settled in. Once she found a man, she moved out but that mansion was still there. I won't ever put it up for sale; it will be around even after I'm dead.

"How did you get involved?"

"Montell is my uncle." He smirked, jumped in his ride and pulled off. If that man was his uncle, why didn't he know about me. Instead of standing there tryna figure it out, I left as well.

Two days later, Montell called me over to his home out in Maine. It was his main place and I've only been here twice. I can't lie, the house was huge and held security as if he were the President.

Long story short, I learned Montell was indeed, Block's uncle. His mother was Montell's sister, and Mariah's father was their brother too. The guy he had me kill for my first job was their father, and had been cheating on their mother for years. They blamed her suicide on his infidelity and decided he had to go too.

I ended up staying over Montell's for a few days, which was how me and Block became closer. Montell said in order to work as a team we had to know everything about one another. As hard as it was to relive some painful shit, it felt good speaking to someone else who wouldn't judge.

Little did I know, Montell knew my past and it was the

exact reason he chose me. His famous words to me had always been, *"There will come a time where you will have to make a choice between a loved one, and the woman you love."* At the time, none of us knew I'd marry Mariah but as the years passed and we got together, what he said was slowly coming together.

"You good, bro?" Block brought me outta my thoughts.

"Yea."

"You sure cuz you ran two lights and almost crashed into my truck." He pointed to how close I parked in his driveway. I don't even remember driving or anything. It's as if I were in a zone but still able to get to my destination.

"I'm cool. I'll see you Saturday." Mariah wanted to have a gender reveal at the house for her and Arabia.

Since her man passed away, my wife made it her business to include Arabia in everything. Not that she wouldn't have been invited if it was just for her but no one wanted her to go into depression or lose the baby.

After Block got out, I headed home but made a stop at the store to get some swishers. On the way out, I saw Salina hugged up in a man's embrace. If my daughter wasn't at my house, I would've had a problem because her momma ain't shit either and that's who she always left her with.

Getting in my ride, I made a mental note of dudes face. My ex may be pretending not to see me but I know for a fact she saw my car because she was only a few feet away. Salina not speaking only verified to me that she's up to something. That bitch will speak no matter what; even if she was sitting on his lap. They say things happen for a reason and this stop at the store was to make me aware.

* * *

"I can't believe you're having a boy and Mariah, a girl." The chick River spoke with excitement as she sat next to Arabia. They were in the family room with all the women.

"Onyx loved being a girl dad. I'm happy but all the boys better get ready because he'll be ready to kill for those girls. Ain't that right, Laila." Mariah chimed in. She tickled my daughter, making her laugh. Their bond was so tight not even Salina could break it and she tried a few times.

"Yo, who is that?" Block walked up behind me drinking a beer. He had just gotten here and hour ago.

"Who?" He knew everyone here.

"The chick with her hair down by her shoulders." I looked at him and then the woman.

"You don't know who that is?" I questioned because to my knowledge he bothered her any chance he got.

"I saw her from a distance when y'all did the gender reveal but I don't know her." I was at a loss for words right now.

"Nigga, you serious?" The expression on his face told me he really had no idea.

"Bro, that's River." He almost spit his drink out.

"What? Nahhhh. That chick don't have on bifocals and she dressed in a catsuit like outfit with heels. River broke as fuck!"

Now it was time for me to spit out my drink. Arabia turned around to see us standing there and got up.

"Block, did you see, River." She smirked, folding her arms. He took another sip, walked in the room where River sat, stood in front of her and stared. Janetta was laughing and both my mom and Mariah's had a grin on their faces. All the women in the family wanted him to find someone.

"That nigga crazy." I shook my head.

"What? You better not call me names." River stood, moved him out the way and left the room. Block was mesmerized for the moment which had all of us laughing.

"I'm gonna go." River told Arabia who was still standing next to me. Block finally snapped outta whatever trance she had him in and came in our direction.

"Ok. Thanks for coming." She appeared to be off balance walking to the door.

"You ok? Block, you should give her a ride home. I think shorty had too much to drink." I said, trying to get him to take her.

"I do not want him taking me home. I'm fine." She barely drank anything but the wine can affect people later.

"River, you were drinking a lot of wine. Block take her home." Janetta chimed in.

"No, thank you." She was adamant about him not driving her. He finished his beer, grabbed her hand and opened the door.

"I wish you would pretend like you don't want me touching you." River turned around.

"Can someone else take me?"

"We all drunk." Arabia responded making all of us laugh again. Her, Mariah and the kids were the only ones not drinking.

"Really?" Block basically yanked her out the door.

"Those two fucking tonight." I closed the door after they pulled off. Everyone went back in the living room.

"And what are we doing later?" Mariah wrapped her arms around my waist.

"We doing some nasty shit when they leave." I leaned down to kiss her.

"Well, let me tell everyone to go home." She smiled, grabbing my hand to follow. Needless to say, the house was empty an hour later and my wife was definitely nasty.

Chapter Seventeen

BLOCK

River could pretend she wasn't happy about me driving her home but we both know it wasn't true. I'm not gonna lie, her outfit enticed the hell outta me. Everything about her was different; it was as if her being dressed up brought out something she didn't know she had.

The catsuit was dark blue and she wore a thin sweater around the waist. It didn't hide the shape she had been hiding from the world. River wasn't very skinny, but she was short and thick in all the right places. The heels gave her some height and surprisingly her toes were painted. Her hair was down and the glasses were missing.

"I can walk from here." We were at the corner by her house that she didn't know I was aware of.

"Relax." She pouted.

"Stop acting like you don't want me to know where you live." I turned down her street.

"How do you know?" She turned toward me with her arms still folded.

"This chick who sucked my dick real good stay a few houses down." River rolled her eyes.

"What? You asked?"

"It still doesn't explain how you know where I live."

"Duh! She didn't move. I saw you here two nights ago and when did you change your style." I flipped her hair.

"I thought she only sucked you off."

"She does that first to get me in the mood." I shrugged before continuing my statement.

"Her pussy just ok so she gotta do something good to keep me there. I'm surprised you didn't hear her yelling. As loud as she was, I assumed all the neighbors knew my name." I could tell River was sick of me by her facial expressions.

"You're disgusting." I pulled up on the side of her house. Putting my truck in park, River opened the door and hopped out too fast. She ended up on the ground.

"Block are you gonna help me?" I heard her yell. Luckily the music was off, otherwise I wouldn't have heard her. Slowly getting out, I stretched, closed the door and walked around the truck. River was sitting on the ground nursing her ankle.

"I think it's broken." Bending down to her level, I unwrapped the strap on her ankle and lifted her foot.

"It looks swollen but there's no bone poking out and you're not whining when I touch it." She gave me a weird look.

"I had enough broken bones, fractures and sprains growing up. You'll be fine." Placing her foot down on the ground gently, I removed the other shoe, lifted her up and carried her to the door. Her scent was turning me on and it didn't help that the outfit was thin so I could feel how soft her body was.

"Thanks." I let her down and watched her stand on her tippy toes with the other foot. Once she opened the door, she hopped in.

"You can go now."

"I ain't going nowhere until you thank me properly." Moving past her, I maneuvered through her apartment as if I've been here before. The set up was quite decent for someone who recently moved in.

"Aye, where all this furniture come from?" There was even a king sized bedroom set in her room.

"Excuse me. I had money saved up." She felt insulted.

"How? You broke as hell and you damn sure wasn't making money at the salon washing bitches hair." My delivery may be wrong asking those questions but again, she broke and now all of a sudden she had all she needed. Granted, that Scooby Doo truck still at my cousins house which was how she probably got there.

"You know asking questions instead of being rude and ignorant may get you the answers you're searching for." River sat on the couch with a Ziplock bag full of ice on her ankle that was now wrapped in an ace bandage. She must've did that while I went through her house.

"Or you could just tell me if you have an Only Fans or not."

140

River fell into a fit of laughter.

"I haven't worn clothes like these since my junior year in high school, and even then, they weren't this revealing." She pointed to her outfit.

"Then why you have it on and where are those thick acrylic bifocals?" She laughed.

"Your sister thought it was a great idea to give me a makeover. She stopped by hours before and brought me this outfit and shoes to match. Trust me, I declined to go but she begged me." She removed the ice off her ankle because the bag started to leak.

"As far as my bifocals go, these contacts were as close to my prescriptions that I could get on short notice." She explained how Arabia picked her up and they went to the eye doctor. Because she didn't have an appointment they couldn't see her because they were closing. However, one lady did tell River she could take the prescription she wrote down and go into the eye glass place at Walmart or Target.

"I can see but things are cloudy at times." She limped past me to go in the kitchen. Looking at the text that came through, I wasn't paying attention to River standing in front of me.

"What type of compensation you looking for, for giving me a ride and helping me in? I have soda, juice, animal crackers and chips. My food stamps kick in tomorrow so that's all I got."

"Let me find out you have some Scooby Snacks in your cabinets." If she could kill me with her eyes, she probably would.

I hated that she wasn't well off with money but respected

the hell outta her for not being ashamed of who she was. Most women would do anything possible to make themselves something they're not. Putting my phone away, I rose up out the chair and towered over her.

"You can't afford what I want."

"And what's that? Steak and Lobster? Caviar and Escargot? Ace of Spades? What?" I laughed at her tryna name expensive things.

"Nah."

"Then what." She now had an attitude because I turned down her snacks.

"Good pussy."

"What the heck does that have to do with being able to afford you?" Invading her space, I tilted River's head back to look in her eyes.

"Good pussy will make a nigga go crazy over a woman. He'll do any and everything for her, and I'm not just talking about upgrading her life materialistically. I'm talking about showing her things she's never seen, taking her places she's never been and making sure to treat her like the queen she was." River took a deep breath.

"Making love to her mind, body and soul. Letting her know that no bitch could ever compare or break our foundation and lastly—" I stopped speaking for a moment. River was hanging on my every word too.

"Lastly, a woman with good pussy would never have to worry about anything because if she could get me, I would give her the world."

"Wow. Ok."

"I would also let the woman know that once she had my heart, no one could take it from her." I placed her hand on my chest.

"It may not make sense to you, but it makes perfect sense to me." I may be a hood nigga but I've always been a romantic at heart. I leaned down to whisper in her ear.

"You ever had a man make you cum so hard, your body shakes violently, and the blood feels like it's gonna come out your body." She closed her eyes as I spoke.

"You'll feel as if nothing can top that first orgasm until another one comes and then another. You try to get up and can't walk because you're completely drained and the only thing to quench your thirst, was some dick penetrating you. Your eyes roll in back of your head with each stroke, driving you more insane." My hands found the zipper on the side of her catsuit. As I pulled it down, River opened her eyes and kept them on me. She wore no underclothes which had my dick waking up.

"Has a man ever sucked on that clit until you begged him to stop?" I helped her step out the outfit. My head was close to her pussy and the peach scent began to seep out from in between her legs. Spreading them wider, I could see her clit starting to peek out. Placing a soft kiss on top of her shoulder, she turned to me and our tongues collided. We weren't rushing or even trying to outdo the other; the kissing was sensual, erotic and passionate as if we were lovers.

"You like this, River?" I pulled away to ask when my fingers glided up her leg and delved deep into her tunnel. I lifted one of her legs on the couch to push in deeper.

"Yesssss." Her juices were streaming down my hand.

"Show me what that body can do." I went a little faster and watched River's body succumb to a powerful orgasm. Removing my hand, I slid my fingers inside her mouth and then mine. She had a distinctive taste which made me wanna go down. I took my shirt off, sat on the couch and pulled her in front of me. She was nervous when I put both legs over my shoulder but all that went away as my tongue latched onto her clit.

My back was against the couch as she gyrated her pussy on my face. Squeezing her ass and pushing her closer as if she weren't close enough, I ate that pussy like it was my last meal.

"Oh, gawdddddd. I can't cum anymoreeeeee." She pounded her fist against the couch as another one ripped through. Kissing her inner thighs, I freed my dick with one hand while keeping her in place with the other.

"You ready?" River stared down at me. Without saying another word, my hands went to her waist as I had her slide down my dick slow.

"Shittttt." She gripped my neck and after a minute, she touched the base of my dick with her pussy.

"I guess you weren't lying about the size." She joked, moving slowly in circles. I stopped her for a second to take my sneakers, jeans and boxers completely off.

"Take your time. I wanna enjoy fucking you." She smirked, placed her hands on the couch behind me and rode the fuck outta me. My ass fucked up and let out a few moans.

"Get up. I'm about to cum." We had switched positions a few times and she was now riding me in reverse cowgirl. My toes were about to snap by how good it felt.

"Let me know when."

"Fuck, right now." She hopped off, quickly turned around and sucked every drop of my cum. The way she moaned and got nasty with it had me releasing harder than ever before.

"You taste good." She placed kisses all over my body turning me on again.

"So did you." She was on my lap facing me and this time, she wanted me to lie on the couch so we could do a 69 position.

By the time we finished it was after three in the morning and we turned each other out. We fucked in her bed, the shower, the couch and I ate her pussy and ass while she was bent over in front of the dresser. I'm not even sure why when I never go down on a chick unless she was mine.

Neither of us wanted to move so she pulled the covers up and snuggled under me. Knowing this was only a spur of the moment thing, I managed to get up and put my clothes on to leave.

"Hey." She turned over to see me about to walk out the door.

"What's up?" I grabbed my phone.

"There's money on the dresser for you." I looked and sure enough there was a knot on there.

"I ain't no, ho." That shit had me hot. Slowly, River got out the bed and made her way to me. Her ankle started bothering her again but it didn't stop her from fucking the shit outta me.

"You're my ho now." She wrapped her arms around my waist.

"That's the money you tried to give me for doing, Arabia's hair." She reminded me. I'm surprised she didn't spend it.

"Why didn't you go shopping?" Most women would've ran to the mall.

"I went there as a favor for you and her. There was no need for a payment." I moved her off my body.

"This was a one-time thing, River."

"Sure it was." She grabbed a robe to put on.

"Let me walk you out."

"You heard what I said." I was serious about it only happening this one time. She needed to be clear as well.

"I heard what you said, Block. Just so I'm clear, there's no more sex between us, right."

"Long as you know." She opened the door after I said it.

"Long as you know." Was all she said as I left. Walking to my truck really had me in my feelings because why didn't she ask me to stay. Why didn't she ask for money to shop like Melanie did after sex? And why didn't she ask for my phone number? How would she get in contact with me? River had me feeling like a used bitch right now and I wasn't appreciating it at all.

"Block, what's wrong? Your dick not getting hard." Melanie complained, still jerking me off. It had been a week since me and River slept together and I hadn't heard from her. I know the dick was good because she told me verbally and through her moans. She may not have my number but she had, Arabia's.

"I'm not in the mood and I told you that but you had to beg me to come over." Melanie ignored me and decided to suck me off. Closing my eyes as her warm mouth started to wake my dick up, River came to mind.

"Mmmm, there you go, baby. Nice and hard the way I like." Melanie moaned. I opened the box of condoms, put one on and fucked the hell outta her with thoughts of River. I knew the women were different but the flashes of River's face kept me going.

"I'm about to cum." Melanie yelled. When she did, I pulled out to do the same inside a condom. Walking in the bathroom, I did my usual by removing the condom, flushing it and washing my dick off to make sure no remnants of my sperm was on it. Women do the craziest shit when they're tryna keep a man and Melanie fell into the crazy category.

"I'm out." Throwing my clothes on, Melanie laid on the bed watching.

"Are you leaving me money?" She reminded me of what I'm used to doing.

"It's on the dresser?" I left her and went home to pack for my trip. Me and Onyx had a job to do and distractions couldn't happen. Maybe it was better for me and River not to link up after all.

Chapter Eighteen

RIVER

I experienced everything Block said I would when we had sex. The mind blowing orgasms, body shakes, blood rushing through my body and lastly, the way he made love to me had me confused. I'm not saying the first two times we had sex wasn't good because it definitely was. But the last time, we went all out for one another. It was no longer just fucking; his touch became different, his kisses were more intimate and the number of times he had me yelling his name should be against the law.

I caught an attitude when he mentioned it being a one-time thing but never let him know. I refused to show any sign of weakness. He was already full of himself and that would add fuel to the fire. I did want to tell him we should at least stay in touch with one another but he left before giving me his number.

In a way it made me feel like a ho, because what we shared shouldn't have been an, *I'll see you later* moment. Then again, I never had a boyfriend or a man. Ryan and I were friends with benefits, where Brandon was just there for money. Having an actual man never happened for me so maybe that's why I assumed Block would want more.

The connection was there and everyone saw it. All I can assume was that he didn't want a girlfriend and that when he said it was just sex, that's all it was. Next time a man comes around, I definitely won't allow his sweet whispers to make me drop my drawers.

"Mommy, someone knocking on the door." Jasir ran in the bathroom to get me. I just stepped out the shower and was getting ready to put my pajamas on. Making sure the towel was tight, I slid my feet in the Nike fur flip flops and went in my room to check the Ring doorbell. No one really knew where I stayed and the ones that did never mentioned stopping by.

"What the hell?" Shock was an understatement to see Block standing there.

"Who is it, Mommy?" Jasir jumped on my bed. Grabbing a robe, I threw it on and walked to the door. Removing the dead bolt, as well as the chain, I opened it.

"Let me find out you waiting on a nigga." He let his index finger open my robe. Once he undid the towel, I had to catch myself.

"What are you doing here?" He pushed me inside, closed the door with his foot and hoisted me in his arms.

"You want me to leave?" His lips touched my neck and goosebumps formed all over.

"Jasir in the other room." Rushing to put me down, he adjusted himself.

"Why you tryna fuck when your son here?" I busted out laughing, fixing my robe.

"Mr. Jerome. What you doing here?" Jasir ran from out the room to give him a high five.

"Didn't you ask me to come over to play a game?" Jasir grabbed his hand and led him inside the room. Usually, no man would meet my son but since they became acquainted at the diner, it was if Jasir knew him well.

Locking the front door, I went to throw my pajamas on and noticed my cell going off. It was an unknown number and the person hung up before I could get to it. Seeing the caller would've been Brandon, I was happy not to have gotten it. He was becoming a stalker. A message came through as hung the robe up.

Brandon: *When you letting me come by to fuck?*

Me: *Never. Don't text or call me again.*

Brandon: *Oh, you moved so now you're too good for this money.* How did he know I wasn't there any longer? Did he stop by?

Me: *Bye*

Brandon: *If you don't let me fuck, I promise to let whatever* *nigga you sleeping with know that you're a ho and will do strange things for change.*

Instead of responding, I blocked his number. Brandon was really acting like he couldn't find someone else to harass. This was the first time he called himself texting something like that and I'm hoping it's the last. Putting my phone on the dresser, I went to check on Block and Jasir.

Standing at the door, I watched them go back and forth about who was winning in a Mario game. With the money I had saved up, I purchased Jasir a PlayStation 4 at Game stop, along with a few kid games. That store really was a good place for people who couldn't afford high priced games.

"Aye! Order us some pizza. We gonna be here for a while."

"I don't get paid until next week." Ms. Rogers was able to get me in for orientation right away. Because Ryan still had custody, we didn't have the childcare for him to attend after school due to his income being too high. Therefore, the set up was still the same. He went to regular preschool but there was no before or after care. Ryan said he wasn't wasting money on those programs when he could pick him up.

"Here." He reached in his pocket and handed me a hundred dollar bill."

"Save your money. We're having tacos. You're more than welcome to eat that." Block gave me a weird look. I walked out and went to start dinner.

An hour later, the three of us were at the kitchen table eating and cracking jokes. Jasir really got a kick outta him as did

I. Afterwards, I helped Jasir shower and get ready for bed. By nine, he was knocked out snoring.

"Let me talk to you real quick." Block led me in the bedroom, helped me outta my pajamas and stared.

"What?" He removed the glasses from my face.

"I can't fuck you with those glasses on. I'll think you're Velma and my dick won't get hard." He was a fool. I made sure my bedroom door was locked.

"How about I don't want you to fuck me." I made my way over to him and started unbuckling his belt. Squatting down, I was at his dick level pulling down his jeans.

"Then what you tryna do?" His dick damn near popped me in the face once his boxers were down. As he stood against the wall, I had to stare at how magnificent his body was. The muscles, tattoos, and his six pack was enough to drive any woman crazy; especially if he had sex with them like he did with me.

"I'm tryna take your soul tonight." He removed his shirt, kicked his sneakers off and the rest of his clothes hit the floor. Block reached in his pocket for something. When I saw the lighter, I knew it was to smoke while watching me do him. He told me how sexy I looked the last time.

"When you're done, I'm gonna take yours." He blew smoke in the air and allowed me to do exactly what I said. His knees buckled when my tongue went to that sensitive spot under his balls.

"What the fuck, River. Shit." His body was stiffening up.

Once my nose touched the base of his dick and I started purposely gagging, he grabbed my hair.

"Mmmm, you taste real good, Block." I was spitting the cum on his dick, then licking it off. He was losing control; his body shook for a few seconds before he went limp. Watching him trying to catch his breath, I stood admiring the stage he was in.

"My turn." He lifted me on his shoulders and ate my pussy very well. For the rest of the night, he took total control of my body and I must admit, my soul was snatched. He had me at a point where I didn't even care if he used me for sex. It was that fucking good.

"What's going on, River?" Ryan asked, when I dropped Jasir up. The judge set up a custody hearing for a month away but Ryan let me keep him full time. He got him on the weekends or whenever Jasir called.

"What you mean?"

"Who is this, Jerome, guy, Jasir talking about? I thought we agreed not to let him meet anyone unless we're serious." Over the last three weeks, Block was at the house all the time. He claimed I was his and he was mine, yet we never went anywhere together to show off our relationship.

"I was going to speak with you today about him." He offered me to come in.

"Jasir, let me talk to mommy real quick."

"Ok. Love you, Mommy and tell, Mr. Jerome, I'll be back in two days." He hugged me and put up his two fingers before running off.

"Soooo." I rubbed my hands on top of my jeans.

"His name is Jerome, but he goes by, Block." Ryan began rubbing his temples.

"Please tell me you're not talking about, the guy, Block that everyone scared of." How did he know him? Ryan wasn't a street dude and always stayed away from that area even as a kid.

"I'm not scared of him and you know I'm not in the streets." Ryan put his hands under his chin like he was about to say a prayer.

"I can't tell you who to date but make sure to keep our son safe." He spoke like he had an attitude.

"Ryan." I took offense to him saying that because of the past.

"I'm sorry, River. I wasn't referring to what your mother did. He a street dude was all I meant and dealing with someone like that, you have to be careful." He hugged me and apologized for how he worded it.

"Daddy, when is, Chana coming over? She promised to watch a movie with me." Now it was my turn to question him.

"She's a nurse at the hospital. Her and her pops just moved back from what she said." We both went back and forth about the people we were now dealing with. We did make plans to meet the other person soon.

After saying goodbye, I walked to my van and pulled off.

My cell rang when I was halfway home. Seeing it was Block, I smiled before answering.

"Aye! I'm sending you my location. Meet me there in ten minutes." He didn't even let me respond. He disconnected the call and shortly after the location popped up. It was to the same diner me and Jasir saw him at. When I pulled up, he walked out to get me.

"I'm happy as hell you didn't wear your Velma outfit today or those glasses." I pushed him on the arm. I had on some fitted sweats with a V-neck shirt and a pair of Air Max that Block brought me for the security job. He said I had pretty feet and didn't want bad sneakers fucking them up. I wasn't about to complain because Block knew how to suck some toes.

"You still sexy though." He leaned down for a kiss.

"Whatever." He held my hand in his and led the way into the diner. I was surprised to see, Arabia, their mom, Mariah and Onyx, her mom and a few others I didn't know.

"Oh, shit. You must've threw it on my son if he bringing your poor ass out in public." Sticking my tongue at his mom, she flipped me the finger.

For the next few hours we sat in the diner, having a blast. Block's father and other uncle showed up and they started a spades game. It was fun and Mariah seemed to loosen up around me as well.

"Hey, your phone keeps ringing." Arabia passed it to me. I was coming out the bathroom.

"Hey, what's up?" I answered for Ryan. He was so

distraught, I couldn't make out a word he was saying. Block took the phone.

"Wait! What?" Block's entire family began staring at me because panic struck instantly trying to understand him.

"Ok, where are you?" Not sure what he said but the look on Block's face said something was terribly wrong. Once he hung up, he made his way to where the guys were. All of them turned in my direction.

"What's wrong? What happened?" I questioned but he wouldn't answer.

"Let's go." Without another word, Block lifted me up.

"Did something happen to my son? What's going on?" My vision was becoming blurry from me about to cry, one of the contacts fell out and now, I really couldn't see out that eye. Block saw it, placed me in his truck, went to my van and returned with my purse and glasses. I brought them wherever I went just in case the contacts irritated me. I've worn them a lot more since the gender reveal and now that my eye doctor gave me a new prescription for it, my Medicaid covered it.

"Block, please tell me what's wrong." Focused on the road, he had me scared by how fast he was going.

"Block, please."

"Your son was at the park with his father and something happened." My heart started racing faster. As soon as I went to ask another question, we were pulling up at the emergency room. I didn't wait for him to park and rushed inside.

"Ryan! Ryan! Where is my son? What happened?" There

was a woman standing next to him. She must be the chick he was seeing.

"I don't know, River. We were at the park and outta nowhere there was a drive by. Him and two other kids were hit. River there was so much blood. I don't know what I'll do if he doesn't make it." My life flashed before my eyes when he said my son was shot and the amount of blood he saw.

"No. No, no, no. Don't tell me someone shot my son. Don't you tell me that. Ryan, say you're lying." I started punching him in the chest. He tried grabbing my hands.

"River, I jumped on top of him but it was too late." Tears were streaming down his face and the chick was crying as well.

"I got her." Block picked me up.

"River, you gotta relax. He's gonna be ok." My body was shaking so bad, I started hyperventilating. My lips were trembling and my glasses kept sliding down.

"Block, my son. Oh, God. Please don't let him die. I need to get in the back to see him. He's gonna want his mother." I did everything possible to break free but he wasn't letting me go.

"What the fuck?" Ryan barked. I turned to see him staring at the last person who needed to be here.

"Where is he?" When she went to the nurses station to ask questions, I couldn't believe my eyes.

"Who the fuck are you?" Block shouted and I couldn't answer him. Why was she here? Who told her what happened?

"I'm River's mother and that was my grandson who was shot." I couldn't believe she was in my presence. But what really took the cake was Ryan's friend knowing who she was.

"Louise?"

"Who the fuck are you?" My mother snapped.

"I'm your daughter." I could see my mother's face. It wasn't scared or mad but more or less nervous about what this chick would say.

"Do you have a sister?" Block asked and Ryan stared at me too.

"Not that I know of." I asked him to walk with me closer so I could hear clearer. The chick moved in close as well to finish what she needed to say.

"Get the fuck away from me." My mother was adamant about not hearing anything else.

"Oh, you don't remember the daughter you gave away." I gasped at the woman's revelation.

"The family of Jasir Rogers." A doctor came out from the other side.

"Yes. I'm his mother and he's his father." Block started to walk away but I grabbed his hand. He probably didn't think I wanted him to stay but that was far from the truth.

"I need you." He nodded and wrapped his arms around my waist.

"Let's go in another room. There's a lot going on out here." I noticed Block's family walking in.

"Charlene?" The chick knew Onyx's grandmother too. I'm not even sure why she came here.

"Why you here?" Block asked her on the way in the room.

"My great nephew was shot." It was like a nightmare that I

couldn't wake up from. This chick continued unleashing bombs.

"Go inside, River. I'll be in shortly." Block attempted to push me inside but I froze when the chick said her last statement.

"So, you're Charlene. The bitch who forced my mother and father to have sex, knowing they were siblings." *What the hell did she just say?*

"River, it's Jasir." Ryan ran out the room crying harder.

"What? What did he say?" I couldn't worry about Louise or the other chick.

"He said..." Before he could relay what the doctor said, I heard a gun.

CLICK!

"Bitch, I've been looking for you."

Chapter Nineteen

ARABIA

"Hello. Hello." I could barely hear Deray's mom on the phone. There was so much going on inside the hospital, I had to step out.

"Hello." No one answered but she was in the background screaming.

"Hello. Hello." I kept yelling in the phone but she wouldn't answer. Rushing to my car and being careful on the way, I sent Mariah a message letting her know I'm going to see Deray's mom to make sure she was ok. They stayed in Staten Island which wasn't too far from New Jersey.

After the shooting with him, they've been nervous about someone returning to try and get them. Being around my family had me very secure besides the time dumb ass Huff stopped by. In my opinion, the person was there for Deray because I had no beef with anyone and who would follow me.

I pulled out the parking lot and hit the turnpike. It was nerve wrecking that when I tried to call back again, the phone kept going to voicemail. All I could think of was someone may have found and hurt her.

Finally making it to her house, I saw Tricia's car and two other cars in the driveway but no cops. Maybe someone arrived and helped her. Putting my gun inside the back of my pants, I kept my phone on me and stepped out the car. Nothing was out of the ordinary and since it was still daylight, I could see kids playing in their front yards.

It made me wonder if River's son was alright. When the guys told us her son was shot at the playground, we paid for our food and rushed down to the hospital. They may be in a new relationship but all of us knew the two were feeling each other way beforehand. We wanted to be there for her especially after learning some of her past regarding her son. Block found out and told us to let her tell when she was ready.

Slowly walking up the pathway, the door was opened and you could hear voices coming from inside. The screen door happened to be unlocked so I went in and headed straight to the bathroom by the door. I saw his mom standing in the kitchen with his father talking which put my mind at ease for the moment. And besides, it didn't sound like anyone was in danger, and laughter could be heard as I sat on the toilet. My phone vibrated on the counter. I saw it was Mariah and answered.

"Hey, did you get there." I had the phone on my ear while I finished using the bathroom.

"Yea. How is River's son?" I flushed, washed my hands, and checked myself over. Right before she answered, a voice was very familiar outside the door. The person was asking about a ball that used to be in the closet by the front door.

"Hold on, Mariah. I know I'm not bugging."

"Bugging about what?" The second I opened the door, our eyes met.

"Deray."

"Deray?" Mariah questioned on the other end of the phone. I hung up to make sure I'm not dreaming.

"Arabia? When did you get here?" I felt his body to make sure it was real, then smacked fire from his ass.

WHAP!

"What is going on in there?" His parents came in the foyer area where we were.

"When did you find out he was alive?" All of them froze when they saw me.

"Deray, Amani wants you to push her on the swing again." Tricia came from around the corner smiling. She stopped short seeing me.

"All of you fucking knew?"

"Arabia don't get mad at them. I—" He tried to speak but I cut him off. How could he tell me not to be mad when they all knew he didn't die?

"Don't tell me what the fuck to do. Move." I pushed him

out the way and wobbled my pregnant ass to the car. I turned to see all of them standing there.

"Your mothers phone called me and I heard yelling. Thinking she was hurt, I rushed here to help, only to find that my man who I thought was dead, was alive."

"Arabia, aren't you happy?" His mother had the nerve to ask.

"Hell no, I'm not happy that you let me believe your son was dead. You let me believe you were dead. I mourned over you for months. Why, Deray?" I was at the driver's side of my car. There wasn't anything he could say.

"You know what? I don't even care. Stay the fuck away from me. Ahhhh." An excruciating pain shot through my stomach.

"Arabia, what's wrong?" I saw the fear on Deray's face.

"None of your got damn business." Getting in the car, another pain shot through my body. It was like nothing I've ever felt.

"Let me take you to the hospital." He was now on the driver's side trying to keep me from closing the door. I pulled my gun out and pointed it at him.

"Get the fuck away from my car because my shot, is a kill shot and you won't survive." He backed away with his hands up. I hated to be that bitch but fuck him and his family. How dare they not tell me.

Driving to the hospital that the GPS said wasn't far, the pains were coming more and more frequent. I said a prayer to God asking him to save me and my child.

I pulled up close to the door and blew my horn hoping someone would come out. Instead of waiting, I got out and heard tires screeching.

"Move out the wayyyyyy." I heard someone yell as an out of control car hit the curb and hydroplaned in my direction. All I could do was close my eyes and wait for the inevitable to happen.

To Be Continued....

Coming Soon!!

Temptation

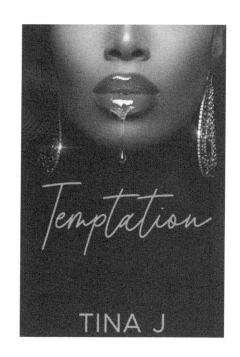

Now Available On Amazon

Bossed Up With A Billionaire: A BBW Love Affair

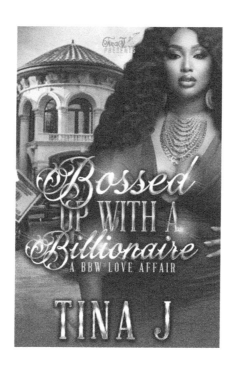

A Kingpin's Dynasty

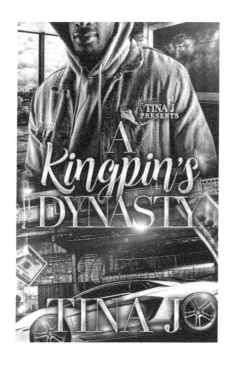

Made in the USA
Monee, IL
06 October 2024

67281712R00098